Good Guys Finish Last

By

Lonz Cook

Lonz Cook

© Lonz Cook 2006

All Rights Reserved

Published by: Elevation Book Publishing
Atlanta, Georgia 30308
www.elevationbookpublishing.com

Cook, Lonz, 1960-
Good Guys Finish Last / by Lonz Cook
ISBN 978-1-943904-02-0 p.cm. (pbk)
BISAC FIC027020
BISAC FIC008000

Acknowledgement

It's a pure blessing to get Good Guys Finish Last republished. This novel was my first attempt at sharing a story from a father's perspective, to his daughters about loving the right guy.

Was I successful in telling the story? Well…that remains to be seen. However, this book is an entertaining path of knowledge being passed to those who indulge between the book's covers.

I'm happy that many people believe in my writing and have faith in my ability to keep this dynamic story spreading across multiple books.

Look for the sequels When Love Evolves, Against Conventional Expectation, and The Predictable End. I am grateful for your support and interest in reading my passion … writing good stories.

Happy Reading,

Lonz

Table of Content

Chapter 1

In Passing

Rodney saw her enter the art gallery. His glimpse sparked an immediate "oh my" expression. He stood across the store and observed every move of the lovely woman. Simone was casually dressed for the office; her taste was exquisite. She wore an outfit with key designers bearing the name Ann Taylor and Donna Karen, with a touch of her own touch of magic, a scarf she loved. Her black pants loosely fit her body, hiding her true curves. Her top was silk which her jacket displayed just enough to enhance her color coordination. She wore her "lucky" perfume, which was sprayed just enough to give a refreshing odor to a passerby. Rodney felt pleased in her presence, grateful for breaking his normal routine by visiting the art gallery. Instead he would have gone to the gym during rush hour in Richmond. He thought working out was a better use of time than fighting downtown traffic. This day, he felt an urge to enjoy the evening, and indulge his interest in art.

The gallery was in an old brownstone warehouse building used as merchant store front when side stores were front entry way to shipping warehouses during an earlier century and located in Shockoe Bottom, the center of the town's revitalization. Since it was on the first block of regeneration, because of construction, there wasn't much sidewalk for pedestrians, limited parking, or open lanes for traffic, but the location was great for Rodney; it was walking distance from his office. Once entering the gallery, one could see that paintings flowed gradually from eye level to the open ceiling, where large scale pictures of were showcased. The gallery staff was exceptionally supportive and responsive to any customer inquiry, which created a positive and enjoyable environment. Their southern charm and professionalism was a true reflection of the owner, who was a friend of Rodney.

Rodney was dressed in his casual business attire. He wore a shirt jacket, a nylon/silk blend shirt, and pleated slacks. His shoes were immaculate, stylish, and clean, but not extremely expensive. Rodney was a classy guy and he took care in his appearance to project that image. Rodney stepped lightly throughout the gallery, periodically glancing to see if this mystery woman moved in his direction. Simone seemed also to slowly gravitate towards his direction. Finally, while observing a particular painting, Simone stood next to Rodney. "This painting is so colorful and full of life. It's as if the artist wanted us to change our moods from dreary to excitement," Simone mused in a soft but audible tone.

"Yes, it is quite colorful and full of energy. It's like a bright moon on a dark night giving life to whatever the light touches," Rodney responded.

Simone took a quick breath and started blushing; she was happy he responded even though she hadn't entirely intended for him to hear. She glanced demurely to get a better look at him. *My, he is absolutely a handsome man*, she thought. *He is better looking close up. Oh and he smells great.* "What cologne is he wearing?"

Rodney turned to her with a smile.

"Oh, did you hear me? I didn't think I spoke that loud," admitted Simone.

"Allow me to introduce myself in case I hear something else.". He extended his right hand as a proper introduction. She took his hand and smiled as he touched her. "I am Rodney Witherspoon and it's my pleasure meeting such a lovely art connoisseur."

"Thank you kindly for the compliment, but I wouldn't call myself a connoisseur. I enjoy interpreting what I think the artist had in mind. I'm Simone. It's nice to meet you."

"Do you come here often? Wait, that sounds like a horrible pickup line," he laughed.

"No, not often. I come in from time-to-time to see if there's something eye catching. And to gasp at some of the prices," she giggled. "Looking at art helps me relax after a day at the office ...and escape the brutal rush-hour traffic."

"Oh yes, you too. Traffic is terrible during this time of day. It's funny we haven't met sooner."

"I'm not a regular, so I can understand how we may have missed one another."

Simone started moving on to look at other paintings and sculptures. She slowly stepped away and subconsciously waited for Rodney's movement to follow her. At first, she wanted to be inviting, but then she decided to reserve her quick encouragement. Simone turned back to him and said, "Well, it's nice to have met you Rodney," and she walked to the next painting.

"Again, the pleasure is mine. I hope we see each other again really soon." Rodney's thoughts began to race through his head. *Am I just being polite? Perhaps I do hope we run into each other. She is fine and I bet intelligent too. Dinner and wine with a woman who can hold her own? She seems like the perfect candidate. Should I make a move?*

"Didn't you say your name was Simone?"

"Yes, I did."

"Please take my card. If we don't run into each other, feel free to contact me." Rodney presented his business card and excused himself; he walked to another section of the gallery and signaled her to call him with a smile and a wave.

Simone turned her focus back to art. She observed another painting near the vaulted ceiling and found that though the colors didn't catch her eye as others, but vivid, with the right lighting she could see something promising. Simone looked for the curator, and glanced about the room. Her eyes captured Rodney's presence once more. For a second time she noticed his physical attributes; that he was well dressed and in great shape which peaked her interest. She then assumed that meant he was vain and self-centered. The last guy she dated with a great shape and good taste in attire was so narcissistic that he didn't have room for her in his heart.

Simone made her purchase, spending quite more than she had intended. The painting was captivating and Simone a needed focal piece for her office, which was stuffy and begging for a change. *Perhaps the painting will spark some inspiration for another venture for the business*, she thought. Simone took the painting to her car and found herself struggling to fit it into the trunk.

Rodney, seeing Simone struggle, began to walk in her direction, but she swiftly closed the trunk, entered her car, and drove off. Rodney observed her leaving the parking lot in her late model IS 250 Lexus sport sedan (insert car brand/style name here). *What a nice car, a really nice car. Man, this woman could be high maintenance!* He returned to his original path and found his vehicle. After starting the engine, his thoughts returned to her. *Simone seems to be a very nice woman. How fortunate I am meeting her today.*

Simone continued her commute home to the West End. Rodney definitely seemed like the type of man she would like in her life. *Maybe I should call him later... No, it would be too aggressive or way too soon.* If Simone called, she feared he'd think her being overconfident.

Three hours had passed since he was talking with Simone in the art gallery and for some reason, Rodney could not get her off of his mind. The few moments they spent together intrigued him to his wit's end. He began to regret not getting her number or having any means of contacting her. *"If our paths should ever cross again or if she*

8

calls, I'll be ready to seize the opportunity, he admitted before ending his day.

Rodney used positive-thinking to motivate him for a morning run the next day. It was the middle of spring and the weather embraced you with the comfort of the warm sun and a cool breeze. A perfect day. Rodney gave thanks by saying "thank you, Lord" before tying his shoelaces. He psyched himself up in the hallway mirror before walking downstairs to the door. It's a routine he performed before running three miles. "It's going to be an easy run. I'm going to feel great." Opening the door, he noticed the street was silent. He looked at his watch and realized it was still quite early. He envisioned his regular course, started his warm-up, stretched muscles, and felt slight pains. "I am not getting younger and I need to do this for my health. The last thing I want is an injury. I have to make it all the way." he said, motivating himself.

Running on the street, he observed the awakening population. Every step on the course, he noticed something different. The surrounding trees, the squirrels and birds, the parked cars, planes flying low in the sky, and people leaving their homes. As he ran, he noticed the increase in movement around him. He occasionally spoke to passersby while maintaining his pace. One street seemed particularly quiet, and upon further observation, he noticed a person laying on the sidewalk. *Probably some homeless person, but I better check it out.* Rodney ran to the prone body and saw the person was dressed for colder weather than the warmth for the day. When he got closer, he realized it was an older woman, in her late 70s or early 80s. He stopped and bent over to see if she was okay. He touched her lightly. No response. He nudged a little harder, and still no response. He then checked her breath to see if she was breathing and concluded yes. He could see her chest rise, not by much, but was happy for the sign of life. He tried to find a pulse and heartbeat, then repeatedly tried to wake her. Still no response, he immediately ran to the house in front of him and knocked on the door. A man answered the door.

"Yes, what can I do for you?" asked the man.

"I need you to call 9-1-1 please."

"Why, what's the problem?"

"A lady is on the sidewalk. She has a faint pulse and needs medical attention. I'm no doctor, but she is alive. She is breathing but unresponsive. You've got to call 9-1-1. Please hurry."

"Right, I'll get my phone and meet you outside."

"Thanks." Rodney returned to the older woman and nothing had changed. *It seems she's in a deep sleep, won't respond or maybe she's deaf. Either way, she shouldn't be on the street!*

The man who answered the house door arrived and he was on the phone talking to the emergency dispatcher. "The address is 793 Dover Place. It's a lady in her…oh my God, it's Mrs. Blaine! Please hurry she is laying here and there is no telling how long she's been here."

"What's your name, sir?" the dispatcher asked.

"Dan Slocum," he answered in frustration. "Why does this matter? Can you get me an ambulance?"

"Sir, does she have any noticeable injuries?"

"No, not than I can see." Dan turned to Rodney and shouted, "Hey, do you see any other injuries?" "No," replied Rodney. "She is still breathing, how long until the ambulance arrives?"

The dispatcher heard the question over the speaker phone and responded, "An ambulance is on the way and will be there shortly; do you know anything of her medical history? Is there anyone who knows of her condition? Does she live with someone? Is there anything you can tell me about her that I may pass on to the medical technicians?" asked the dispatcher.

"No, there isn't anything that I can help with. Wait, I hear sirens. I guess that's the ambulance," Dan acknowledged.

The dispatcher told Dan it couldn't be there so fast and that a different team was dispatched. "Your ambulance should be there within the next five minutes."

A few moments later, Dan heard a second siren and told the dispatch that it's pretty close in proximity. Meanwhile, the dispatcher inquired of Mrs. Blaine's condition in an attempt to gather more information. "Has anything changed since you've called?"

"No, not at all," replied Dan. "She is still breathing on her own and isn't responsive to calls. She hasn't moved since I've been here."

Rodney, who was still attending to Mrs. Blaine, noticed track marks on her arm after he pushed her coat sleeves to get a better pulse. "Hey, guy," he shouted, "do you know if Mrs. Blaine is a diabetic?"

Dan shrugged his shoulders and answered, "Your guess is as good as mine."

The ambulance finally arrived, after what felt like a long wait, and the EMT team asked multiple questions. They searched for the same vital information as the dispatcher inquired about earlier. Right off, they started an IV, checked all vital signs, and tried to wake Mrs. Blaine. Mrs. Blaine opened an eye and moved her head from side to side. Not realizing anything happening at all, she felt pain engulfing her body as if a large truck struck her while she crossed the street. She recognized the EMT uniform and fell back into a deep sleep. The EMT team transferred her to a gurney and then to the ambulance. One team member asked if there is anyone who knew this lady and Dan jumped in and acknowledged that he did. The driver instructed him to come to the hospital with them and tell them as much as possible. Dan pointed a finger to Rodney and told the EMT tech that he was the one who found her and stayed by her side the entire time.

"You did a good thing with the patient," said the EMT to Rodney. "We can take it from here."

"Okay, glad to help," said Rodney.

"What hospital are you transporting Mrs. Blaine to?"

"Henricos Doctor's Hospital Emergency Center."

"Thanks."

The ambulance drove away and Rodney returned to his run. He looked at his watch and concluded it was time to return home. He cut his run short but knew he'd make it up later in the evening.

***

This morning Sabrina moved slowly in her wakening routine. After she dressed, the phone rang.

"Hello."

"Hello. May I speak with Sabrina Willingham?"

"Yes, this is she. May I ask whose calling?"

"This is Henrico Doctor's Hospital. You were listed as the emergency contact for Mrs. Blaine. A Marge Blaine."

"Yes, that's my aunt."

"Well, we have her here and need you to come in. She is in intensive care at the moment but stable. She is…"

"Oh my god, I will be right there!"

She quickly grabbed her purse and left for the hospital. Sabrina just saw her Aunt Marge yesterday and she was doing great. They did their usual weekend errands and everything seemed fine. The last time they were together was in the living room having tea. Sabrina reminded her to take her medicine and to call before she went to bed, which she did. *Why is she now in the hospital? I need to call my sister. But I better find out what's happened first!*

Meanwhile across town, driving to the office and in a great mood, Simone sipped her morning coffee. After parking her car, she stepped lively to the bagel shop. Simone spoke to the counter clerk and ordered her routine bagel. While waiting for the bagel, she thought of

12

her morning objectives. *It's a challenging job staying on top of things especially with the tough economy; tomorrow will be a better day once we find out if we won the latest contract,* she admitted to herself. The contract was needed to save so many jobs, especially Simone's. Everyone was on the chopping block if business didn't pick up. Simone wished she had partner to support her while she ventured into something she loved to do. Right now, it wouldn't be the right time for Simone to start her own company. There are too many things she needed to support first before stepping out on blind faith.

Chapter 2

Understanding the Value

"Aunt Marge, are you feeling better?" asked Sabrina. Before Aunt Marge could respond, she turned to the doctor and asked, "Doctor Smith, will she get better or is it something more?"

"She is going to be fine," Doctor Smith reassured Sabrina. "One of her test readings isn't quite exact, but it's in the normal range. I think we should keep her under observation for one more day so I can run another test. You know it's better being safe than sorry."

Aunt Marge opened her eyes and saw Sabrina. "There's my favorite niece. How wonderful it is for you to visit. Is it the weekend, baby, or is this special?"

"Aunt Marge, it's a special visit. Do you realize where you are?"

"Sure I do, baby, I am in my bed and that's why I am surprised to see you. It's Tuesday and I have to get ready for my meeting at the church."

"No, Aunt Marge, you aren't heading off to the church right now. Look around the room. This isn't your home. It's East Memorial Hospital. You forgot to take your medication. If it weren't for the neighbors, you'd still be lying on the street. It's so nice of them to look out for you."

Confused Aunt Marge explained, "Dear, dear, now I know I took my meds before walking out of the house. I know for sure because I recall you reminding me to. Didn't you ask me before leaving for your home? I suspect I took them all... I remember getting dressed. I even put my large coat on for the cold. I walked out of the door and started up the street. That's the last thing I remember before waking up here."

"There you go, Aunt Marge. You have something troubling your health. I can see why the doctor wants you to stay for another test."

A nurse entered and checked vital signs. "How are you, Mrs. Blaine?" she asked.

"Oh, I feel pretty good now. I am ready to go home," replied Marge.

"The doctor may let you go home tomorrow. You are scheduled to have blood drawn and have a scan done. You will be discharged once you complete those two things. And the doctor will call you with a follow-up appointment to discuss the results of those tests."

"Aunt Marge, I will be here for your discharge tomorrow morning. You don't have anything to worry about. I will take care of your things." Sabrina walked out of the room while the nurse performed her duties. She went to the waiting lounge and used her cell phone to inform relatives of Aunt Marge's condition. When she called her sister to share the news, Simone broke into a frenzy, worried about her favorite aunt. Her anger and tears raged as she blamed herself for not being there when Aunt Marge needed someone the most. Sabrina had to help Simone find a calm spot to face any diagnosis Aunt Marge received.

Marge at age 23 had married Arthur Blaine, the brother of Sabrina's mother when she was twenty-two and a recent graduate from Sweet Briar Women College. A cultured woman and a lover of clothing styles from France, Spain, and Portugal. insert age and other details here]. Marge was an only child and always dreamed of having a large family. She never had children of her own even though her and Author made numerous attempts to get pregnant for the first three years of their marriage. Their success came with joy during their fourth year. Marge carried the baby up to the third trimester. Then it happened, she fell from the stairs as she stepped over a domestic animal. Her fell caused blood hemorrhage and forced the doctors to deliver the baby at an early trimester. Marge survived the surgery but the baby was lost. The emotional impact was devastating to Marge and Author, however their failure to give birth didn't discourage Author from being the loyal husband, nor give up on family with kids as he encouraged Marge to embrace every niece or nephew as an extension of themselves and showered them with love. Sabrina had been Marge's favorite niece since [the age of four. She was the flower girl at her and Author's wedding] and they created a bond closer than mother and child. Sabrina pressured her parents to stay with her favorite aunt, and on occasions she camped in Marge's family room where her uncle and aunt entertained throughout the night. Sabrina loved her private sanctuary and especially being the focus Author and Marge which she didn't have to compete for sister Simone.

When the kids grew older, they would visit Aunt Marge whenever they made the trip to Richmond. Aunt Marge's was the first place they stopped before heading to their parents' home. Great nieces and nephews followed their parents' belief that Aunt Marge was an matriarch in the family. Every year Marge made it a point to send all her famous oat mill raisin chocolate chip cookies, a recipe she grew to love as a child. Her mother baked them for her during those sad days, where her father failed to visit. Those cookies became her lifeline to happiness multiple times. And with love for all, and her deepest emotions wrapped in memories how those raisin chocolate chip cookies saved her, she placed extra effort in perfecting the recipe, baking and sharing those cookies for every celebration. She made them her family trademark.

Her cookie recipe holds secret to this day. In addition to her family famous oatmeal raisin chocolate chip cookies, Marge supported every child through college, military events, weddings and every kid's coming of age accomplishment. One year, Sabrina faced a hard decision to either drop out of college or after a surprised selection, capitalize on a modeling opportunity. Before she thought anyone knew of the situation, Aunt Marge called for full disclosure. Their discussion led to a debate of pros and cons. Sabrina couldn't believe getting a call from her aunt so quickly. It was as if she had magical insight.

On a different event, Marge called her nephew Thomas informing him of a college scholarship, before the organization awarded it. She had inside information on multiple things, and she kept it positive. It's why all the kids kept her close and admired her consistent involvement. Family members wondered how she managed to do it. Her way of communicating was remarkable, it was as if she was the touchstone connection between generations where her intuition validated to do the right thing when most least expected it. She could feel strife from others long before it became a reality. And with such knowledge, Marge prevented greater hardships by her actions. She knew what to do, when to do it, and where to send it.

Panic stricken Sabrina called her sister Simone, and other cousins to inform them of Aunt Marge's hospitalization. Simone took it as a shocker, self-destructive and critical because guilt of not visiting much tampered her. Though Aunt Marge was her favorite, Simone didn't outwardly share because of being self-absorbed, first in achieving her career and focused on anything that made her marketable, and second for giving her the hardest time during those teen years. She completed certifications, achieved higher education, and did anything constructive to enhance her professional status.

It had been several years since the family last came together. Now, in light of the news of Marge's health, niece and nephews' pulled together and planned a large get together for their angelic Aunt Marge. Sabrina started planning with her sister, Simone. "You know, Simone, we should have the family show love for Aunt Marge all week. It would be great to give her something special. I know how she loved hearing us sing. Remember how we use to sing for her when we were kids?"

"Sure, I remember," replied Simone. "We used to start singing and any relative would join in, and sometimes she would help us along. We even made up tunes and lyrics causing her to laugh for hours. Especially Thomas, he was so silly with his lyrics. It's a wonder he didn't become a comedian."

"We should see if Thomas' kids could do something like that for Aunt Marge."

"That is a good idea. The kids may not sing well, but Aunt Marge would love hearing them. She is so fond of little children."

"What about having something at the civic center? Do you think we can afford it?"

"No, I don't think we should get ahead of ourselves. I am sure Aunt Marge would like whatever we do without being elegant and expensive."

"I know, but she did so much for us. She deserves whatever we can do," sniffled Sabrina as tears filled her eyes. "Who knows how much longer she will be with us? Simone, if she died, what are we going to do?"

Hugging her sister, Simone gave reassurance, "Sabrina, you know we've had the greatest time with Aunt Marge. We spend quality time with her at every chance. We support her unconditionally because she'd done so much for every one of us. We are here for her with our hearts and minds. And besides, the tough lady will not give up without a fight. Our love will heal her wound. So don't worry about losing her; she will be with us for many years to come."

Sabrina tried to help Simon understand, "Her dying isn't the only point I'm concerned about, it's not that we may lose her, but her quality of life. I know she wanted to live a long and rich life, and I worry about her. Ever since she lost Uncle Arthur she's been alone."

"I guess that's why she is so active in church and with the community."

"It does take much of her time, but her health is what bothers me now."

"You shouldn't worry so much. It's going to be okay. Aunt Marge will pull through like a trooper," Simone said with hidden fear.

"That's easy for us to say. I plan on staying with her as much as possible. I hope you are willing to share some of the responsibility with me. I don't know about the others helping out since they live so far away."

"You know my schedule is hectic, I have meetings throughout each day because of a new assignment. I'm in the executive development group and they keep me busy. During the evening I'm with Women In Business group, and the sorority leadership this year. Whatever I can adjust, I'll be sure to give a portion of my time as much as possible. One of us should be with her most evenings."

"Sis, no matter what others may say, you're a sweet person. Just kidding! I am glad we had this chat. I hope we have someone to look out for us when we're older."

"If we ever have any kids," Simone said, with a doubtful grimace. "So what about the reunion? Do you think we can do it at her church?"

"You know she would love for us to include her church family. That's not a bad idea." Sabrina looked for a phone book. She left the hospital room and headed down the hall towards the nurse's station. She noticed the back of a man's white coat standing at the counter. She approached with a sense of urgency.

"Excuse me, doctor, is there a phone book available that I may use?"

The young man, with piercing brown eyes, smooth skin, and an inviting smile, turned around and sparkled with excitement. "I'm not a doctor, well, not yet, but thanks."

Taking a quick breath and thinking of a stronger comeback, opportunity knocked and it's been a long time between dates. I have to impress this lovely woman who shared in looks of what her voice projected. "Impress her," he thought as he looked down at the counter for the phone book, grabbed a medicinal reference book instead and gave it to Sabrina. Not realizing the book wasn't in fact the phonebook, he handed it to her and slyly said, "If I give you this, it will cost you. Have dinner or coffee with me, tomorrow night?"

"Oh, a phone directory is costly these days? Too bad it's a medical reference book, or I'd have to say yes!"

"What? It isn't the phone book? I am so sorry, wait." He reached behind the counter once again, this time grabbing the correct book. "Here it is, sorry about that. So this means tomorrow night we're on, right?

"All right, but I should wait to see how my aunt is doing first. So why don't you give me a way to contact you?"

"Sure will." The young man pulled a business card out of his pocket, looked on the back of it making sure he didn't pass anything embarrassing, and gave it to Sabrina. "You can contact me at either of these numbers. I am glad you accepted my invitation." Smiling, he turned, carrying a clipboard and headed down the hall.

Sabrina found the phone number of the church and recorded it on the back of the young doctor-in-training's card: Dr. Lorenz Maynard]. She walked back to Aunt Marge's room to hear the sounds of laughter. "What are you two laughing about?"

"Child, your sister is just as silly as ever," replied Aunt Marge.

"I'm glad to see you in better spirits and feeling energetic, Aunt Marge."

"Laughter is good for anyone, even when it hurts. It helps keep the spirit positive and alive."

"Your spirit will be alive and well for years coming, I am sure of it."

Sabrina commented, "Yeah, your spirit will be here long after our spirits leave us for that long journey down the Mississippi."

"Baby girl, she laughed, I'm still on the Chattanooga rolling with the current."

"Aunt Marge, you are a riot."

***

The apartment was warm and cozy when Rodney returned from his run. He rushed to get dressed, as he was far behind schedule. While tying his tie, he remembered the image of Ms. Blaine collapsed in the middle of the road. *I hope she makes it. I'd hate to see the lovely elderly woman with no family fall by the wayside. If anything, I should check up on her health.* As he headed to the office, he stopped at the local coffee shop for his usual cup. After his coffee order, Rodney winked at the counter clerk. He and she always flirted at every opportunity. Even though they had only exchanged names, they were warm and comfortable enough to enjoy each other's antics. Debbie loved to see Rodney come into her coffee shop. She thought of ways to catch him off guard with her flirtatious remarks. She chided her way into his day, starting with a quick comeback to his morning greeting.

"Good morning, Debbie."

"You got some, didn't you, Rodney?" she asked as she poured his coffee.

"Got what?"

"You know exactly what I'm talking about. Was it creamy and smooth too?" laughed Debbie.

"Like when you dip your finger in my coffee," Rodney smiled with a gleam in his eye.

"Yeah, you're all talk. You couldn't handle what I have to give."

"Ha, ha, ha, you got something going on this morning too."

"Will that be all for you today?" asked Debbie while passing his coffee.

"Just the usual and nothing more, thank you." Rodney dropped a few dollars in Debbie's hand, smiled, and left the coffee shop. His office building was relatively close; it was the first door on the right just after the side road entrance. The tall skyscraper with dark mirror windows was full of different businesses and human traffic. There were people going in and out at all hours of the day, especially for his modeling agency on the 7th floor. They had a 24/7 studio in full operations with multiple photographers. The studio was rented out to thrill seekers, novice photographers, and any photo-related work. Rodney was one of three senior marketing account executives who handled multiple major magazines and photographers. He didn't mind the photo lab being rented for extra income; it helped when the business lost an account or dropped a millionaire model because of her harsh behavior. Besides, Rodney didn't mind as long as he got a chance to work with those expensive models. He knew they would never talk to him; however, one day, bam, he thought, he'd get to smile with a jewel on his arm. If that ever happened, he'd lose his stature in the agency and exposure to all those attractive models.

The 9th floor was where the action was for tomorrow's executive. They seemed to have a training program for all the employees. It was a great network full of surprises. Unfortunately, Rodney hadn't been invited there, but he thought it would be nice to work there one day. Rodney often imagined being selected for the right manager position, attend the proper training, and with a wave of the wand, have an office on the 9th floor. Rodney worked on the 25th floor of the company, in one of those worker pool locations with multiple cubicles. He enjoyed working with a lot of everyday people. His floor was where people interacted without fear. Sometimes Rodney wished they had some fear before they opened their mouths. All in all, things seemed pretty good on the floor, and full of life – the focus was in the right place. Realizing that it was pretty late in the morning, Rodney hurried and logged in to his email account.

"Hi, Rodney, what's the latest?" shouted Dan.

"Not much, Dan. I suspect things are going as planned," Rodney spoke as they walked to the elevators. "Sure, things are as expected. The agency sent another model yesterday who had multiple looks for the McKenzie shoot. Man she's one knockout and with a wonderful personality!"

"It's nice hearing about sharp women in the business. It's always challenging working with egos. Unfortunately for me, that's the majority of women I deal with. What's her name?"

"Sabrina Willingham."

"I haven't heard of her before. Is she new to the business?"

"No, she has a strong portfolio and has worked with top photographers. She started this shoot and was interrupted because of a family emergency. Because she has a certain look the magazine wanted, they changed schedules to accommodate her. We tried to replace her, but McKenzie wouldn't allow it. What a departure from past shoots!"

"She's got to know someone in the right places; it's the only way a model doesn't lose a shoot."

***

Aunt Marge sat up bedside and placed her feet on the floor. "Lord, this floor is so cold. Don't they ever consider having rugs or mats by each bed?" Sabrina looked at Aunt Marge, jumped from her seat and in haste grabbed Aunt Marge's arms to help her stand.

"Aunt Marge, where on earth are you trying to go?"

"I need to get out of this bed and try to make it to the bathroom."

"Why didn't you just call me? I could have gotten your bed pan."

"Why on earth would I want to do that when I am capable of going myself?"

"You aren't in the best shape right now, Aunt Marge. You have to rest and get your strength back."

Aunt Marge took slow and deliberate steps toward the bathroom. Sabrina walked with her, adding a secure brace to withstand any unsteadiness. Making it through the door, Aunt Marge grabbed the sink, turned to Sabrina and said, "Child, I am not the little one as you were, I think I can do the rest from here. I'll call you if I need help."

"Yes ma'am, go right ahead and do your thing. I will be here if you need me. Please yell loud enough to wake up the next room."

"Sabrina, you're such a smart ass. That's one thing that will never change. Cute but smart mouthed as heck."

A nurse entered the room just as Sabrina returned to her seat. "Where is Ms. Blaine?" she asked.

"Oh, she made it to the bathroom," replied Sabrina.

"That's a great sign. I think the doctor will release her in the morning after her test results come back. You should think of heading home. I know it's been a long day for you. I will be here all night and you can call me anytime you feel the need. She's in good hands."

"Is it still okay to stay the night? Either it will be me or my sister, Simone, who will return in a few minutes."

Aunt Marge entered the room without assistance. She slowly walked to the bed, saw the nurse and greeted her, "How are you sweetie?"

"I'm doing quite fine, Ms. Blaine. I see you are doing pretty well too."

"I don't plan on being here very long. There are things I have to get back to."

"The way you're showing improvement, I bet you will be out of here tomorrow. As a matter of fact, you'll be discharged tomorrow after the doctor briefs you with the test results." Simone entered the room just as the nurse told Marge of the discharge plan.

"Aunt Marge, that's great news."

"Yes it is, Simone. I am ready to go home and get into my own bed."

"You haven't been here for an entire day yet. How can it be that bad?"

"Hey, Sabrina, is this what you wanted for dinner?"

Sabrina took the bag, viewed its contents and said, "Yes it is, sis, it's just the way I wanted it. You know, we have to decide who is going to stay for the night."

"No problem, I can stay for sure. My office doesn't expect me in tomorrow."

"Neither of you have to stay," said Marge.

"She's right," the nurse commented, "We have it under control and it's what we do best."

"Well, I'm sorry but it's a plan. Simone, you stay here tonight and I will stay with her at her house tomorrow evening. I'll be there right after my shoot," said Sabrina. "Sorry, nurse, it's for our sanity that we have to look out for our aunt."

For a short period, the three women watched television. The network show was one of Aunt Marge's favorites. Comforting as it seemed, those hospital chairs were too uncomfortable to really relax. Sabrina showed discomfort from being in the hospital all day. She started fidgeting enough that Simone nudged her.

"Sabrina, do you have to?"

"No. Well, yes, I do. These chairs are so uncomfortable. Do you think you'll need anything from your apartment tonight?" asked Sabrina.

"No, I'll be fine."

The nurse walked in with a blanket for Simone. "Here you can use this and since the second bed is empty, you can sleep here tonight."

Sabrina stood up, took the blanket and replied, "Thank you very much. You're too kind."

Sabrina ended her call and wondered if she'd done the right thing. *Whatever it is, I put my desires up front with him. Any man can handle being told what do to, or given the opportunity to think he knows what to do. I'm proud I picked up being direct and forward in college. It paid off quite well, though it didn't help my image with the other girls on campus, it was great with the fellas.* She finally listened to her phone messages, she tapped the play button. "Beep! New message, called today at 11:00 a.m. Hi, Sabrina, it's Marie. I'm calling to remind you of your shoot tomorrow afternoon. I scheduled the shoot for 1:30 so you can visit your aunt first thing in the morning. Call me if you need anything. End of message. Beep! New message, called today at 11:15 a.m. Sabrina, I heard about Aunt Marge. Call me when you get this message. Love much and hang in there. End of message." *You can count on Dale to find out things so quickly. I wonder if Simone called him.*

"Beep! New message, called today at 12:00 p.m. Hi, Sabrina, this is Dan from the McKenzie shoot. I hope things are going well. We are very sorry to hear of your family emergency. If there is anything we can do, please don't hesitate to call, but of course go through your agency first as a courtesy. Hope we'll see you soon. End of message. No new messages…beep."

Sabrina sat in her bedroom at home, looking at family pictures as tears rolled down her cheeks. The concern for Aunt Marge suddenly hit her when the picture of Simone, Aunt Marge, and Sabrina seemed to glare back at her from the dresser. She couldn't hold those tears in any longer. She cried with fear and pain, a true concern for her loving aunt who is supposed to be healthy. Even though the doctors for caution's sake advised to have a test done tomorrow morning, she wanted them over with and for Aunt Marge to get a clean bill of health. Sabrina dropped to her knees on the side of the bed and began to pray in between sobs.

"Lord, I know you are the almighty powerful one who bestows blessings upon all who seek your will. I ask that you look over one of your loving and faithful servants, my Aunt Marge. I ask that you watch over her and wash away her illness. Please give her the health to live a good life. She has been good to all and a true blessing to this earth. For all things and in your name I pray. Amen."

Chapter 3

Worth the Chase

Three days passed after Aunt Marge's hospital visit. Doctors insisted she stay for observation after the results of her scan and blood test. The girls alternated staying overnight even though the medical staff would inform them of any changes. One evening, Sabrina stepped into the hospital corridor with the intention of meeting that handsome guy she met. She looked left down the hall and hoped that he'd entered the passage way so that they might continue flirting. Not seeing any sign of him, she stepped lively towards the nurse's station. During her approach, Sabrina looked in each direction as if the doctor might appear.

Faint noises echoed the halls, giving her a creepy feel. Even though it was past 10 p.m., Sabrina's hopes of running into the doctor held her close with anxiety. She remembered the business card he had given her, pulled the card out of her purse, read it again, and contemplated calling at this late night hour.

Lorenz arrived to his station and exited the train. He walked upstairs to the street, turned left, and dodged people along the path to his apartment. In front of his apartment building teenagers were hanging out on the sidewalk. Across the street was a playground where younger kids could enjoy themselves.

Early summer mornings, Lorenz went to the park to watch the sunrise or take in the new day. That is if he returned from his shift at a decent hour. He normally took time to meditate and contemplate on his activities to achieve his plan. By visiting the park, he met a lot of the neighbors, many of whom were mostly nice people. And as usual, once they discovered his plans and marital status, they always seemed to set him up on a blind date. Either she was a near relative or a close friend. Fortunately for Lorenz, he had little time to venture on a date and seemed to have too much on his plate. He focused on multiple activities and was too busy to notice women during public service programs or amongst the staff at the hospital.

Today was very unusual for him because of free time. He reminded himself of beautiful and impressive woman he met. Headed into the apartment building, he walked up to the second floor, turned right, and headed to the last apartment on the left. He unlocked the door, entered, and heard his answer machine beeping, indicating new messages. Having thoughts of Sabrina, he'd forgotten to stop at his mailbox, which was outside of his normal routine. Then the phone rang.

"Hello."

"Hi, Lorenz, how are you," Sabrina asked. "Or should I say Doctor Maynard?"

"Hi, is this Sabrina? You can call me anything comforting to you."

"Good, I'll call you Lorenz." She smiled and chuckled. "Did I catch you at a bad time?"

"No, actually it's good timing. I just walked in. I was wondering if I would be hearing from you."

"I don't mean to be forward or seem aggressive. I would like to get to know you better."

"Actually, a woman making the first move is refreshing."

"Thursday 7:30 sounds like a charm. Will I meet you and do you like chivalry?"

"Chivalry of course, but if the activity you choose is convenient for us to meet, then I am open to either. Your call; let me know where. Let me give you my cell number."

"Okay, let me write it down," Lorenz recorded the number on a business card in his wallet. He highlighted it by writing Sabrina with a 1 centered in the circle. Repeated the number to Sabrina and asked, "When is the best time to contact you?"

Sabrina answered, "Anytime. Leave a message if I don't answer. Talk to you later, I have to go."

"Bye, and thanks for calling." He placed the phone back on the stand, walked to the calendar and highlighted Thursday by writing "7:30 date/Sabrina." Lorenz recalled he needed to retrieve the mail. He left the apartment headed for the mailboxes on the first floor. While opening his mailbox, a neighbor walked in.

"Hi, Lorenz, how's it going?"

"Hey, hey, Robin, it's going pretty good today."

"Wow, that's the most you've spoken to me on any occasion. It must be a great day for you."

"Yes, it is. It was a great day," he replied with a dimple-accented smile on his face.

"You know, it would be nice hearing what made you so happy. Care to visit for a while?"

"No thanks. I have some studying to do," Lorenz hesitated and then responded, "Actually, sure, why not?"

Robin smiled as she led the way to her apartment, the one adjacent to Lorenz. They never got a chance to share in conversation as Robin always observed Lorenz in passing. Today, her excitement flourished a long desire was finally answered. Robin kept tabs on his activities and then how he'd arrive late and leave early. She also noticed how Lorenz rarely had few visitors. Maybe one or two of his fellow interns would drop by, and on one occasion she took over baked goodies. Lorenz's friends seemed more grateful even though he said thank you. Robin was excited to finally get an opportunity to get close to Lorenz. She opened her apartment door and invited him to sit on the couch. He entered the apartment, picked up a magazine, and thumbed through the pages. Robin left the living room on the way to her bedroom. "Let me get comfy and I'll be right back. Make yourself at home." Lorenz took a seat on the couch and picked up the picture album and shuffled through the pages. He saw Robin youthful poses with her friends and family. Robin then returned, dressed in sweats. She observed his interest in her photo album and quickly asked if he'd like anything to drink, breaking Lorenz's concentration. "Sure," Lorenz said.

"I have juice, tea, and water."

"Water is okay with me. Thank you."

Robin returned to the couch and placed a glass of water in front of Lorenz. He put the album down and took a sip from his glass. "You have some interesting pictures."

"Yes, I like the camera," Robin giggled. "I don't think it shows how much fun I had taking them."

"Where did you take most of those pictures as a kid?"

"I grew up near District of Columbia. It was fun growing up in Northern Virginia. We always had something to do. How about you? Where did you grow up?"

Lorenz took a moment before answering. He knew it wasn't a straight answer as most civil service and military kids moved a lot. "We moved quite a bit when I was a kid. My dad was a civil servant and moved us where there were opportunities for his career. We lived in nearly every military city on the east coast. My siblings and I used to joke to start packing after two years."

"That must have been hard making friends."

"No, not really because we kept each other entertained. I have a cousin who is one hell of a character. You know, the kind of person who keeps you laughing."

"I know the type you're talking about."

"Besides, he's more like a brother than cousin. We visit my parents in Carolina every so often."

"Is that where you finally graduated from high school?"

"No, but I attended undergrad at a small university in North Carolina, Campbell University. It is a school close to the Triangle near other major North Carolina universities."

"Smaller schools have better student-teacher ratios."

"I think so, it's why I got into medical school."

"Was being a doctor something you always wanted to do?"

"You know," Lorenz paused before answering, just to gauge where he'd like the conversation to go. Things were getting a bit personal but he decided to answer. "Yes, I think so. It's like we do things as a kid and it falls into place. I watched my brother, Dan, punch our father with such force that he knocked him to the floor. My other siblings couldn't believe it and just stood there. I had taken a class on vital signs and how to find them. I took Dad's vital signs just like I was taught. He was knocked out, so I woke him up. Man, that guy didn't mess with Dan anymore. It was kind of funny, but scary. I guess it was a combination of drinking and Dan's punch that knocked him out."

"Oh, those drunken fighter types."

"I watched a few of those as a kid. But when Dan knocked Dad out, it was no more of those. I'm grateful for him doing it. I never wanted to be one like that. Dan ended up in the Marines."

"Marines? I guess he had no fear."

"Actually he liked the idea. And so did Dad." Lorenz laughed with the comment as he recalled his father being happy that Dan left home. "It was different without Dan around, and yet Dad changed his ways. He stopped drinking, which alone is another story."

"Interesting. My parents didn't drink or smoke. I can only imagine how you must have been with your dad."

"Actually, it wasn't bad except for those days he was in a drunken stupor. Otherwise I had a great relationship with my dad."

"So the incident with your father sparked your interest in becoming a doctor."

"Yes, that and one in school when I resuscitated a kid on the football field. He was hit pretty hard and it knocked him out. Once everyone got up, he didn't move. I ran over and checked his vitals and resuscitated him. I did what any kid would have done. By the time the ambulance arrived, he was sitting up. Not moving, but breathing freely and coherent as if nothing happened. The guy quit the team that day."

"Sounds like being a doctor was your calling."

"I didn't have any other idea of being something different. Enough about me, what did you do in your younger years?"

Robin paused before responding by taking a sip of her water. She wanted to impress Lorenz, but her life was pretty simple. She was the typical middle sibling with two brothers. She wasn't an athlete, but she played sports with her brothers in the yard and playground. She didn't date much in high school, nor was she the popular one amongst teenage girls, but what she wanted to keep his interest. "I'm a simple girl with lots of friends. I think I was pretty normal."

"Really, I bet, as nice as you are, you were the center of attention."

"No, not the center, but nice is something I'll accept." Robin smiled after her response. "You know, one kind person finds another in turn."

"I believe so."

"So, is that why you're nice to me?"

"Actually," Lorenz hesitated for a moment, "I didn't realize how nice you were until some of my classmates talked about coming over and asking if you'd bake. The embarrassing thing was I couldn't answer. Only a kind and thoughtful person would do such a thing."

"You know I love baking! I'm watching my weight and since no one else is here to eat it, you are always welcome to anything I pull from the oven."

"You can drop your baked goods by any day. I can even take them to the hospital and our staff will gladly devour whatever you bake."

"You wouldn't think I am being too forward?"

"No, not at all. I hope to someday repay the kindness."

"I'm sure there will be a time."

"Let me get this straight: all you did in high school and college was bake?"

"No, not at all, I was involved in a few clubs, like drama, Spanish, and the arts. When I got into college, I decided to follow my parent's advice. I followed with accounting and finance. I really wanted to pursue art, but that major didn't seem to offer a career. I kind of did what I was told to, so I'm working as an accounting clerk."

"Oh, well, one day you'll get to do what you really like."

"I don't think so. I'm not talented enough at painting."

"Talent is in the eyes of the public and not yours. It's just my opinion. I have to get going, lots of studying to do. I'll catch you around." Lorenz said goodbye and headed to his apartment, mail in hand, and thinking of what just happened. Without a second thought of Robin, he skipped right to Sabrina and this coming Thursday. *What am I going to do for this date? I know she's probably spent a lot of time with better eye catching, classier, profound, and pretty financially stable men, but that doesn't matter. I know exactly what to do, so if my plan works, it will be one evening she'd always remember.*

Robin found a card in her mail, just after Lorenz left the apartment. She didn't read a return address and upon opening the card she smelled a wonderful fragrance. Without knowledge of who sent the card, she excitedly retrieved it from the envelope. The card cover was beautifully covered with a floral print and a heart in the center. She opened it and began to read:

> If one-night mist is not the time
> Then morning dew delight
> My wish or may to be with you
> Will come when time is right
>
> Admiration near but far
> From one with focused eye
> Tempest of the heart's desire
> Calmed by colored sky
>
> You are the one I wish to see
> Silence golden not true
> When the chance presents itself
> The one becomes the two

Without a signature on the card or return address, the sender was a total mystery. *Could Lorenz have sent this? No, he couldn't have. He didn't mention it while he was here. Maybe he did it to thank me. Could the next step be inviting me for a date? Oh, that will be a day to remember!*

Lorenz finally opened his mail. Not noticing anything out of the ordinary, he placed the mail on his desk. It was his normal routine – pay bills, study, shower, and sleep. While in the shower, he thought, *Tomorrow is different. I have to plan my date with Sabrina.*

Chapter 4

Health and Romance

In the early morning, Aunt Marge awoke to Simone's light snore. It reminded her of when Simone's mother brought the young girl to visit the first time. Simone had snored all night and woke Marge with a frightful yell. "Simone!" yelled Aunt Marge. "Simone, wake up. Wake up, you snoring hen. Why are you making all that noise so early in the morning?"

Simone answered, "Huh?"

"People are walking the hall trying to find where the loud noise is coming from."

"Aunt Marge, you can't be serious. I don't snore and you know it!"

"You are here for me, right? And since I am up, you should be too."

"You haven't changed a bit, Aunt Marge. Still as crazy as ever. You never allowed us to sleep in when we visited as kids."

"You know it isn't good to sleep your life away. When the sun comes up, you should be too. Didn't I teach you anything at all when you were a child?"

"What time is it, Aunt Marge?"

Marge turned the television on and searched for the information channel. The nurse entered the room, softly speaking, "I thought I heard talking. Good morning, Ms. Marge."

"Good morning," Marge replied.

"Good morning," Simone whispered. "What time is it?"

"It's nearly six-thirty," said the nurse.

"Six-thirty in the morning? That's impossible. I feel like I just fell asleep."

"Well I am glad you are up, Ms. Marge. Your first appointment for testing is at eight-thirty and all should be done by noon. I think you should try to have breakfast and be ready for the technician to take blood by eight-fifteen. Is that okay?"

"That's all fine, but I am ready to go home now.

"Stop being cranky, Aunt Marge," implored Simone.

"No problem. I get that all the time. I know you'd rather be in your own home than a hospital," responded the nurse as she exited.

"Well, at least the nurse understands the importance of comfort," replied Marge.

Marge moved her legs off the bed. She hesitated to stand, completely overcome by feeling, dizzy and shaking hands . She waited by the side of the bed with her feet on the floor. Simone jumped to her aid. "Are you okay, Aunt Marge?"

"Child, I am fine, when you're as old as I am, you'll move slower and shake too."

"I don't think that's all it is, Aunt Marge. Look we are here to ensure we know the condition of your health. If you don't tell us, we won't know the extent of your illness."

"What gives you the impression that I'm ill?"

"We are here, aren't we? You were found in the street by some man jogging by your block. If it wasn't for him, who knows what would have happened to you. Let me help get you to the bathroom." While Marge was in the bathroom, Simone took the liberty of ordering breakfast for her. Reading the menu card, she decided on two eggs over easy, cereal, juice, and hot tea and left it for the nutrition clerk who visited during meal times. Simone would pick up a bran muffin from the cafeteria later for herself.

Aunt Marge was a harden warrior at fighting ailments. She used home remedies to settle any sickness, but when things got out of hand she would visit a doctor. This time she thought it was best to try herbs and Oriental medicines because she experienced similar symptoms some time ago. Marge didn't believe that doctors knew what they were looking for testing or why they wanted her to stay for observation. She thought her condition was from a cold she was fighting.

At 6:30 in the morning and Rodney was back at his exercise routine. He stepped outside the door to start his morning run. After the routine stretching, he took off on his second route, a total of six miles today. Rodney was feeling good and it was time for a heart-pumping, lose-a-few-pounds run. Turning the first corner, he passed oncoming pedestrians as they approached. Many people were walking their dogs, sitting out on the stoop with coffee, or picking up the newspaper. Huffing and puffing through the first quarter mile, Rodney began to have second thoughts about his six-mile attempt. Pain crept up through his legs, breathing was difficult, and his lower back is prickled with pins and needles. *Gotta keep going.*

Just as he finished his first mile, a drastic pain shot through his chest. Slamming into the ground, Rodney fell. He landed right on the grassy knoll next to the cement sidewalk. He rolled to his back and felt the pain grow in his chest. He could only manage short, shallow breaths and almost hyperventilated as his heart raced. Lying there, facing the morning sun, he grasped his chest from the pain and tried desperately to breath and stay conscious. The pain was crushing and his arm started to numb. *I am too young for a heart attack!* Summoning all of his strength, he rose to his feet to walk home. He sat on a street bench for a minute or two before trying to make it back to his apartment. When he walked in, he immediately called his doctor's office for an emergency appointment.

"Hello, Doctor Tyler?" he shouted with panic.

"You have reached the office of Doctors Tyler and Willis. Our office hours are…"

Rodney decided to call his friend Dan. He fumbled the phone in his fingers. As he was gripped by chest pain, he slammed his fist on the desk to catch his fall.

"Dan, I need you to take me to the hospital."

"What happened?" asked Dan. "Are you okay?"

"No, I have this excruciating pain in my chest and it's getting worse. Hurry!"

"On my way! Keep the door open."

Within minutes, Dan arrived. He entered and found Rodney laying on the floor, still breathing, but faintly. Immediately he checked for a pulse and Rodney opened his eyes.

"Dan, you made it. Help me up."

"Sure. Hang on, man, we'll have you in the car in no time." They entered the car and took off down the street. Racing to the emergency room, Dan ignored the speed limit and dodged traffic as best as possible. Not knowing for sure how dangerously ill Rodney was, his increased urgency helped him decide to drive faster with hopes of getting a police officer's attention. He sped through busy streets of Richmond, screeching tires at every turn. Within another block, they arrived at the hospital. Dan jumped out of the car, grabbed Rodney and placed him over his shoulder. He ran into the emergency room and captured a nurse's attention. Rodney, slumped over Dan's shoulder, nearly passed out because his lungs were pressured. He gasped for air and whispered, "Put me down."

Dan did just that…hastily flopped Rodney down in a wheelchair. "Sorry about that, but my friend really needs attention. Can you help him?"

"Yes," replied the nurse. "What's the problem?"

"His chest, he's in dire pain, he can barely breathe, and he nearly passed out."

"Is he allergic to anything that you know of?"

"I don't know; you'd have to ask him."

"Who knows his medical history?"

"I guess his family will know, but unfortunately I don't have the number."

"What's your friend's name?" the nurse asked Rodney.

"Rodney, Rodney Witherspoon."

"Are you allergic to any type of drugs?" asked the nurse.

"No, but can you help settle my pain??"

"I hope so, if you help me. Did you take anything within the last 24 hours?"

"No," Rodney answered while holding his chest.

"When did the pain start?"

"This morning during my run. The pain stopped me dead in my tracks."

The nurse rolled Rodney into an emergency bed section for doctor's review. A young doctor entered the room. Dr. Lorenz Maynard started his review of Rodney and performed routine checks. He asked Rodney, "What's your name, sir?"

"Rodney Witherspoon," he replied.

"Does your family have a history of heart trouble?"

"No," he answered softly.

"Are you taking any medications?"

"No."

Lorenz ran through the routine screening of Rodney. He ordered an EKG and fluids. He then told the nurse to give Rodney a couple of Tylenol; a strong dose to stop the pain and decrease the swelling in his chest. Before continuing to his next ER patient, Lorenz said, "Nurse, please set up an EKG and call me when the results are back." As the nurse left, he turned to Rodney and said, "Mr. Witherspoon, we have to test your heart and see if you suffered a heart attack. It seems like you had an angina pectoris event. The right thing for us to do is run the EKG to make sure of my prognosis. After the EKG, I will give you further instructions. Everything should be fine."

Rodney replied, "Okay, doc," as he settled down and his breathing improved.

***

Walking down the hall from her aunt's room, Simone was headed for the cafeteria. To avoid a bustle of patient traffic, she had taken a detour to by passing through the ER hallway.

At the cafeteria, Simone ordered a ham and cheese omelet, lightly browned toast, and two slices of bacon. When she received her order, she paid the cashier and rushed return to Aunt Marge's room. Earlier that morning while passing by the ER, Simone had seen a man who looked like Rodney slumped over the shoulder of a friend, *That guy looks really familiar*, she had thought, *I wonder where I've seen him.*

Now, Simone, carrying her breakfast, encountered the man she guessed was Rodney's friend just as she reached the elevators. The man asked, "What's for breakfast?"

"Hey, didn't I see you earlier with a guy over your shoulder?" asked Simone.

"Yes, you did," replied Dan. "It was my friend Rodney. He felt chest pains while running."

"Does he run a lot?"

"Yes, nearly every morning. He's nuts, but you have to admire his discipline. Why do you ask?"

"Well, he looks familiar, so I wanted to see if my memory was right. Does he work downtown?"

"As a matter of fact, he does. He works at the advertising agency near the center of town. You look like someone I know... Are you related to Sabrina Willingham?"

"She's my sister. I'm Simone," she answered.

"You two have a great resemblance. You wouldn't happen to be a model too, would you?"

"Most people recognize me as Sabrina's sister all the time. It happens when you have a popular sibling. No, modeling is not the life I'd like to have or profession I'd care to venture. So what about you? What is it that you do?"

"I am at the advertising agency as an account specialist. The name is Dan. I'm so sorry to cut this short, but I need to go and speak to Rodney's doctor," Dan started down the hall. Looking back, he said, "It was nice talking with you and I hope your breakfast isn't cold."

"Nice chatting with you, Dan." *At least I know it was Rodney for sure*, she thought while strolling back to Aunt Marge's room. Stepping off the elevator to Aunt Marge's room she walked with thoughts of Rodney and her conversation with Dan. *I hope he gets better*!

***

Sabrina woke early morning for her routine Pilates class. She bounced out of bed, dressed in her workout clothes, and headed to the 5:30 a.m. session. The gym was relatively full this morning. Just in time for the class, she quickly found a spot on the floor and waited for instructions from the instructor. After her workout, Sabrina went home and changed, ate a quick breakfast, and headed for the train station to the hospital to visit Aunt Marge. It was 8:00 as the train stopped at the hospital transfer point. Sabrina walked through the corridor directly in front of the nurses' station and entered Aunt Marge's room.

"Hello, pretty lady," Sabrina spoke to Aunt Marge.

"Good morning, my little angel," replied Aunt Marge.

"Hey, girl, how was your night?" asked Simone while she munched on breakfast.

"There's nothing like sleeping in your own bed. And speaking of that, when are you ready to get out of here, Aunt Marge?"

"I have a few more tests this morning and then I should be allowed to leave. God knows there's nothing like being home."

The nurse entered the room and asked, "Ms. Marge, are you ready for your first test?"

"Yes, I am," replied Marge. She moved from the bed and settled into the wheel chair.

"Aunt Marge, would you like me to come along?" asked Simone.

"No, I think the nurse and I will be just fine. Simone, you should go get cleaned up and get some rest. Even though you slept here last night, I know you didn't sleep well. I will see you here this afternoon. Love you two very much!" she shouted while being rolled out the door.

Simone, yawning from an emotional draining night, gathered her things before heading out. "Sabrina, are you going to work now?" Simone asked.

"Yes, that's the plan."

"Can I ask you a funny question? Are you working with a guy named Rodney?"

"Ah, I think so. Is he like an account manager or something for the Sapphire Marketing Agency?"

"Yes, that's the guy. He's here in the hospital for chest pains. His friend Dan told me about it. I ran into him when I headed to the cafeteria this morning."

"Really, he is so young and in good shape too. It would be horrible to be in a medical condition so young. I should drop in on him and see how he's doing. Want to come?"

"Oh, I'd love to, but I look so horrible. You go ahead and I'll call you later and see what we should do to pick up Aunt Marge and get her home."

"That's a great idea. Let's talk later and I'll tell you how things went with Rodney."

"Why would you do that?"

"Let's face it, you only ask about a man if you are interested in him. I don't think you've met the guy, sis."

"Well, I met the guy in the parking lot nearly a week ago and got his card, but I haven't called. I'm waiting for him to call me."

"That's a little old fashioned. How do you know he isn't waiting for you to call him?"

"I am sure he is sitting by the phone every night just waiting to get my call. Surely he must have things going on or he would have called me by now."

"You assume a lot of things, don't you? He should be calling you right as he leaves the hospital. Just you wait and see. Remember the guy you were interested in back in high school? You waited for that phone call and it never came. Years later you ran into him and the first thing he told you was how much of a crush he had on you the entire senior year. But as usual, you never made a move. You're repeating that mistake again. I think you should just call him and see where it goes. Better yet, why don't you go see how he's doing and get a read off of him? You can do it on our way out."

"That sounds a bit bold. He's in the hospital, for heaven's sake."

"No, that's just following your gut. Go on, sis, you can do this. If he isn't interested, at least you'll know and be able to move on."

"Ugh. We can talk about my love life another time, Sabrina. Now what are we going to do about the reunion?"

"Oh, that's next on my agenda. I think we have to get a letter out to the family. I'll construct a sort of 'scare them to come but not in grief' letter, if you know what I mean. I don't think we can pull everyone here without it. Family normally comes together only when there's a death or a wedding. And I want them to come while Aunt Marge can still enjoy seeing them."

"If you send that kind of letter, they are going to think the worst. Aunt Marge does not accept sympathy. Let me think of another way to invite them. You start planning the entertainment. Let's make this reunion an event that Aunt Marge will never forget. Well, I have to go home and change before heading into the office. Are you okay here with Aunt Marge?"

"Sure, you go ahead, I have everything covered. I'll call you with an update if something comes up."

Simone left the hospital and set out for home. She intentionally strolled past the emergency area hoping to see Rodney or his friend. She scanned the room, but unfortunately she didn't see either of them there. Deflated, she walked out of the hospital. *I wished at least one of them were around. I could have reminded Dan to tell Rodney to call me, she thought.* Arriving at her car, she noticed a piece of folded paper tucked in the wiper blade of the windshield. She grasped the note, unfolded it, and began reading:

Simone,

> Thanks for asking about me. It's nice to know you remembered me from weeks ago. I guess you too left an everlasting impression. I'd love to ask you out for milk (doctor's orders to cut down on the caffeine). Please call when you can.
>
> Rodney
>
> P.S. If this isn't Simone's car, please accept my apologies.

Smiling, she started the car, buckled her seatbelt, and put the car into reverse. Holding the brake, she turned around for a good look before pulling back. Just as the car began to move, she wondered where she might have put Rodney's information. Reaching for her purse, she slammed on the brakes, stopping the car short of hitting a passerby. She rummaged for any loose business card, but none was Rodney's. *Why didn't he write the number down? That would have been so much easier! I don't recall throwing that card away. It must be at the office.*

***

Rodney and Dan drove back to Rodney's apartment. "Dan, do you think it was smart to leave Simone a note like that?"

"I guess we'll have to find out! It was a little enigmatic. Do you think she still has your number?"

"Well this will be a true test to her interest. If she's really interested, she'll have to find me. And when she does, it will be an award for us both. I think asking her out for milk was smooth. I thought she'd get a chuckle out of it."

"But, man, that is a serious game you're playing. Do you really think it will work?"

"Believe me; a woman loves a challenge. And if she doesn't, then it's not worth the effort for me anyway."

"Okay, you may have lost a great woman there because of that silly note. What will you do if she doesn't call you within a week?"

"I may call her and invite her to lunch."

Dan sighed and makes a face of confusion as he listens to the latest groove on the radio. "Man, you are tricky. I don't get it. I don't understand why you make it so challenging. Most women I know would toss the note without a second thought."

"You know, the kind of women you date aren't really, well, they seem kind of short on the intellect."

"Rodney, that's cold, man, that's real cold."

46

"I'm only kidding, Dan. It's a fact that you have wonderful taste. Look at your last girl, she was wonderful and funny. She held her own."

"That didn't last. She sort of fell off the fun wagon. The theater and museums were a little too inactive for me. And she asked so many 'what are you thinking?' questions. She would get furious with me."

"I understand to some extent. So you keep the simple and interesting women close; easy to entertain, right?"

"I see them being much more fun and less pressure. I still think I've found some bright women. Remember Crystal? She was fantastic! A great cook, loved the outdoors, and was very athletic. I just couldn't take her to an office event. I don't think she would do well in those business crowds. She would not think before commenting on a subject. She's really opinionated without tact. I would have to interrupt any conversation and be a watch dog for damage control."

"She was a looker too."

"And that she was. A fine woman who hopefully isn't dating anyone. I shall call as soon as I get back to my apartment."

"You do that, but keep it simple - just joking."

***

Minutes later, Sabrina called her agent for her shoot schedule. No answer. She left a message for a return call. Aunt Marge returned to the room for her discharge after all those tests. While waiting for the doctor's visit, Marge prepared for the trip home. Packing everything she can, she placed all clothing items in a bag that Sabrina brought with her on the first visit.

"Sabrina, aren't you going to help me?"

"Sure, Aunt Marge. What is it you'd like me to do?"

"Grab the flowers and all those cards for me, sugar child."

"What are you going to do with those dying flowers?"

"Child, don't you know flowers can be dried and used for very lovely decorating? You'll see when we return to the house. Make sure you put them in the bag and don't damage them."

"Yes, ma'am, I will take care of these flowers." The phone rang. Sabrina answered.

"Sabrina, it's Phil, how are you?"

"Fine, Phil, it's about time you called."

"I wanted to contact you this morning. There is nothing strenuous or exciting happening today, but you have one shoot scheduled that's no real challenge. It's a basic studio shoot for a perfume account. I'm sure you'll look your best as you always do."

"Well, nice hearing it's something easy. What time and where is this shoot?"

"It's off Simmons and Yorkshire Streets, call Jamie at 555-949-1112. Make sure you call him early enough and confirm your time. I'd hate to pay a fine for bungling the shoot with a no-show. Don't be late either! Last time I had to pay homage favors for a sick guy. It was gross as hell too."

"No doubt, a fine is the last thing I need these days. I'll call him as soon as we hang up."

"You do that. Do a bang-up job and it'll open doors for in the future. Talk to you later, good luck."

Sabrina fumbled with her notes for Jamie's number. She looked at her writing and couldn't make the last number. *Was it a five or two? I wrote it down so fast I didn't write clearly enough. Five, it's five. I'll try this number first.*

***

Lorenz tried his best to communicate with the young group of how to distribute donated flowers to senior citizens. Every week or so, a local florist group donated flowers to the community health center. The youth group took the flowers to multiple senior citizen homes throughout the community, and sometimes there were extra flowers for other locations. Senior citizens love to see the kids and especially spend time with them. As each child showed up with flowers, the residents had smiles and hugs to share. There is warmth for both the child and seniors. As a matter of fact, the children often spend time reading and playing games with those who seldom have visitors. It's a fantastic trade-off as each person entertains the other and friendships are born.

Such great friendships that people entertain each other in between the floral deliveries. Lorenz takes time out during his community services and in between studies to supervise multiple deliveries, communicate with kids on positive lessons of life, and encourage entertainment. During one visit, the kids started racing wheel chairs around the retirement homes. The funny thing was seniors were in the chairs enjoying the race. It was difficult to stop the action, but Lorenz felt responsible if something happened, so he stopped it after only a couple rounds. Just short of someone starting to complain about the races. "Doctor, you should be ashamed of yourself! It's dangerous for the kids to race around the building with the patients!" said the on-duty nurse, barely containing her smile at the rule-breaking fun.

"I understand, nurse. It's my mistake to let the kids have so much fun with the senior citizens. Thank you for correcting me. I don't think the kids did any harm and, of course, I think the patients loved it."

Lorenz walked over to the administrative office to schedule future visits from the community center. Since the kids were having so much fun with the inhabitants, he thought it was fantastic for the home to adopt some of the kids for their patients. It helped most of the elderly with their health and emotional stability. He walked into the office, and heard a conversation between an administrator and a perspective inhabitant. *That voice sounded very familiar.* He approached closer to the receptionist desk to listen in on more of the conversation.

"I think it's an amazing place you have here. How do you select your patients or residents? What is it that you expect from them as residents on rules and behavior? Is it only the cost identifying who you allow here?" confusing asked Simone.

"It's a combination of many things besides money and character. It's a combination of residents interviewing new prospective people and having them select their neighbor. It's amazing how patients feel contributing to their living conditions when they help choose their neighbor. And it's a happier environment for every individual," explained Ms. Whitmore.

"I see, it's a great way to have others come in and feel really accepted once they complete the interview process. I think Aunt Marge may be happy here if we present it well enough."

Immediately Lorenz recognized the voice once she mentioned Aunt Marge. He recalled the fantastic patient who responded to his care. It's nice to remember patients that embraced him, but most of all, its great how the patient has a wonderful attractive niece. *I need to make myself known to Simone before she leaves*, he thought. "Hi, Simone."

"Hi, do I know you from somewhere?"

"Sure you do. I attended to your aunt during her stay at the hospital, and your sister and I are supposed to have a date really soon."

"Oh, I remember Dr. What are you doing here? Are you visiting patients?"

"No, I'm here trying to set up this home as one of the regular visits with the community service I support."

"Oh, it's nice you do community service."

"Yes, it is. I love doing the service and finding great people whenever I can. What are you doing here, if you don't mind me asking?

"I am looking to see if it is appropriate for my sister and I to place Aunt Marge in this home. She's getting older and we can't help her living the way she did before she was found on the street. We can't be afraid to live our lives without thinking of her welfare. It just isn't possible for us to look after her as busy as we are."

"I understand, but how do you think she'll feel once you tell her of your idea? My impression is she wants to continue her life style and be the happy woman she is."

"Yes, Doctor, it's going to be challenging for her to accept. It's something my sister and I need to discuss."

"Your sister, now that is a very energetic woman. When will you talk to her again?"

"Later today we are meeting for dinner. Right after she leaves Aunt Marge with the nurse we hired."

"She and I are going out soon. I am excited about it too. Its like a date that's needed, greatly needed."

"Yeah, she told me about your date. I hope you two have fun. What are you planning?"

"I can't tell you, but I will tell you its simple and nothing extravagant. Heck, I can't afford anything beyond simple. Just can't do it right now."

"She knows, since being an intern brings limited funds. Don't worry, I am sure she'll like whatever you decide to do; no doubt."

"I have to get back to the kids. Please tell your sister and aunt hello for me. It was nice seeing you again."

"It was nice seeing you too, Dr. Lorenz. Nice talking to you."

Lorenz walked towards the lounge room where large noises of laughter were. He walked into the room, watched the wheelchair race, kids dressed like clowns in old clothing the citizens allowed them to use, a couple card games like black jack and poker, and a two fellas dancing the swing with a couple of elderly women. "*These kids sure know how to have a great time with senior citizens. I hate to end all the fun, but it's time for us to leave. We promised not to overdo it this visit*," he thought and said, "Sorry folks, but the fun has to come to an end."

Immediately the kids knew what to do. Without additional guidance, the kids and elderly began saying their goodbyes, cleaned up the mess, and started out to the center of the facility. The kids waved to the elderly as they walked towards the exits and told them how much fun they were today.

"We'll see you again soon," said Lorenz. "Let's get in the van, kids, and head back to the community center. We haven't much time."

Everyone climbed into the van and found their seat. Lorenz took the helm and started down the road.

"Hey, Lorenz," Rick called.

"Yes, Rick?"

"I hear you have a date. Considering how rare that is, I want to know, is she really pretty?"

"No," Fred jumped in. "She's just a girl that he likes. Looks have nothing to do with it, right, Lorenz?"

"She's awesome looking, smart, and I think a little sassy. She's the kind of girl you definitely take home to your mother."

"What type of girl is that supposed to be?" asked Elaine.

"Um, you know, the kind of girl you want everyone to like. You'll understand as you get older and start dating Elaine."

Almost in unison, Fred, Rick, and Elaine asked, "What's the plan for your first date?"

"You know gang; I really haven't thought about it yet. It can't be something fancy. I am not at the point where I can afford the great fun things. I guess it's got to be something simple, a little romantic, and of course cheap." They started laughing and snickering about being cheap for a first impressionable date. Elaine whispered to Rick, "You know we can help him out. I have an idea, are you game?"

Rick answered in a low tone, "Sure if it ain't gonna cost us too much. Fred, are you in?"

"In what?" Fred replied.

"Not so loud, silly. Are you helping Lorenz on his date?"

"Are you crazy, I don't have the money to help him. He's going to be the doctor and all. He can handle his first date impressing the lady."

"You know interns don't make much until they become doctors. Didn't you know? So, are you in or not? We want to do something nice for him."

"I'm in. So what do you two have in mind?"

"We can talk about it after we get to the community center."

Lorenz stopped the van in front of the center and instructs everyone to get out here so he can park the van in the drive. The kids jumped out and headed into the center. There was nothing exciting at all when they headed to the meeting room except the receptionist holding a note for Lorenz.

"Didn't Lorenz drive you guys today?" asked Jalissa.

"Yes." replied Fred, "he's parking the van and will be right in."

Lorenz entered the center and immediately handed a note from Jalissa. "You had a visitor today and she left this note. She was very nice and really interested in you, and she asked a lot of questions too. I didn't think she'd ever leave."

Chapter 5

Bringing Things Together

It was early evening when both Sabrina and Simone arrived at Marge's house. They entered, sat in the family room, looked at each and other allowed their silence to share personal disbelief. "I'm going to keep my mouth shut on this one. I can't believe we're thinking about it," said Sabrina.

"You know, Sabrina, the family will not like Aunt Marge in a home. They will be outraged if we place her there," said Simone.

"I know, but it's for the best. Who is going to look after her now? Are you going to schedule your work and life around her? I can't do it. I don't see any of our relatives jumping to her aid. And why should it be us who steps up and take the lead on these things anyway?"

"Did you call anybody about the reunion? I didn't get a call, e-mail, or letter from anyone."

"I don't think it's a good idea. You know, we're putting Aunt Marge in the grave before we even know if it's happening or not. I don't like the reunion idea anymore." She touched her forehead and shook her head. "I'm not for it like before. It sends bad vibes like we're losing her."

"Did you call anyone at all?"

"I called Diane but didn't tell her the entire picture."

"We've got to bring the rest of the family. What if she doesn't make it? And the more they know, the better it is. I always say, the sooner the better."

"Let me talk to Diane about it first. Maybe we're jumping the gun." Simone left Marge's house for Diane's apartment."

***

Rodney stood at the door of his apartment and watched his neighbor fumble with her keys. She seemed so distraught that she dropped the keys three times from her hand. "Hey, Diane, what's wrong? Can I help?"

"Nothing is wrong, Rodney," she said between sobs and sniffles of frustration, "nothing is wrong. It's been a bad day and I am ready for a serious wind down; a glass of whiskey has my name on it."

"Can I help you with the door? It doesn't seem to cooperate with you." In a swift move, Rodney picked up the keys, and with a nod from Diane, he inserted one into the lock. The door opened and he led Diane into her apartment. "Please have a seat, I'll pour you that whiskey and you can tell me about your day." Normally Rodney would share his frustrations with Diane on occasion. He would gripe about losing accounts or not making a marketing impact as he desired. Diane usually listened and gave simple advice, but this time Diane shared her conflict.

"Thanks, but I don't feel like talking about it. I appreciate your help. Could you do a favor and have some whiskey with me?"

"Sure, I don't mind. Whatever it takes to get you on track; what's a neighbor for?"

Rodney poured two whiskies, handed one to Diane and sat squarely in the recliner. Diane sat on the couch with her head in her hands, fraught with drama and confusion. "Rodney, I had a hard time at the office. I received a call from my pain in the ass boyfriend starting another fight. He canceled our weekend for a game with his friends. I hate going to those damn games. Then my cousin Simone called about our aunt being in the hospital. She said she would tell me about it later. When she called it didn't sound good. All I need now is for my best friend to share more bad news. You know, a person can only handle so much in a day."

"Sometimes it's just bad timing and things seem to happen all at once. It doesn't mean it's the end of the world. You have to find a way to cope with rough times." They sat there for a few minutes, said nothing, and sipped a swallow or two. In no time the whiskey glasses were empty and Diane said, "Thank you for being here for me. I appreciate it so much. I'll return the favor one day."

"You are welcome. Its what friends do." Rodney got up to leave and gently kissed Diane's forehead. "You'll get your chance. I'm sure I'll cry on your shoulders like all of the other times."

When Rodney stood, she gave him the look of contentment. "Thanks, Rodney, I really needed this. You have no idea."

"No sweat. Since you're feeling a little better, maybe we can head over to my place and I can fix dinner for us. You're in no mood for cooking."

"Ah, that's nice, but I have to take a rain check. I have too much to do this evening and besides, I still don't think I will be great company. My cousin is visiting and we need to talk."

"Tell you what, my door is always open if you change your mind. Just give me a ring."

"Thanks again, Rodney. You are too sweet."

Rodney left Diane's apartment for his place next door. He entered the kitchen, poured himself a glass of Chardonnay, and started his creation. Rodney was a master at work in the kitchen or, better yet, the wizard of creation. He cooked chicken and rice, strawberry and nut salad, and a green veggie. He made chocolate pudding with whipped cream. He would flair the chicken and rice with certain spices for the veggies. He enjoyed cooking for women. It motivated him to think of Simone, whom he expected to call later. Dinner was complete in 20 minutes. Rodney heard a knock on his apartment door. He laughed out loud that Diane changed her mind after she smelled his cooking.

"Just a minute, be right there," Rodney said.

"Okay," Simone said.

"Who is it? Is it you, Diane?"

"No. Is she home?"

Rodney opened his door and said, "I guess so, but she isn't here." He gasped as he recognized Simone. "Well, I'll be a lucky son of a gun." A smile cracked across his face and he gleamed from ear to ear. "I must have wished you up. I was just thinking about you," said Rodney.

"Oh, my goodness, you live in my cousin's apartment?"

"Diane is your cousin?"

"Yes, has been all of her life."

"Wow, you're cousin 'Simone,' right? What a coincidence! No, this isn't her apartment. It's the one next door."

"I didn't mean to disturb you. It's obvious I get confused which apartment is hers. You can tell I don't visit too often. I'm so busy with my job I rarely get out. I'm sorry to bother you." Simone said before turning towards her cousin's door, "I should check up on her. She didn't take the news of our aunt too well."

"Diane mentioned she had a bad day. Maybe you can get her to have dinner with me, and please include yourself as my guest. I'd love you to taste of my cooking." Simone turned from Diane's door and said, "You cook? Are you a good cook?"

"No doubt, one of the best if I have to say so."

"Okay, I'll try to get her to your place, but if all else fails, I'll come back and take you up on dinner. I wanted to talk to you anyway."

"Sounds like a plan to me."

Simone left for Diane's apartment and Rodney returned to the kitchen after he closed the door. Rodney filled an ice bucket and placed a bottle of Zinfandel he pulled from the wine rack in it. He put three wine glasses in the freezer. Rodney made an effort not to appear feminine so he set the table with simple tools of the trade. From napkins to dishes, he coordinated his presentation with quality. He kept his unique decorating taste a secret amongst his male friends. They thought everything in the apartment was selected by a former girlfriend or his mother.

The adobo chicken and wild rice dish gave a mouthwatering aroma, which filled the apartment. Rodney cooked with such talent that many asked if he'd open a restaurant. Back in the kitchen, Rodney took a sneak peek at the veggie dish. He added a little zippy hot sauce for flavoring and turned the fire down a little. "It's just about ready. I hope Simone and Diane comes over soon." The phone rang and Rodney said, "Hello."

"Hey, Rodney, we can smell dinner and it's making me hungry. Diane and I will be over in a few minutes if that's okay."

"Are we on the same wavelength? That was my thought just before you called. Dinner is ready and come quickly before it gets cold."

"We'll be right there. Bye."

Simone put the phone receiver down and gathered her things to head next door. Diane stood from the couch and placed the last glass of whiskey down on the coffee table. She slightly stumbled as she went to the bathroom to freshen up.

"Diane, you know, Aunt Marge will be fine but we have to think of a way to take care of her. You surely aren't available to come in every day. Sabrina and I think we, all of the kids, should place her in a senior citizen home," Simone said.

"No way, it just isn't like her to want something like this," said Diane.

"Well, it's not what she wants, but it's something we have to do. We all have our own lives."

"I can understand," water from the bathroom sink made a loud noise making Diane nearly yell her response, "but maybe we can share the responsibility or work some sort of schedule to maintain her home and support her." Diane splashed her face with water.

"That is a good thought, but our dependability isn't the greatest. And the object is to share our time and not take one over the other doing our own thing. Which of us is willing to start sacrificing our careers?"

"I see your point." Diane walked from the bathroom into the living room, "But she is so sweet. You know we love her to death."

"Are you ready for dinner? Rodney finished cooking and we need to head over right now."

"Yes, I'm right behind you. I need to lock the door."

"I hope dinner tastes as good as it smells."

"Oh, girl, Rodney can seriously cook. You won't be disappointed."

The girls headed for the apartment door when Simone made it to the hallway and the apartment's phone rang. Diane said, "Hello? This is she. No, I will not accept the charges." She shook her head, hung up, and made her way to the door. "Some people never give up."

"Oh, was it someone you're trying to get rid of?"

"Yes, it is just that. A dead beat I should have never gotten involved with. We can talk about it later. But right now, let's go! I'm famished.".

"Ok, let's knock on the door and hope for the best."
Simone on Rodney's door. Rodney yells, "Just a minute," and placed finishing touches to the dinner table. Ok, all set for three. I hope they are ready and just in time too. Rodney briskly to the door and turns toward his counter and grabs two lilies from the flower arrangement. He opens the door and says "welcome ladies to my humble abode, presenting them with the lilies."

"Thank you for inviting us to dinner. We really appreciate it and the timing couldn't be better."

"Anytime, what are neighbors for?" smiling Rodney.

"Its nice having a great neighbor that looks out for another. You are so sweet. Where should I sit?"

"Simone, you sit here", Rodney pulls out the chair and places her at the east side of the table. "Diane, you are here" and he repeats the courtesy and places Diane at the opposite end of his position at the table. "I have wine prepared for you. If you don't mind, I'd like to serve the wine first and you two can sip on it while I prepare the plates."

"Sounds good to me" said Diane.

"Yes, its darling for me too", answered Simone.

Rodney gets the chilled wine glasses from the freezer. He places the glass in front of each person and then opens the wine for consumption. He pops the cork and pours each glass to the near rim. He places the wine in a chilled bucket for later. He then runs over the entertainment center and starts his music. All CDs were planned to provide a not too funky crowd or atmosphere, but one of true relaxation and enjoyment. Numerous love ballads start playing over the air as each song has a hint of island flair.

"Rodney, this is a nice CD. Did you compile it yourself or is it something you picked up?" asked Diane.

"Still in the kitchen preparing plates," Rodney answered, "Something I picked up from a friend. He dabbles in mood settings."

"Oh, this is supposed to set our mood to eat? I don't need to be in a mood to eat, just be hungry enough and you don't care about the music," said Simone.

All three chuckled to the Simone's comment. Rodney moves back to the kitchen and retrieves the plates. He places each dish in front of each of the girls and returns to the kitchen to get his. Returning to the dining area he takes his position at one side of the table. Sitting at the table, he asked, "Is there something else you need?" Rodney said.

"No," they answered in unison.

Settling in, he raised his hands asking the two to join him in dinner grace and with one motion, he grabbed their hands and said, "Father, bless this meal as it provides the goodness of the earth, the multitude of strength through the fuel for energy, and one connection of three spirits as we enjoy the savory taste of your creation. Thank you for my guests and their hunger, and may work in the kitchen please the hunger pain of the day. With all things of your grace and goodness, we pray. Amen."

"Amen," they said in unison.

Together they picked up their forks, filled them with food, and began to eat.

"Umm, if it were any better, we'd have to hire you," said Simone.

"I told you he could cook," said Diane.

"Thank you for the compliment, but you haven't gotten to the good part yet, wait until you taste the main course."

"Is that something you made especially for us?" said Simone, favoring him with a smile.

Taken aback by her quick comment, he thought hard to come back with a remark that didn't seem overly confident. "Ah, that's a sure thing. I want you to open your arms for every time I prepare a meal. I need you to want more at the drop of a hat and at the mention of my name. When you get hungry your mouth should water at the thought of my cooking."

"As if I don't every time I smell your cooking in the evenings," said Diane.

"You mean he cooks all the time?"

"I try to cook as often as possible, but my schedule only allows certain nights. I try to be creative as I consider my next move in the office. You know what I mean, don't you, ladies?"

While eating the meal, drinking wine, and enjoying the moment, Diane and Simone nearly finished while Rodney talked about his cooking. Rodney noticed how they both were such quick eaters and commented, "No one has ever eaten my dinner so quickly. Did you taste it all?"

"Of course we tasted it!"

Laughing, Rodney finished the last of his chicken adobo. He started on the vegetables and just before placing the next forkful in his mouth, he looked towards the kitchen for another bottle of wine. Simone saw him and immediately moved closer and sensually placed his fork in her mouth. "Mmmm, that's great for a second taste of those veggies."

Looking surprised and stunned, "You know, you took the best bite!" he said with a smirk.   Diane looked stunned and extremely surprised. "Simone, uh, we need to talk," she whispered.

"No, not now, later," she whispered.

"Simone, you know we should talk, now!"

"Okay, okay, let's go into the hall."

They both stood and walked across the apartment into the hall. Rodney rose to his feet and looked puzzled by their act. "Hey, is there something going on?"

"No, just a moment," they both said in unison.

"Oh, okay, I guess."

They made it into the hall way and immediately Diane touched Simone's shoulder, looked into her eyes and said, "What are you doing?"

"What? I see someone very interesting and I'd like to snatch him up. Isn't he fine? The man can cook and keeps a clean apartment."

"He is a great catch. But should you throw yourself on him? You just met the guy."

"Oh, no, I met him a few weeks ago. He walked in the art gallery and we hit it off. I know he remembers, but I'm going to remind him of our encounter anyway."

"Then you do what you have too. He is a great guy and let me warn you, there are women dropping by here all the time."

"Shouldn't we talk about this later?"

"Yeah, we should get back. Just remember to take it easy and not be too aggressive. He can be a player, so watch your step."

"You sound as if there's history between the two of you."

"No, no history, just observation."

"Sure. Thanks for the info. Let me work my magic. By the time I get my hands on him, he won't need another woman in his life."

They returned inside the apartment, they found Rodney had just finished cleaning the kitchen. "I didn't know you two were coming back."

"We were in the hallway. We weren't gone for too long. Besides your cooking is fantastic and I wanted to finish the rest of my food. Not to make a pig out of myself, it's a compliment to your cooking," said Simone.

"Thanks, I appreciate the compliment. And since I didn't put everything away, I can make you a plate to take home."

"Thanks. What about that desert?"

"It's not included, because I'm not sure what you liked. I'll have to make you something the next time. Do you like soufflé?"

"Yes sounds good. Is there more wine?"

"It is," said Rodney as he retrieved the new bottle from his carafe in the kitchen. "Let me know what you like, and I'll get it together for the nest time."

"Any soufflé will do Rodney," Simone said. "I like a good soufflé."

"Good to know," Rodney said.

Rodney returned from the kitchen and poured wine in new glasses. He looked into Simone's eyes and said, "I hope you enjoyed the meal, the music, and the wine. Is there something else I can do for you to make your evening better?"

"Yes, you can," said Simone.

"No, you can't, everything is fine. Actually, it was excellent," said Diane.

Simone gave a look of disgust to Diane that signaled for her to head back to her apartment. Diane looked back and winked, shook her head from side to side indicating 'bad move.' In a heated whisper, Simone said, "Are you sure there's no history between you two?"

"No," she whispered.

"Rodney, everything was great. Your meal hit the spot. It was wonderful. When can we do it again?" said Simone.

"For you, it's just a phone call. As a matter of fact, I have an opening for this weekend. What's on your schedule?"

"Let's say my schedule matches your weekend of events."

"Okay, we're on. Let's make it Saturday night."

"Saturday night it is."

Diane took the last bit of her wine, stood and walked towards the door. She moved with a frustrated face, and thought, *It never fails, nothing changes with Simone. Every guy has to be someone she dives for. It didn't matter if I had my eyes on Rodney. She always moves on a notion and throws her claws at him. It could be a hundred guys in a room and she'd always go for the one I like. Never fails.* "Good bye, Rodney."

"Good night neighbor," said Rodney.

"Simone, are you coming?"

"No, I want to talk to Rodney for a moment or two."

"Okay. The door will be open. Just walk in."

"Thanks, Diane, I'll be right there."

Simone picked up the wine glasses off the table, and walked toward the kitchen. Rodney met her at the kitchen entrance and grabbed the wine glasses from her hand. In one smooth motion, he positioned himself for a quick, brisk kiss on her cheek. "Thank you for the glasses." Rodney moved to the living room. "Won't you join me?" He pointed to the couch and within an instant Simone took her seat opposite end of Rodney. "When did you realize you enjoyed dating?"

"That is an unusual question." Simone said as she looked at Rodney with a curious face. "If you want to know."

"I want to know."

"I was 14 when I had a crush on a boy in school. He was atrocious but I didn't realize it. I guess I liked him just because he gave me the right attention."

"The right attention? I guess most men would be lucky to spark your attention some kind of way. Has anyone done so yet?"

"Are you asking if I'm dating someone?"

"I'm asking."

"No, I'm too busy. The last guy was not quite my cup of tea. He didn't have the quality I wanted in a man, but he challenged my mind. I liked that about him."

"What did you do for fun when you were a teen?"

"You ask a lot of questions."

"How do you get to know someone if you don't ask?"

"I did a lot of things. I learned a lot, especially since my parents died when my sister and I were young. I zoomed through elementary school, I was a brownie, and by junior high, I was a junior achiever." Simone continued sharing her childhood with Rodney. By the hour, the two had covered their first dating rituals and even gotten to their hardships on finding a mate. Rodney shared his latest girl friend who didn't meet his expectations.

"You are something, aren't you?"

"Something?"

"Yes, different from other men, I sense there is much more to you than you reveal."

"There is always something special to every person. And showing all your cards at one time leads to a boring life."

"A boring life, you mean showing all leaves little to the intrigue of finding a lifelong partner? You know how challenging that is in today's society."

"Intrigue, you mean finding someone that you have a connection with on a mental level instead of the usual physical one?"

"Yes, finding that one. You have an idea of what we have to go through. Aren't you tired of searching?"

"Searching is half of the fun. The problem is the players expect too much too soon."

"You mean committing before you know the person?"

"Yes, you do look for that commitment and partnership in every person you date, don't you?"

Rodney moved over to the sink to begin washing the glasses. Not saying much, he contemplated his answers and Simone took notice. "Don't think too hard on that last question. You know all of us seek one special person to spend the rest of their lives with," said Simone.

"No, it's not what you think. It's different for me. Or should I say for guys in general. I don't see every woman as a potential lifelong partner. It's just not my way and I do believe most guys don't see it that way either. I mean, when you find the right one, you immediately know."

"That leaves room for a question or two. It also leaves room for assumptions. You have an idea of what type of girl is your dream woman, right?"

"Yes, I have an idea, but nothing I'd like to share with you tonight. I'd like to take time and find out more about you and our start is Saturday night. That way we can ease our way into something if we are compatible."

"Oh, I get it. Keep it as interesting as ever and the more you keep in the dark, the better it is at finding out. Isn't that a game people play?"

"No, no game. You don't lay all your cards on the table unless there is something specific about the guy you like right?"

"Ah, right. You are right. Let's keep this conversation open for the weekend."

"Exactly, let's keep this open and our eyes keen on each other."

"One day at a time and build on this night."

Moving closer to each other, Rodney embraced Simone, gave her a tender kiss on the cheek and said, "Here is the beginning of tomorrow and a step on a journey to the rainbow."

Simone said, "As long as we walk hand in hand, explore with an open mind, we'll laugh and play along the way, and fly the big blue sky."

"Fly the big blue sky?"

"I couldn't come up with anything else that quickly, but it works for the moment."

"Great," he agreed with a laugh.

Simone walked towards the door when she looked back and smiled before she said, "Bye Rodney and I look forward to Saturday night."

"I can't wait." Right after Simone walked out, he closed the door. *What did I just start?*

It wasn't long before after Simone left Aunt Marge's house, Sabrina sat in the parlor listening to her cell phone messages. She speed dialed a return number and waited for the ring. "Hello," Jamie said.

"Jamie, is it you? Thank goodness. I thought I misplaced your number, I wasn't sure I saved it right on my phone," said Sabrina.

"Sabrina, it's about time you called me. I've been patient for a while and you are pushing it so close to your next shoot. You need to be at Market Square, 9:30 in the morning, and meet the photographer today, seven o'clock at the bottom park by the lake. He's doing a shoot there and wanted to meet you and review the shoot strategy."

"Why tonight?"

"I don't know. I'm just the messenger. You need help getting there?"

"No. I can make it. Just don't understand those strategy meetings."

"You know, it's a part of the deal and profession."

"No, it isn't. Every time I see a photographer in the evening, it turns out to be some kind of sexual advancement. I am so tired of this. I can't wait until I find the one guy who respects me."

"Don't worry about this one, Sabrina. It's going to be different. Trust me on it."

"You say this-every time, Jamie. Don't worry, I'll be there."

Ending the call, Sabrina turned to her calendar for notes to her shoot. It was a shoot for a charity organization. *I see, so why should we have a strategy meeting for a charity shoot? It can't be something out of the usual charity organizations. I hope it isn't for hunger as I am sure going to eat at the restaurant.* She turned to her wardrobe and selected her outfit for the meeting. *Nothing seductive, nothing too plain, but something enticing and comfortable will do the trick.* She chose a pants suit.

***

Lorenz arrived at Market Square around 6:30 p.m., walked in the door and scanned the room for a table. He found an empty table, moved towards it and dodged other people at the door. "Excuse me," he said as he bumped one gentleman. The gentleman nodded and said, "I'm sorry, excuse me." Lorenz pulled out the table chair for one beautiful woman with a camera around her neck. He looked at ther closely and compared her to models; her face was very unique with luscious lips, eyes of gold, and a proportionate build most women would envy. Her skin was olive, and seemed smooth. Her hair was dark, brunette. Needless to say, guys gawked in awe in her presence, and as he looked around the restaurant, that's exactly what he saw men are. A waiter approached Lorenz' table and said, "Welcome to Market Square," as he handed Lorenz a menu, "May I start you with a drink while you look over our menu?"

"Water is fine. I'm looking for a photographer named Mikel, do you know of him?"

"Yes, and it's a woman, not a man. She is right over there," the waiter pointed at the lovely woman.

"No way," said Lorenz.

"Yes way. Is there a problem with a woman being a photographer?"

"No, no problem. I just didn't expect Mikel to be a woman."

"Most people don't. Should I bring your water to her table?"

"Yes, that will be the right thing to do. Thank you."

Mikel left her table and made her way through the restaurant, waving at multiple people. Lorenz observed her as she proved being a regular patron. Multiple people smiled and waved at her as she moved about the place and conversed with a select few. Mikel stopped at a specific table, large enough for six people. As she sat in the same location Lorenz assisted, two other guys walked up to the table and immediately sat after their artsy air kiss near each cheek greeting.

Lorenz thought, *I sure hope she doesn't expect me to do the same as those two. It might be fashionable, but it's not in my circle of things just yet.*" Mikel placed her camera on the table and reviewed the menu. "I guess I'll have the usual," she told the other two. Her usual was a calamari appetizer, blackened salmon steak, steamed vegetables, and coffee as her dessert. The guys nodded and turned to a waiter who stood by. They ordered and the waiter walked away. Lorenz walked toward Mikel and her friends' table. Just before he arrived the waiter who took Lorenz's drink order dashed to the table and placed the glass of water on it in front of an empty place. "Who is the drink for?" asked Mikel.

"It's for him, the guy walking to the table," said the waiter. "He said he has a meeting with you."

"Thanks, Tom."

"You're welcome," Tom said.

Lorenz sat at the table. "Hi folks," he said. "Mikel, I'm Lorenz and I represent the community center. I am supposed to be a part of the advertisement you are shooting. The director asked me to meet you here."

Mikel took his hand, looked him over and said, "They made a good choice. As soon as the other model arrives, we can get started. Please take a seat and give Tom your order." Lorenz ordered a salad and asked that it comes out with the main meal.

Sabrina walked in the door of the restaurant in a silky pants suit. Nicely fitting, and showed her features but conservative to reveal her skin. She stopped a waiter and asked for Mikel. The waiter directed her to the table in the rear of the room. She saw one woman with the three men. Sabrina arrived at the table and said, "Which one of you is Mikel?"

"I am," Mikel replied.

Shocked and surprised she started to giggle, "You're a woman."
Lorenz saw Sabrina's smile and immediately stood.

"Yes, I am. Most people find it shocking," said Mikel.

"Sabrina," Lorenz smiled.

"Lorenz?" she replied.

"You two know each other?" Mikel said.

"More of an acquaintance," Sabrina said.

"Not for long I hope," Lorenz said with a hint.

"Please have a seat. I can get a waiter for your order". Mikel
waved her hand and signaled for a waiter. "One is on the way; shall
we get started with the meeting?"

"Sure." They agreed in unison.

"This shoot is for the community center. I hear they are doing a
great job, but they need our help in raising funds. It's that time of year
when we have to give back to the community and I have support from
your organizations to do this shoot. My objective is to make it simple,
clean, and interesting. So I've asked you here to discuss how we may
present the community center. First, let me introduce everyone.
Sabrina is our model from the agency, Lorenz is a representative from
the center, Ted is a writer for a magazine, and Paul is a marketing
director for one of the agencies. We are all here to pull this off with
minimal funding."

"They didn't tell me I am doing this as a contribution," said
Sabrina.

"I don't think you are making a contribution, your agency is
contributing," said Mikel. "We can start with Lorenz telling us about
the community center."

"First let me tell you my activities at the center. I contribute time
and medical skills to the center. Therefore, my exposure to the entire
program is limited. So I can only tell you about the things I see.
Twice weekly I hold a health clinic, once a week I drive the teenagers

around to senior citizen homes, and that's the extent of my exposure. All other things you'd have to get back to the director."

"You give three afternoons to the clinic?" said Sabrina.

"Yes, I do and it's worth every minute."

"We can get enough ideas from you for the shoot. Just your activities will be a start," said Mikel.

The waiter returned to the table and took Sabrina's order. She ordered Calamari, salmon steak, and a dish of steamed veggies. Mikel looked at her and winked "Good choice."

Ted said, "Lorenz, do you mind if I follow you around on your days at the center?"

"Sure, I don't see why not."

"Good, this will give us an idea what the public will embrace as a campaign. It will also give Mikel an eye to some great snapshots of common people and where to throw in Sabrina."

"Paul, are you open one night this week to meet at the center?"

"Sure Ted, just give me a call when you're ready. I only need a tour of the facilities and one day of observation to create a marketing scheme."

"Then we are looking at next week as our time of discovery and the following week to have a complete package. You guys are wonderful. Let's agree that all questions should come to me as the coordinator. I want to make sure we stay on the same page for this fund raising commercial shoot." said Mikel.

One after the other, they all agreed to Mikel being the coordinator. After the agreement all meals arrived to the table. "Dinner is served," said Tom as he smiled with enthusiasm.

"Sabrina, it's surprising to see you?" said Lorenz.

"Same here and I look forward to seeing what the center is all about."

"You're going to love being with the kids there. Once you get with them, your world changes."

"What about the others? Isn't there some training classes for a change in professions?"

"I am not sure about that, because I focus on two areas, the kids and the health clinic."

"So what do you do for a living when you aren't at the community center?" asked Mikel.

"I'm a medical intern at the hospital near the clinic?"

"Yes, that's where we met. My aunt took ill and he gave me a phone book." Sabrina giggled.

"A phone book?" Ted laughed.

"It was to dial a doctor right," laughed Paul.

"No, no, Sabrina wanted the phone book for another reason."

"Don't get angry Lorenz, we are only kidding," said Mikel.

"I know, I know," Lorenz mumbled as he shook his head from side to side.

"He's a good intern there. My aunt liked him and so did my sister."

"Oh really, and what about Sabrina, does she like him too?" asked Mikel.

"Let's just say opportunity is knocking."

"Opportunity knocks loud but will the door open?" Lorenz said.

"Sure, it's opening for dessert right now," said Ted.

The dessert cart came around the table. Ted chose a pudding dish, Paul a cake, Lorenz asked for coffee, and Sabrina rejected it all. "Mikel are you ready for your coffee?" asked Tom.

"Yes, would you please bring me a cup? Sabrina, are you sure you don't want anything else?" asked Mikel.

"No, I'm fine."

Small talk between the men occurred while Mikel and Sabrina had a woman to woman conversation. "You know Lorenz is drop dead gorgeous. You better get on him."

"Yes, I know. I am on it believe me. We are supposed to go out this Friday night."

"You mean the date is set up and you two didn't know you'd be working on the same project?"

"No, I didn't know it was shoot for the community center. I know it's a shoot coming and we needed to meet tonight."

"You know what this means don't you?"

"I think I do, but tell me your thoughts."

They looked at each other and lipped the word "fate," smiled at each other and then glanced at Lorenz.

"He's too good looking to be alone. Is he alone?"

"Yes, he doesn't have time to do much of anything. I wonder how he gives three evenings to the community center."

"You do what you can to get him off the take. I have an idea to help you if you need it."

"I need all the help I can get."

Ted, Paul, and Lorenz called the waiter over the table. Mikel said, "I have these guys."

"Thanks, Mikel" they said in unison. Ted and Paul stood and motioned for the door. Mikel rose repeated the cheek to cheek greeting as they said good bye to each other. Lorenz looked over to Sabrina and said, "Do you have a ride home or can we share a cab?"

"I have my car. Do you need a ride somewhere?"

"As a matter of fact, I do."

"Are you ready now or do you have a few minutes?"

"I have a few minutes. Only a few minutes because I have to be at the hospital, with a glance at his watch he adds in six hours. I need to get some sleep before the shift."

"If that's the case, we should leave now. Mikel, do you mind us leaving?"

"No, go right ahead. I will be fine." said Mikel.

Lorenz and Sabrina both rose from the table and headed for the door. Sabrina led the way and Lorenz followed, he gazed at her luscious body. "Stop looking at my ass, Lorenz" Sabrina said while giggling.

"But a nice ass it is. Lovely specimen, if I have to say so".

Through the restaurant doors, they headed to the parking lot for Sabrina's car. Sabrina suddenly stopped and turned towards Lorenz. "Are you sure you want us to go out this Friday? Or was that a conversation piece?"

"Sabrina, I seriously want to take you out this Friday. I've thought this over a number of times. I see us having a good time together."

"Then why haven't you confirmed a time and place for us?"

"You know, I am very limited until I complete my internship. I am trying to find a place suitable that I can afford for such a lovely woman."

"You shouldn't worry about impressing me, I'm very simple. I'd like to get to know you, soon-to-be doctor."

"Okay, we are definitely on for Friday. Can we get to your car now?"

"Oh, I'm sorry. Yes, we can."

They entered Sabrina's car and she started the engine. As she backed up, she said 'Where do you live?"

"You know where the community center is?"

"Yes"

"I'm two blocks from there. I can show you once we get near the center."

"Okay." Sabrina pushed a few radio buttons to find a soothing channel. After finding one, she looked over at Lorenz to ask if he liked the music and saw Lorenz had fallen asleep. A few miles later, Sabrina arrived at the community center and woke Lorenz. Lorenz directed her to the next block and asked her to stop the car there. He exited, told her good night and he'll be in touch. Before Sabrina pulled away, Lorenz disappeared into the darkness of an alley.

Simone returned to Diane's apartment and knocked on the door. Diane opened the door, waved her in, stepped aside and said, "Are you that desperate?"

Simone entered saying, "Desperate? I don't think so. You know, Rodney is a great guy and when you have an attraction that's all there, then why play around. You have to go for it. Obviously he has the same idea, as we have a date this Saturday night."

Both girls sat on the couch, Simone stretched for a magazine from the coffee table.

"Look Simone, Rodney is a great guy, very good as a matter of fact. He is worth taking care of. He is considerate, helpful, focused, and on top of all, attractive. He is all of that and I know how you like to go after the opposite type of guy. He isn't your norm so please try to control your emotions."

"Like you control yours?"

"What do you mean? Of course I control my emotions and I always find the right one."

"Like the one who called before we left for Rodney's apartment."

"Simone, he is not the one. You know, you think you have one and they either hide something from you, pretend to be someone they aren't, or just play on your emotions."

"Then your choice of men happens to be someone like Rodney. Why didn't you try to date Rodney?"

"I thought about it, but it was too close for comfort. And besides, he is too good of a guy in my eyes."

"That's what this conversation is all about. I thought you had something for him and wanted me to back off."

"No, I'm just doing the family thing, We have to look out for each other even if we aren't sure what they are about to get into."

"Then tell me everything you know about Rodney. Start from the first time you met him."

"I told you earlier. He is all and everything I'd want in a man. No, I haven't seen many women come by. He had a girlfriend, but something happened and we never talked about it. Or, let's just say he didn't spill the beans when I tried to get it out of him," Diane said with a mischievous grin"

"You sly woman. It's amazing how investigative you can be at times. Is that the good ole college training? Or is it just being interested enough as a good neighbor?"

"Just interested as a good neighbor, and could have been more she added with a wink at Simone.

"So there is interest. I thought you just said there weren't any physical or mental attraction."

"No, I didn't say it wasn't. I said he wasn't quite the type of guy I normally date. But I almost got him to tell me about his past." *A quick way to cover up my comment without revealing my actual thought; whew that was close.*

"So you wanted to but didn't have the opportunity. Are you sure we aren't trampling on each other's ego or turf?"

"No Simone, we aren't traveling down the same path. You go have fun on this date. But, don't expect me to be a spy for you since he's my neighbor."

"Don't worry, I'll only ask sensible questions and you will tell me," said Simone with a wink. I better get back to my place. We can talk about Aunt Marge later in the week. I'll call you. Thanks for everything tonight. Thanks especially for letting me hang with you at

Rodney's apartment. I'll let you know about the date." Simone tracked to the door for a quick exit. Diane moved right behind her to lock all the locks on the door once she exited. "Good night, cousin."

"Good night, talk to you soon."

***

Rodney called to make reservations at Restaurant De Marco for Saturday night dinner. The restaurant has an Italian cuisine, is fairly romantic with its booths, tables, and showcased a relaxing atmosphere. It is not too ritzy, but perfect for conversing and setting the right impression. "Hello," Rodney said.

"Hello, thank you for calling De Marco's. May I help you?" said the receptionist.

"Yes, I'd like to make reservations."

"Sure, reservations. Please hold while I transfer your call to reservations."

"Reservations, may I help you?" said the clerk.

"Yes, I'd like to make reservations for two on Saturday night around 6:45pm. Is there a table available?" asked Rodney.

"Yes there is. I have a booth or table. Which do you prefer?"

"I prefer the table near the east window overlooking the city lights."

"Sir, 6:45pm will barely be dusk. Would you prefer another table since the view will not be as expected?"

"No, that's the table I want and with reason. Tell me, is Tyrone working now?"

"The table is yours. Can I have your name to hold the reservation?"

"Sure, it's Rodney Witherspoon."

"Thank you, Mr. Witherspoon. Yes, Tyrone is here. Would you like to speak to him?"

"Yes, please and thank you." Rodney waited for Tyrone, Rodney thought of ways to really impress Simone. *I can order one dozen*

roses and have Tyrone place half of them as the table decoration. The
second half I'll tip him to have one of his waiters bring and present
them to Simone. I hope he allows me to bring over the dessert and
keep it especially for us. What else will impress Simone? Let me think.

"Hello, this is Tyrone."

"Hello, my friend."

"Rodney. What a surprise? We haven't seen you around the restaurant lately. How are things?" said Tyrone.

"I have been quite busy, had a health scare, and met a beautiful woman. Can you help me out with a date this Saturday night?"

"Sure, no problem, are you well enough for a date?

"I'm more than well, I'm excited. If you saw her you'd have the same enthusiasm as I do."

"From the sound of it, I'll see. I can do your favor but remember you'll have to make some advancement in our marketing scheme this summer. If you give us your all with the advertisements, I will help you with your date. Is that a deal?"

"No problem. Your food is so excellent, that you don't even need my marketing help. Working for you is a no brainer. Just display a photo of one of your popular dishes and everyone will drive thousands of miles to eat there."

"You're still funny, Rodney. What do you need for your date?"

"First, what do you think of this? A dozen roses, six for the table arrangement and the other six you have delivered to the table once we settle in. Second, allow me to store her dessert in your fridge. And third, is there a violinist available for hire? Do you know him very well? If so, can you coordinate the violinist for me for two songs once the dinner comes to the table? Is this too much?"

"She must be a special woman for you to go out of your way. Are you popping the question?"

"She is, but I am not asking her anything. It's all very new."

"What's so different this time, Rodney?"

"This woman has something more. I just have a gut feeling about her. Are you okay with my request?"

"I've got the request down. When are you bringing the roses and dessert?"

"I will have them there around two o'clock on Saturday. Will you be there or will you leave a note with the receptionist?"

"Don't worry about anything. Everyone will be instructed to look out for you and we'll take it from there," said Tyrone.

"Great. I will see you at two o'clock on Saturday. Thanks, you guys are the greatest."

"You're welcome, and remember our deal; a discount for our advertisement on the next shoot."

"Not a problem, Tyrone. I have it under control. Talk to you later."

"Have a great one, Rodney."

"You too, Tyrone, see you Saturday. Bye," said Rodney.

Rodney was happy with his planning for Saturday night's dinner arrangement. He thought of a concert being the way to go, or a show at the theater would do the trick. He pictured doing a slew of activities that would impress and show his charm. It was his first date to impress and that was his focus. Minutes into his stampede of thoughts, Rodney walked to the closet and picked his clothes for the night. His selection gave him the final idea of what they would do for the date. *Jeans are out. Suit, over dressy. Sports coat, ok. Black slacks, black shirt, blue sports coat. River Cruise Jazz seems to fit. No, maybe not have to check show times.* Rodney continued contemplating his selection until he realized simplicity works best. *After dinner we'll head to the Cloak Room with a drive through the park by horse and buggy. The Cloak Room for sure.*

Chapter 6

She's Sick

Sabrina, after making it home safely, looked to find Lorenz' phone number to confirm Friday's date. She found the number on a folded piece of paper torn from the local telephone book in her navy blue jacket. *It's late, and it wouldn't be a good time to call. I know he's asleep for the night for sure. He was so cute sleeping in the car. I know he has much to do in the morning. What a coincidence being on a shoot together? Is this fate or what?*

Smiling, Sabrina prepared herself for bed, still thinking of Lorenz and their opportunity. After she completed her nightly routine, she prayed. *God, please allow Aunt Marge to get better. And please get Lorenz and me together. Amen.* Then she set the alarm, cuddled under the covers, and found her perfect position. Trying to fall asleep, she continually ran over the dinner conversation and the upcoming event with Lorenz. Pictures began to snap in her mind of Lorenz and her at the community center presenting the great work that goes on there. She imagined Lorenz wearing nice slacks, no shirt, and a white lab coat unbuttoned to show off his chest. Herself wearing a tight white blouse with the bottom tied at her waist, pushing her breast up to fully expose her assets to Lorenz, a nice dark colored short skirt exposing her legs, and the makeup of angels to really indulge his attention. Eventually Sabrina fell deeper into a trance and off to sleep.

***

Lorenz woke to his alarm fully clothed from last night's dinner. He reached over to the alarm, turned it off, and placed his feet on the floor to sit up. He pushed his hands against his forehead in exhaustion and rose to his feet to prepare for the day. Running in his mind is last night's dinner and something else but he cannot remember. *Oh my, what was it? What else? I know there is something else.* Moving about the apartment he found all that he needed for his day. After a quick breakfast bar from the kitchen, he grabbed his pack and headed for the door. Looking back, as he opened the apartment door to exit, his thought returns to something he has forgotten but cannot place what it is. Nothing comes to mind so he closes the door and exits, locking the door behind him.

"Good morning, Lorenz." said Robin, she smiled as if her sun just rose at the sight of Lorenz.

"Hey, Robin, how are you?"

"Good. Are you going to the train station?"

"On my way there now, do you want to walk together?"

Smiling, she answers, "I thought you'd never ask".

They left the apartment building heading North on the main road. The train station was four to five blocks. Every morning, the same people were out and about. The traffic picked up as life comes to this part of the city. "Robin," called Lorenz as they continually walk to the train station.

"Yes, Lorenz."

"Have you ever thought of something you are supposed to do and just cannot for the life of you remember what it is?"

"I've done that a few times".

"What did you do to get your mind to remember?"

"You go through a checklist of events that either you talked to someone about, or you wrote somewhere as a reminder."

"A checklist; let's see. Appointments, Community Service Center, Spokes Person, Emergency Room. So far nothing comes to mind."

"Don't worry it will come."

"Yeah, let's hope so. I don't like dropping the ball on anything."

"Remember, you normally don't. Don't worry about it, it will come."

"I have too as it could be very important."

Step-by-step they paced towards the train station. Robin thought of the opportunity as it presented itself. *We shouldn't be so quiet while walking to the station. Now is my opportunity to get his attention.* "Lorenz," called Robin. "What does it take to create interest from a man?"

"What?" answered Lorenz. His mind wondered about her question as if it were a slap to the cheek. *Is she actually thinking about someone I know?*

"You know. What does it take to get interest from a man?"

"I guess its dependent upon a number of things. First it is the man and the opportunity." *Why on earth would I answer her like that?*

"That doesn't tell me anything. What do you think will get attention from a man? And be honest."

"Attention from a man. Let's see. There are things you can do with appearance. Does he see you often?"

"Often enough, but I know he doesn't recognize me."

"Well, some men like the way a woman dresses. Some men like the way she smells from her perfumes. Some guys don't mind being the recipient of gifts and messages. Some men like to be plain told about a woman's interest."

"So you are saying it could be a number of things to get a specific guy's attention."

"Yes, you can say that. Watch your step."

"Thanks."

"It's too vague to get a guy's attention when you don't know the individual and what he likes. What do you think would get his attention?"

"Well I can use the seat to write a note when we get on the train."

"Okay, a note is a good place to start."

"Sounds like you have a plan or two. Does he have any idea to your interest?"

"No, I don't think so. He is kind, very nice, has a great physique, and is very smart."

"Seems like a nice guy so far. What does he do for a living?"

"He's in school and plans to graduate with a purpose."

"Oh really, he's in school. Aren't you in the last year of your undergrad?"

"Yes, my last year. But my guy is in graduate school."

"Oh, really. What does he study?"

"Yes, really. As a matter of fact, he is in graduate school for a specific profession."

"What profession?"

"Something in the medical arena, like a doctor or surgeon specialist."

Upon both reaching the station, they walked through the gates and submitted their electronic pass for entry. Each one walked in sequence to the exact bench location perfect for waiting on the next train. Lorenz sat on the left side opening a book to review a chapter before hitting the hospital. Robin sat on the right and glances at Lorenz as if they were the only two at the station. She glanced at him from head to toe, from toe to head, sighed and stared exactly at his features. She sighed louder and faked a sneeze to get his attention. "Ah Chew!" sneezed Robin.

"Bless you," Lorenz exclaimed.

"What are you reading?"

"My study guide to emergency room operations."

"Is it a hard subject?"

"It's challenging. But not too difficult since I'm applying everything right now."

"Do you perform any operations yet?"

"No, not yet. I am generally helping patients with all sorts of emergencies, from applying band aids to saving lives without intense surgery."

"Oh, that sounds exciting."

"It can be at times. But I know my work helps a lot of people. And it's rewarding, tiring but rewarding."

"Can you tell me something else?"

"Depends on what it is."

"When do you have free time? You never seem to be home, not that I am watching, and I never see you with friends or girls. Do you go out or have a social life?"

"I get around and free time is limiting. As a matter of fact, I have a date coming soon. I don't know what I'm going to do just yet, but there is a girl who's interested."

"Do I know her?"

"Oh, you might."

"Does she know about the date?"

"What kind of question is that? Do you think I'm imagining a date to appease your conversation?"

"Oh no! Don't get angry. I just never saw you with anyone. Where did you meet her?"

"I think at the hospital."

As the train signaled its arrival, Lorenz stood while Robin found a seat. She tried hard to get close to Lorenz but decided to back off since their last conversation   didn't go so well. Lorenz stood holding the top rod that's attached to the cab's roof. He looked around the cab at the various faces as they ride the train to their destination. Riding from station to station, the driver announced every stop just before arriving. People constantly moving on and off at each location. The train moves quickly and pauses just enough for people to exit and enter. Bells rings as an alert for the train's take off. The train driver announced the next stop, "Medical Center is the next stop. Please exit on the left side of the train."

Lorenz prepared himself for a quick exit. He looked for Robin in a seat near the cab's rear. After spotting her, he nods his head upwardly indicating a farewell. She waved back just as Lorenz moves towards the exit. He stepped quickly onto the deck just as the cab doors closed. Stepping lively, Lorenz moved immediately towards the stairs leading to the street. He maneuvered around others moving slower and each step brings him closer to the open exit and to the hustle and bustle of the street. He moved into the flow towards the general hospital area. Routinely there are multiple people who seemed to arrive on his schedule. He waved his hand greeting each one of them, and without a sound, they returned the wave as if there was a common language for them. Each step closer to Lorenz' destination, he started thinking of his date with Sabrina. He recalled his ungentlemanly like exit from Sabrina's car. Over and over again, he questioned his intentions with her as if he was the one in pursuit. Not like anything else in his past, he contemplated how to process the actions so he would know what to say to her once he called and made sure they were still on for the coming date.

Arrived at the locker room, Lorenz opened his locker, placed the bag on the bench and reached for the white coat. He placed the bag in the locker, secured the lock, and headed out to the nurses' station for instructions. Without hesitation he stopped at the station, picked up the phone and called the community center to check his schedule. "Hello. Is Mr. Hicks there?"

"Hello, yes he is. May I ask who's calling?" answered the receptionist.

"Yes, this is Dr. Lorenz Maynard. May I speak to him please?"

"Please hold." The receptionist placed Lorenz on hold and announced the phone call to Mr. Hicks. "Mr. Hicks there is a Dr. Maynard on line two".

"Thank you, answered Mr. Hicks" Picking up the phone, Mr. Hicks answered, "hello".

"Mr. Hicks, this is Lorenz Maynard."

"Hey Lorenz. I've heard great things from the kids and other people here at the center. Are you coming by today?"

"That's why I'm calling. Can I change my schedule?"

"Is there something wrong? I know the kids will miss you if you don't come today."

"No, it's not today, its Friday. I have something I need to do that evening."

"Oh, you mean your date. Oh sure you can switch days on your schedule. No problem."

"How did you know about the date?"

"When has a kid ever kept a secret? Did you tell them to keep the date under wraps?"

"The kids? I guess you're right about the kids. However, I didn't expect them to mention the date. Anyway, thanks for understanding."

"I am glad to see you do something more with your social life. You spend so much time here - I can't imagine you'd have a social life. How did you meet the young lady?"

"I met her here at the hospital."

"Coincidence, right?"

Smiling, Lorenz answered, "Yes, as a matter of fact, a nice coincidence. Thanks for understanding and I will make it up to you."

"No problem. You don't owe anything; you've done more than enough. Just enjoy yourself. Let me know how it goes."

"Thanks again. Take care Mr. Hicks." Lorenz disconnected the phone and returned the phone back to the nurses' station, immediately grabbing charts for his round.

Robin walked from the train station directly into her office building. She saw a coworker who arrived at the front doors. "Hey Missy, how are you?"

"Hey Robin, I'm fine and you"

"Great. I had an awesome ride into work today. I got a chance to spend some quality time with my dream guy."

"Wow that can always make a girl's day."

Blushing, Robin replied, "Yeah, it made mine for sure. Now if the rest of the day goes as nice it will be a good day."

"You're smiling and it must be love. Does he make you like this every day?"

"Yes, every time I lay my eyes on him my day gets better. Every time I hear his voice, my day is brighter. Every time I smell him, my day becomes awesome."

"You've got it pretty bad. I'm happy for you. When will I get to meet him?"

"One-day Missy. One day."

They both got to their cubicles and performed the daily routine to start the day. In no time, the office became hustled and bustled. Periodically, Robin found herself in a daze thinking about Lorenz.

Sabrina woke in one of the greatest moods. She recalled a part of her dream with Lorenz as the main character.

He stares deeply in my eyes, as if a message from his heart alludes to his secret desires. His arms are strong, shapely as a Greek god. His chest is muscular in definition. His abdominals are cut like a middle weight boxer. His legs are shaped like a 100-meter track runner. His voice sounds like the melodic whisper of a deep voice radio announcer playing love ballads in the late evening. His touch, gentle, smooth, and effective, coupled with his focus has a tremendous effect on the spots that counted the most. His thrust was consistently smooth as the push rod of a locomotive. His eyes were deeply entranced into mine as he passed multiple messages from his heart. His embrace, strong and firm, holding me in one spot where moving is difficult, like cornering me into a position of pleasure. His move, his touch, his strength, my breathing changes, a moan comes to my throat, and the combination brings me to....... WAKE UP.

No wonder I'm in such a great mood. If that only happened in real life? What a dream, girl what a dream. I haven't had one with such intensity in such a long time. If this isn't excitement before a date, I don't know what is.

Preparing for her day, Sabrina showered, brushed her teeth, put on her makeup. She walked to the closet and selected a cozy dress that's easy to slip on and off for quick disrobing. Afterwards she realized she had about fifteen minutes before it was time to leave, having just enough time for breakfast. As she moved to the kitchen, she grabbed the box of cereal, a bowl, milk from the fridge, and a spoon from the drawer and poured herself a cup of cereal for the morning. As soon as she had sat down the phone rang. "Hello," she answered.

"Good morning, sis," said Simone.

"Hey, you sound really energetic."

"Yeah, I had an interesting last night. I ended up with a date for tomorrow night."

"You too! What a coincidence. I have a date tomorrow night too."

In unison they ask, "Who's the guy?" Giggling, they immediately reverted back to their teenage days. Challenging who goes first.

"Sabrina, you go first. Who is he?"

"Remember the intern at the hospital when Aunt Marge was there?"

"Yes, is that him?""

"He's the one. What about you?"

"It's Diane's neighbor. We had dinner there last night. Girl the man can cook, and cook great. I mean great."

"That's nice. I have to get out of here and head to the studio. Can we finish sharing this later? I want to know all and everything. As a matter of fact, let's just compare dates Sunday."

"That sounds good. I will talk to you then. If you don't hear from me earlier today, you will tomorrow. Ciao"

"Ciao."

Sabrina went back to finish her quick breakfast, and cleaned up soon after. Then she picked up her things and headed for the door.

Simone placed the phone on the receiver and began her morning routine. Her typical habits start from toilet to shower. Right after the shower she prepared her color coordinated clothes in line with her meetings for the day.

What impression she needed to make with whatever client that entered the office suite. She recalled one marketing executive who required the firm's services as the schedule for the day. It's the meeting of the day for the right clothes. Ideally, she made the appropriate power arrangement with her clothing selection.

Dressing, she remembered her conversation with Sabrina. One great smile appeared reflecting anxiety to tonight's date with Rodney. Brushing her hair right before pinning it up, she walked to the compact disc player, pressed play and her favorite singer bellowed the melodic tune. After finishing her dressing routine, she swayed to the music and sang verse to verse of three songs on the CD playing in the background. One more look over before walking out the door, she turned around in the mirror, turned off the music, grabbed her things for the day and headed out to her car. That particular morning, Simone sang happily the rest of the way to work.

Down the street after one intersection there's a coffee shop. Simone normally stops there to purchase a cup of coffee to drink during her 45-minute drive to work. On occasion traffic bogs down the interstates to work but this time Simone was extremely ahead of schedule and had ample amount of time to stop for coffee. Simone Parked her car, walked into the shop, looked at the menu board and made her selection. "Mocha vanilla swirl coffee, specialty coffee instead of black, with room for cream."

Waiting for her coffee, she stood near the window and watched the cars and people pass by. In an instance, she recognized a neighbor out on his morning run. She waved at him and turned back to the call of her name from the coffee shop attendant. Simone grabbed her coffee, picked up a napkin and headed out of the shop towards her car. Getting ahead meant an easy ride to work for once. Along the drive, Simone began to think out her date with Rodney. *I have three dresses that will do the trick. You can never go wrong with the little black dress, but that might be too simple. The red dress with bare shoulders is a knock out, but that might be a little too formal for a first date. The blue dress with a floral arrangement might be the one. Yes, the blue wins. I am sure he'd like that one, it fits well and shows a little of my figure, let's say a little more of my figure and I want him to notice all of me tomorrow night.*

Just as Simone arrived at her office, Simone had a message light flashing on her phone. She immediately dialed in the code to listen to her messages.

Rodney's voice sounded on the answering machine, "Good morning Simone, I am excited about seeing you tonight. I hope you're just as excited. I think we're going to have a great time. Please don't be mad at Diane for giving me your work number. I made a deal that she couldn't refuse. Also, I'll pick you up 7:00 at your place so if you don't mind, please call and give me your address. It's something we left out in our conversation last evening. I think it would be nice and courteous if you'd give it to me. I hope to hear from you soon. Bye for now"

Simone scrambled into her purse for Rodney's numbers. After a few rummages through her purse, Simone dumped the purse's contents onto her desk in search of the card. Still, no card. She realized that she didn't return it back to her purse and figured to have left the card either in her car or her house. Right now, no card and she would like to return Rodney's call. *No problem, I have time I have to get into business and start my day; I will figure out how to contact Rodney later.* And with one thought, the professional Simone returned to her work routine.

***

Rodney started his day with his usual run. Early morning habit followed with the calisthenics and weight lifting. During his run, he contemplated his date for tomorrow night. *I should wear a royal blue blazer, black shirt, black slacks, black shoes, black belt. That is a lot of black, but the shirt will hit it off well. I think it's a pleasant outfit for the occasion. And the cologne, 'what if she doesn't like it?' Maybe I should call Diane and ask her about her taste. No, that's going a little over board with it. I am sure she'd like the cologne I use. I haven't heard anything bad about it yet and don't think it's a factor, unless she's allergic. I don't think she's allergic. I know every woman likes a nice smelling guy. Nice smelling, oh, that could be defined differently with every woman. Heck, it's a chance I have to take and sweating over the cologne is not that important. Let's see, the meal is coordinated, the pick-up time and location. Location, she has to call me for the location. I haven't any idea where to pick her up and I*

93

don't want her to drive. "That wouldn't be much of a date now would it? Of course not, you're too classy to have her meet me" he spoke to himself.

Another quarter mile passed in no time. Rodney continued his checklist for his first date with Simone. "Let's see, what activities will we do after dinner? I think we can listen to jazz in the park after the horse and buggy ride. That's it. We can always go dancing later. This gives me time to explore her mind and not fight to hear every word. Man this woman is awesome, and impressive. She seems to have the right chemistry for me. Only time will tell. It all starts tomorrow night with a little quality exchange of thoughts.".

Chapter 7
The Dating Game

Early Saturday morning, the city is alive after Friday evening's events. City sponsored jazz concerts flared at most public parks. Clubs with Latin dancing, R&B jingles, Rock –n-Roll, in the entertainment district were active for most of the night and until early morning. Traffic with families and friends were headed out for activities, social club, city sponsored races, and of course park games. Sporting games for kids ranging from 5 to 18 bombarded multiple parks and fields, went on for hours with parents in observation.

At the community center, the kids from Lorenz' pre-teen group met to plan his date with Sabrina. The kids jumped at the opportunity to put Lorenz in good standing with his first date. Knowing that Lorenz is not a man of great resources, Fred, Rick, and Elaine came up with a quick plan instead of their routine sporting event. "Let's see," said Fred. "Let's meet at Lorenz' apartment building. I know his neighbor Robin who'd let us use her apartment to set things up. We should meet there around three."

"Three sounds good to me" answered Rick. "What about you Elaine? Are you in?"

"I wouldn't miss it for the world. Besides, you two think you can set up something romantic?"

"Oh heck yes," answered Fred and Rick in unison.

"Oh heck no, and you two shouldn't think you have romance in your heads. Thank goodness I'm here or this date could be devastating. You need a woman's touch"

"You girls think the same thing all the time. We guys don't know anything about romance. It isn't like you know much more than us."

"I know a lot more than the both of you in my pinky finger. Not including the simple things like setting a table."

95

"You may have a point, but we know lots of stuff. We have girlfriends too. Right Fred?"

"Sure, right Rick. We have girlfriends. I remember taking my girl to a burger place for a bite. She was really mad. Does that seem like romance? I thought it did," said Fred.

"Yes, really romantic. That could have been nice if she wasn't led to believe the date would be something more. Didn't you tell me you wanted her to dress nice?"

"Sure did. She looked good too, really good. Nice dress and shoes, I thought she looked very nice indeed. Even had her mother drop us off when I went to her house to pick her up. It was nice of her mom to drive us to the burger joint. She looked funny at me when I told her the restaurant. And as a matter of fact, so did my date."

"Explains it all Fred, you have no idea to romance."

"Yeah, Fred, you have no idea."

"Rick, as if you had a better date. You haven't had a date since…you've never had a date."

"Yes, I have."

"No, you haven't"

"Yes, I have and you know it."

"No, you haven't and I'd know if you had one."

"Stop before you two get carried away" piped Elaine. "Let's get this rolling. Are you going to get the rest of the crew involved?"

"That's the plan. We can get at least five for the chorus and two to help cook" said Rick.

"You leave the cooking to me; it needs a woman's touch".

"Do we have a woman in the group? Do you see one Rick" said Fred.

"Will you cut it out? We don't have time to play around. Let's get serious. The date will be here in no time."

"I'll get the three singers and rehearse one song. I think we can pull that off. You two figure out how to get the meal set up. Fred, you contact Robin and get the key to the roof while you Elaine go to grocery store for the meal. Here is the money we collected from the rest of the community center."

"Okay, we're gone with the winds making this happen," shouted Elaine and Fred.

Rick called Lorenz to find out what time his date is supposed to start, and where they were to meet. "Lorenz, hey it's Rick".

"Hey Rick. What's happening today?"

"Not much. Just thinking of your date tonight; what is your plan?"

"What? I have a date, not you."

"Look Lorenz, you know as well as I that you don't have much money. You borrow from us all the time."

"Don't say that, I never borrow money from you. I make a few dollars here and there."

"You're right. You never borrow money. But I know you are limited as being an intern doesn't pay very much. I noticed you cutting corners all the time."

"Okay, you are right about the funds. But, you still shouldn't try to get involved with my date."

"Look, you do lots of us at the center. Just let us show you how much we appreciate your time and efforts. We promise not to do anything too expensive or extravagant."

"Well, you go ahead with your plan. I will not be home until 6:15 or so. My date is supposed to be 7:30. What do you have in mind?"

"Just something un-costly for you, I am sure she'd like it too. It should be great, don't worry."

"Now I'm worried because you told me not to worry. The last time you told me not to worry, I got my butt chewed out from the center's director. Will it cost me again?"

"No, totally different. Things are altogether different this time."

"Sure, they are. You should be glad I trust you. What do you need from me?"

"I need you to promise to bring Sabrina to your apartment for the date."

"What? Are you serious? Don't you know Sabrina will think of me trying to make moves on her instead of going out to a public place?"

"I don't know about that. I'm only a kid remember. Just get her to the apartment and don't have dinner until after you bring her by."

"Okay, I can pull this off. DO NOT do anything crazy. Remember, I trust you and I know the rest of the gang's involved. So please tell them to take it easy on her. She is important to me."

"Sure, sure, the gang knows to take it easy.'

"No really, I am not kidding, I trust you and this may be the one."

"I got it. Don't do anything crazy. What do you consider crazy?"

"Don't play with me. You know what I mean."

"Just kidding, I know what you mean. Just remember to have her there at 7:30."

"Okay, 7:30. I'll see you then. Bye Rick"

"Bye Lorenz."

Rick walked to the center's game room where the rest of the gang was waiting. "Hey, it's on. Lorenz will bring his date by at 7:30 tonight. We have to get things on track."

"We have a song picked out and practically rehearsed while you talked to Lorenz", said Fred.

"I have the dish planned and collected a few dollars for the meal. Do you want to contribute?" asked Elaine. The money part is repetitive they gave it to her earlier

"Yeah, here is a couple dollars. Man that kills my allowance", replied Rick.

"Don't worry, we are all broke now. But at least Lorenz will have a great first date with this lady. Did you call his neighbor Robin"?

"No, not yet, it's my next thing to do. What time are we meeting?

"Let's meet at Robin's apartment at 5:30 to get things together. As soon as I get her on board with this call we should get out of here."

"Sounds like a plan."

"Yup, sounds like a good plan to me."

"Okay, I need to make the call. See you guys at 5:30." Rick walked to the office again used the telephone. He reached into his pocket for the number. Dialing, he turned to see Elaine talking to the community center's director. Curious, he waved at Elaine with a high signal not to let him in on the plan. Elaine winked back. The phone rang, once, twice, and Robin answered on the third ring. "Hello".

"Hi Robin, its Rick. Rick Hillman. How are you?"

"You mean little Rick from Worcester Street?"

"Yes, it's me."

"How are you? How's your mom and sister?"

"They're fine, doing great. Sis moved in with her friend a few months ago. She seems happy now. Mom is hanging in there; even though she sometimes gets on my nerves. But I seem to stay out of trouble with her."

"That's nice to hear. What can I do for you? I know you want something because you always did when I lived near you."

"Oh, there is something but not elaborate. I just need a favor."

"Nothing elaborate? Money involved?"

"No money involved unless you'd like to contribute. But that's not what I want. I want to use your apartment to prepare a meal and give us access to the building's roof. Can you do it? We are counting on you."

"Give you and your friends access to the roof. What the heck for?"

"You know Lorenz right? Well he has a date tonight with a girl he met. Since he's always doing for us at the community center, we thought it would be nice to do something for him. So we decided to cook, serenade, and create a nice atmosphere for his date. Can you help us?"

"For Lorenz and with another girl. How could you ask me to do this?"

"Is something going on Robin? Did he do something to you? If he did, I know he didn't mean it."

"No, he did nothing to me. I'm sorry for yelling. He doesn't know, I mean he hasn't done anything to hurt me or offend me. He is a nice guy and a good neighbor. I guess you can use the apartment and I will give you access to the roof."

"Great. We, my friends and I, will be there at 5:30 today. Is that alright?"

"Yes, come on down. I'll be glad to see you and say hello to your mom for me."

"Thanks Robin. You're the greatest." Rick ends the conversation and places the phone receiver back on the home base. There is a touch on his shoulder just as he turns to exit. It's Elaine. "How did it go?"

"We are in there. It's set as planned. Did you tell anyone about our plan here at the center?"

"What do you think, I'm stupid? NO!"

"Good. You know it's against policy for us to have activities outside of the center when it comes to a counselor or volunteer. They don't like the possibility of something going wrong."

"Glad to know that. It's a good thing because fortunate for me the conversation was on a ping pong tournament."

"Let's go buy the groceries."

"Let's go." The two walked out of the community center heading for the nearest market. Along the way, they discuss the menu. "Elaine, I thought you had this all together?" asked Rick.

"I have it together. Let's just say I know how to make a quick meal. Nothing fancy of course. But it's going to be interesting."

"Interesting? That's a scary thing to say."

"Are you going to cook?"

"No, that's your area. We decided that you'd handle the food."

"Then I'm handling it."

"What can you cook?"

"Lots of things; the simpler the meal, the better it is of course. So let's see my best dish for the occasion. I can make Mac & Cheese, Green Beans, and Fish Sticks. How's that for a meal?"

"Sounds great to me. I like them all. But fish sticks?"

"Yeah, they are easy to make. Put them in the oven and minutes later they are done."

"I guess you're making the macaroni & cheese from scratch, right?"

"Yes, scratch right from the box. How much money do you think we collected?"

"I see your point. Simple and inexpensive."

"Now your eyes are opening."

***

Lorenz called Sabrina to coordinate the date. "Hey Sabrina, how are you?"

"Hey, I'm doing pretty good. How are you?'

"Excited. I'm really excited to seeing you again. Especially tonight."

"Me too, I was thinking of you earlier."

"Since you know I don't have transportation; do you mind driving tonight?"

"No, of course not silly. I don't mind at all."

"Good, then can you come over around 7:30. The kids at the community center have something up their sleeves. I promised you'd come over at 7:30. They are nice kids and I spend my off time with them mostly. I guess they are trying to impress you for me. Will this bother you?

"They sound very nice. I will be there 7:30 on the dot. You can't disappoint those kids. Or you'd never hear the end of it."

"Right you are. Thank you for understanding. Talk to you later, I have to get to my rounds."

"Bye Lorenz."

"Later, beautiful woman."

***

Rodney called the restaurant to make sure everything is in place. It's nearly 6:00 pm; he selected his clothes, pressed them, and jumped in the shower. He pulled out his best cologne, the one that gets him the most compliments, splashed it on, and   dressed. He checked shoes for shine and a great appearance, and inspected the shirt and pants for additional wrinkles, and steamed his blue sports jacket. He looked himself over once more before he completely dressed. "I'm Immaculate", he thought, "I look great and I hope she sees the same."

Simone arrived   home from the cleaners. She picked up the dress for tonight on the way and hung on the bathroom door as she headed into the shower. Singing in delight, Simone blared her tune as if sung for a church choir. She was excited about t but didn't want to display the entire girl like characteristics; being too anxious. "Why am I so excited about tonight?" she wondered, "What makes Rodney so right for me?" she asked herself. As she toweled off, she found herself in thought while she moved around the bathroom in her preparation. *Is it his charm, or is it my need that's driving me for this? Is it because we've bumped into each other over these past weeks, or is it the intrigue of him being such a handsome gentleman and I just need attention from a man?* she pondered. All of these thoughts haven't been answered, and her motive related to her answer; *Just go and enjoy even though you practically threw yourself at him at his place.* She continued dressing. *No doubt, it's the thing to do. Don't read into anything more, just go and enjoy the date. I don't foresee anything happening between us. Heck yeah, he's a nice man and I want things to happen. Who am I fooling*, she argued with herself.

Simone takes another look for perfection. Her dress was immaculate, a smashing blue color off the shoulders, and tight enough that it revealed her sexy figure. The dress color accented her skin tone and hair. Her shoes were attractive open toes sandals. She made a 360-degree spin in front of the mirror to get the last look over and prepared for Rodney's arrival. Simone walked to the kitchen, grabbed a wine glass, poured wine and turned on nice music to set the tone for the date. At least in her mind being smooth and comforting decreased her excitement to controllable levels. Even though Simone was enthused to go on the date, she didn't want to seem over anxious when Rodney arrived. Simone took a sip of wine, walked r to the door, and peeped for Rodney's arrival. *Not yet, no car in the drive way*, she thought. She looked at the clock in the kitchen and realized Rodney wasn't supposed to arrive for another 20 minutes. She returned to sitting in the kitchen and drank her wine as she waited for Rodney. *No one is here yet, is it me or is the time creeping along. I shouldn't be so anxious but he is a fine man with nice attributes. You know, the body, the mind, and the spirit. The man can cook too, has lots of style and I've waited for him to come in my life for a long time now. Let's hope he continues to show me his true colors. If he maintains what he's showing, life can be really good.* The phone rang. "Hello" answered Simone.

"Hey Girl, is he there yet", asked Sabrina.

"Hey. No he isn't, answered Simone.

"I have to go to Lorenz' place in a few minutes. I hope you have a wonderful time and let's get together after our dates."

"Do you think we are going to be in early or something"?

"Well, let's call each other in an hour and a half to check on each other. If things are going bad, maybe we can use the call as an escape."

"Do you always have to have an escape plan in case of a bad date?"

"You haven't gone out with the guys I have in the past."

"That bad?"

"That bad and you only know the surface. We'll have to laugh at it when we get a chance."

"I don't think we will have to call or at least I don't think I will. But I will call you anyway, just in case."

"You call, I like Lorenz, but just in case you never know when you go out with a poor man."

"I'll call. At least I hope to hear you're having a good time. If nothing else, it will be an experience. Look forward to it and enjoy."

"I'm heading out of the door now. Don't forget to call."

"I will. Bye."

"Bye."

The sound of a car entered Simone's driveway and she gulped the last of wine and placed the glass in the sink. She peeped out of the window to see if it's Rodney standing at the door. She   ran to the bathroom for a once over and to brush her teeth from the wine. Rodney rang the doorbell with a fist full of flowers and he wore his blue blazer. He stood close to the door for Simone to answer. While he waited, he gave himself a once over as best he could. Three minutes at the front door and no answer. He reached for his cell phone and just as he started dialing, Simone opened the door. "Hi Simone", he said, "These are for you."

"Sorry I didn't come right away; it took too long to come to the door. You look great, very nice Rodney"

"It's ok, thank you. You look ravishing yourself. How did you manage to wear blue?"

"I see we have a serious vibe going here. Blue happens to be one of my favorite colors. I always like the way I look in blue. It's a good color on me. And I see it's the same for you. How nice, another thing in common."

"Well, it seems like we have lots of things going on here. Are you ready for dinner?"

"Yes, I'm ready. Let me get my sweater." Simone opened the closet door and reached for her powder blue sweater. She started to place the sweater around her shoulders and Rodney reached to assist. Simone turned and remembered the flowers. "Let me put these flowers in a vase and then we can leave."

"Sure thing, that's a good idea."

Simone moved hastily into the kitchen with flowers in hand, took a quick sniff and grabbed a vase from the cabinet. "These are so nice and how thoughtful" she exclaimed to Rodney.

"Glad you like them. I wasn't sure if roses would do, especially on a first date. They send a strong message.'

"And what kind of message is that?"

"You know, roses claim love and affection. Not quite the impression I'd like to make too soon."

"You think I'm in love with you because of roses?"

"No, just the message of love I'm sending by the roses. I mean to impress not direct emotions. Let me stop before I put my foot deeper in my mouth.'

"You should. Just know I love the roses, not you. Not that falling in love may not happen, but it's the flowers and they do impress me. Shows you are a man of style and class. Thank you again."

Rodney turned, headed for the front door. Right behind him Simone followed. Rodney opened the door and waited for Simone to exit first. Simone pulled her key out to secure the lock. Rodney reached out for the keys. Simone stepped back and asked, "What are you doing?"

"I'm reaching for the keys so I can lock the door. I will return the keys as soon as the door is secure. Please allow me to lock your door."

"This is a first. I've never had a man ask for my keys on a first date. That is different," said Simone and gave Rodney the keys. Rodney took the keys, locked the door and turned for the drive way. He passed the keys back to Simone, stepped in front of her and walked to the passenger side of the car, opened the door, and waited for Simone to enter. After she entered, he closed the door. Simone thought "H*e's laying it on tonight. It's nice he's such a gentleman.*" Rodney entered the driver's side and placed his seat belt in position. He looked at Simone and asks, "Please put your seat belt on."

"You drive that bad?"

"No, it's just a safety habit" he answered while starting the car.

Once the car moved into the street, he changed gears and started the car forward. Music from the compact disc played It's a love ballad by Luther. "Is this music ok for you?" he asked.

"It's nice. I like Luther. I like all of his music. They really hit the spot for all moments in life. Don't you agree?"

"Yes I do. As a matter of fact, I have all of his albums. Luther and I go back for years."

"Who else is a favorite singer of yours?"

"Will Downing. A smooth melodic singer for with a deep voice and it places many in similar moods like Luther. Except Will's albums are not as consistent as Luther's. I think his last album was for true Will lovers."

"I like his music too. But I don't follow him as close as I do Luther."

"What did you do today?"

"My usual weekend routine"

"Yeah, the routine, we all have them. I did the same as usual for a weekend until now. You've made a variation in my routine."

"Yes, you and I both actually since you put it that way."

"Are you famished?"

"No. Just hungry" she answered. They both laughed at her comment.

Rodney drove in silence thinking he shouldn't talk too much too soon as they will not have much of a conversation over dinner. "What are your thoughts on the current economic situation? Do you think it's going to change?"

"Funny you mention this. It's been a subject I've wanted to discuss over some time now. I think we are definitely heading for a recession. I don't know how much of the GNP will impact our current market analysis; however, I do think the local economy will bounce back after the recent spiral and with local investments the city will grow. I heard the city made some deals with a few fortune 500 companies to build offices and assembly plants here. If my information is right, it would be interesting to find a few properties and hold on to them until the change. Now is the time to do it."

"You know, that is a great idea. With information like that, it would be wasted if someone like us doesn't take advantage."

"You have to have money to do so. Do you have money to invest?"

"Now you're asking me about money? I don't have money exactly for a home purchase, but I do have a few dollars stashed for a rainy day."

"Well, it's raining" she laughed.

"Oh, you've got jokes. Yeah, it's raining and I can respect a woman with a business sense. I see if there is a way for people to build a partnership, we could make a large investment and reap greater profits."

"That's the idea."

Rodney pulled into the restaurant's parking lot. He quickly found a parking space, parked the car, and steps around to open Simone's car door. She reached out her hand and he took it to assist her. "I can get used to this," she thought. Rodney held his arm out for Simone to grab and they walked in stride towards the restaurant's entrance. As they reached the entrance, again Rodney showed his consistent charm and gentleman like action by again he opened the door for Simone. "Good evening, can I help you?" asked the Maitre-de.

"Good evening, yes, you can assist us. We have reservations. Witherspoon."

"Yes, Mr. Witherspoon, your table is ready. Please follow me."

Rodney waved his had forward for Simone to follow the Maître-de first. He followed and walked close enough to have everyone recognize he and Simone are together. They reached the table, the Maitre-de pulled out the chair for Simone to take a seat, and placed the napkin on her lap. He walked to Rodney and placed a napkin on his lap while he announces the specials for the day. Immediately after the Maitre-de left, the waiter appeared. "Hi Mr. Witherspoon, may I interest you in a cocktail from the bar or start you out with drinks?"

"Simone, do you have something in mind as a pre-dinner drink?"

"Sure, an apple martini will do for me."

"One apple martini for the lady and a black Russian for me please?"

"Thank you, I'll be right back with your drink orders." The waiter left for the bar , ordered   drinks and headed back to the table with two bottles of wine that Rodney previously coordinated. "Sir, I think these are our best suggestions for the dinner you're having."

"Simone, do you mind doing the taste test and making the selection?"

"How did he know what we're having for dinner? I haven't opened the menu."

"I took the liberty to order for you earlier today. I think you'll like this dish as well as desert. Trust me a little please"

"Okay, then I'll be glad to select the wine."

"Please do."

Simone waited for the waiter to pour a little   wine in a glass. She took it, swirled, sniffed the aroma, and sipped a little. "Ooh, I like this one. But before I say ok, I'll have to taste the other." The waiter repeated the process for the second bottle of wine. Simone did the same as before. "Ooh, this one is nice but the other has it best."

"Has it best? Or the other is better?"

"Then, we'll take the first bottle. Thank you" Rodney tells the waiter.

"Sure Sir" the waiter answered, prepared the bottle and took the other away.

Another waiter returned with their drinks from the bar.

"Apple Martini for the lady and a Black Russian for the gentleman."

"Thank you," they both exclaimed.

"Rodney, this is a nice place. I'd heard about it but never got to try it out. Is it true about the food? I hear it's the place to dine, and the ambiance is touching. Are you planning to ask my hand in marriage?"

"Let's not get silly so fast. Let me answer your first question about the meal. Girl you are in for a treat. How's that for an answer?" he said while he smiled. "Second, I chose this place because of its ambiance and charm, as well as the service. I come here with family and friends on special occasions. And finally getting out with you is a very special occasion."

"Oh really," she smiled "A date is that special to you?"

"It's a first date that's special. You see, everyone in the dating scene has a first date. It's a beginning and we wish to remember our beginning even though we have no idea to what the future holds of this beginning. Yet, we remember important things and I want the first date to be important and have a memory of a lifetime."

"I see your point. So I am to remember this event for a lifetime. You, so far, you've been pretty good at impressing my memory. I think I can relive this so far. But my saying so does include the event that something bad may happen tonight. If the date changes to something bad, then I will definitely remember it as well. It will be the date to remember!"

"Now don't get negative on me," he sipped his drink, "you shouldn't have negative thoughts because it causes bad things to happen, you know, subconsciously."

"Don't worry, nothing bad will happen; at least from my part." Simone's cell phone rang. She reached in her purse for the phone and looked it's face. "I'm sorry Rodney, I need to take this."

"Please go right ahead."

Simone left the table and immediately answered, "Hello."

"Hey sis, it's me. How's it going?"

"Girl I can't talk. It's going really good so far. As a matter of fact, it's going so well that I forgot to call you."

"No problem, I haven't gotten upstairs yet. Lorenz is waiting for me now. I wanted to call you because I am behind time. Listen, you should call me in an hour or so to check on me okay?"

"I'll try, but if I don't that tells you things are going really well and I'll have to tell you about it tomorrow."

"Girl, you better call. You know our pact. Don't let me down."

"I'll call. Bye little sister."

"Bye."

The dinner was served as Simone returned. "Oh my, this looks wonderful".

"I'd hope you like it. I was sure of it after you had dinner at my place with Diane."

"Yes, you cooked a wonderful meal. How did you know I like sea food?"

"I paid attention to your conversation and to your comments about the dinner. You put two together and it made it easy to order for you. Besides, this way our meals are much faster being served the normal."

"I see. Are you trying to get me going here for something else? Or are you doing this for quality time?"

"Its quality, my dear lady, quality."

"Well, it's working for sure."

"Allow me to say grace before the meal" said Rodney. "Father, bless this meal we are receiving as nourishment for the body, mind, and spirit. Allow this fellowship to lead to greater events for two of your children. May it be a beginning of a wonderful friendship and the building of a great partnership for future endeavors. In your name we pray, Amen."

"Amen" said Simone.

In a stroke of the fork, Simone took her first taste of the meal. Rodney looked at her and waited for a response. He then poured a half glass of wine for Simone. "Well, what do you think?"

"It is awesome Rodney. It's awesome."

"Good. Please enjoy. I wanted you to know, since the first time I ran into you, I've wanted this moment."

"You mean me stuffing my face?"

"Yes, exactly, you being in a vulnerable moment where I can take advantage of your heart if I wanted too. I think you have what it takes for us to be wonderful, so I'm breaking away from my old dating habit."

"What do you mean dating habit?"

"I mean; with you I'm going out on a limb without really getting to know you. It's a gut feeling I have about you that drives me   and makes me want a path to us."

"Isn't this a little fast? Don't you want to know more before you get ideas?"

"Like I said earlier, I know you in my heart as if you were there for many years. I cannot put my finger on why, but it's a gut feeling that I've never experienced."

"Ok, I see. I've never had anyone come on to me so strong. Or have I ever had someone go to the extremes for a first date. Even though we are acquaintances, it is still a first time we give time to each other independent of being involved."

"Well, how do you see things now? Is this too much or is it enjoyable?"

"It makes me wonder if this is a show and you're hiding something, or is it schmoozing for an ulterior motive?"

"No, it isn't a motive for anything more than what you see and I am not hiding anything other than fighting the old cliché of "love at first sight."

"Rodney, you are kidding right. Love at first sight. And you let me throw myself at you during dinner at your place. Why would you do so?"

Rodney took a bite of dinner and sipped a little wine before he answered. "You think about that one. Throw yourself at a man who is already crazy about you. Why would he complain or stop you? That would be crazy for him. He'd love   seeing you fit to throw yourself. And why did you throw yourself at me?"

Simone continued eating, all of a sudden; she placed the fork down, wiped her mouth with her napkin and looked directly into Rodney's eyes. "It isn't love at first sight, but its interest beyond the norm. Let's say there is a fantasy world that we often embrace and I'd like to see it come to life."

"Fantasy world? You mean there is a fantasy about me going on in your mind? How could you go there without knowing me? That was a dumb question; fantasy is nothing close to reality, duh," Rodney responded.

"Don't be hard on yourself, I met you before, and I was impressed from the first moment. You've been on my mind ever since. Just so happens I allow you to enter into my thoughts and subconsciously think of things we can do together."

"You know a man can run on that statement as if being a dream comes true," he smiled. "Do you ever understand why women don't share their sacred thoughts with guys? That's exactly why. You run as being a gift to women, and this isn't the case."

Dinner was nearly over and they both had completed the major meal portions. The waiter appeared and asked, "Are you done sir or ma'am?"

"Simone, are you finished?" asked Rodney.'

"Yes, I am pretty much," and reached for her wine glass for a quick drink. Rodney picked up the bottle and poured the more wine into Simone's glass as soon as she placed it back on the table. He turned to the waiter and said, "We are both done. Can you please bring the desert?"

The waiter took both plates and said, "I'll be a moment with the deserts," he replied.

"Did you like the meal, Simone?"

"Sure, it was fantastic. I know desert is going to be exactly that, wonderful."

"I know you'll like it. But meanwhile since we're waiting for the desert, let's finish our conversation. Not to harp on anything, but I'm not the general guy who capitalizes on the dreams of women. Well, let me tell you, not this time. I've been known to jump on opportunities to find short term warmth and affection, if you know what I mean. But this moment means the world to me. And you are much more, much more than a whim of affection, more than a moment of warmth, and more than a fantasy to please. You are…"

Simone looked at her watch and immediately interrupted Rodney. "Hold on a minute. Keep that thought I have to go to the lady's room." In an instance she rose from the table, picked up her purse and left for the lady's room.

Rodney was caught off guard, stood at the table when she stands, and immediately sits down thinking, "Did I say something to offend her? I hope not."

Simone entered the ladies room and quickly dialed Sabrina on her cell phone. Waiting for an answer, she looked into the mirror and checked herself over. On the fifth ring Sabrina answered. "It's about time you called. I thought you forgot."

"I told you I would but if things were going well, you may not have gotten it. It's a good thing I remembered. I walked away from an interesting conversation too. I want to get back so tell me how's your date going?"

"It's really nice and different. I have lots to share and I too want to hurry back. Thanks for calling; I know I can always count on you. Later." Sabrina disconnected without giving Simone a chance to reply. Simone's thought, "She must be having a great time and next time I won't stop in the middle of a date to call her again. She'll have to learn how to escape on her own."

Sabrina returned to her date on the other side of the roof. It is a lovely evening, stars are out and the thick intensity for her and Lorenz is in abundance. She never had anyone so focused on her beyond the physical as she found Lorenz to be. She never had anyone do something simple for a date nor have so many people invested to its success. "Amazing, just amazing and quite appropriate for a first date," she thought on her walk back to Lorenz.

The date started when Sabrina arrived at Lorenz' apartment. When she walked to the stairs a young lady greeted her at the door and escorted her to the elevator. "Are you Sabrina?" she asked.

"Yes, I am. I am here to see…," Sabrina replied but was interrupted.

"…Lorenz, right."

"Yes, Lorenz is he in?"

"Please follow me." The young lady led Sabrina to the elevator pressed the up button, turned and said, "He's expecting you and I want you to have a wonderful time. Lorenz is very special and we wanted to help him with your date, so we'd appreciate it if you'd go along with us. Please go along with it okay."

"Okay, since you put it like that. I think Lorenz is nice too. That's why I'm here."

"Good," she answered. The elevator doors opened. She walked in first and Sabrina immediately followed. Elaine pressed the 12th floor button which provides roof access. "You're going to have a lovely time. I just know for sure. We are really excited to get things going."

"What things exactly?"

"You'll see. Please remember your promise to enjoy it no matter what."

"No matter what, I guess I can, or give it my best shot."

"Please give it your best shot. I am counting on it and woman to woman, Lorenz is a great catch."

"Yes young lady, woman to woman, Lorenz is a fantastic catch and I'll take your word on it," Sabrina winked   towards the young lady.

The elevator arrived at the 12th floor and when the door opened, a young gentleman smiled and said "Please follow me," then turned away from the elevator and headed to the stair way for the roof. He opened the door and waved his hand towards the entrance. Sabrina entered the stairwell for one flight and heard music on her ascent as she approached   the exit. "*Oh my, this is really something,*" she thought, "*he said to be open and there were kids involved.*" She opened the door and saw a different set up.

There was a table for two with a white table cloth, folding chairs, candles in jam jars, and a mixture of flowers as the center piece There was also sparkling grape juice in a carafe on ice, and of course the view of the city with the moon rising and the sun set. "How lovely and impressive," she thought.   Music played soothing melodic tunes and Lorenz was immaculate in his attire; jeans, shirt and blazer that made him look different from his white work coat. "He is a handsome man, I mean really handsome, darn near breath taking gorgeous. His height is just right and his build is slim and muscular, which allows him to dress well. And he has the most charming smile which he shared while he stood and waited for me to come to the table."

Sabrina thought and commented as she approached, "Hi, this is lovely."

"Hi, lovely woman, yes, it is. The kids did it; I give all credit to them. And for our surprise, there is more. Go along with it as I have no idea what's planned."

"More? You mean they did this and you had nothing to do with it."

"As I said, you have to go along with it and just enjoy what we can." Lorenz leaned over the table after he pushed Sabrina seat into position for her comfort. "And I have no idea what's for dinner," he whispered.

"We'll have to take it one step at a time. So how was your day?"

"It was full of anxiety to this point. I want this to go well and have fun all at the same time. Do you love the view?" Lorenz responded as he took his seat at the table.

"Oh my heaven's yes. The view is beautiful and I admire what the kids have done with the table setting. They did a lovely job."

"Yes they did." Just as Lorenz replied, the kids filed into a group formation. Three in the front and four behind, one stood in the very front as a maestro and coordinated the group. The maestro raised his hands in the air and upon dropping them the group sung a harmonizing tune. The song echoed on the roof top and windows opened to hear the melody. People looked from the street towards the building roof to conclude   the origination of the sound. Other building dwellers jumped   to see where the choir sung as their angelic voices heralded the air. Many people in buildings across from Lorenz' gathered at their windows and eyed the romantic escapade the children put together. Sabrina looked in awe at the children, smiled in wondrous agreement and glanced as Lorenz's face as he too embraced the kid's voices. "Wow," he whispered as he looked at Sabrina. "I had no idea they'd sound that good. Or is it because of you being with me?" he asked.

In a whispering tone she answered, "It's because they are just good".

"Aren't they amazing?" asked Lorenz.

"Yes, and for them to do this for us, you mean something to them."

"They are my crew. I spend a lot of time with them during my community service. You have to give back to the community and these kids are the greatest. No trouble from them at all. I love being with them. They remind me of my youth from time to time."

"It isn't like you're far from being like them now. The only difference is that you're an educated kid with a wonderful heart."

"You think I have a wonderful heart?"

"Sure you do. And I'm not the only one who thinks so. Look at what the kids have done for us. If they didn't think you were special, then why would they go to this extreme just to make our date successful?"

"I see your point. I love them too."

At the end of the first song, all people clapping as if they were in a concert. Lorenz and Sabrina joined in accolades, and smiled at them. Just as Sabrina stood to hug them all, two kids approached the table with their dinners.

"Please be seated so we can serve the dinner to you" said Elaine.

"Sure" replied Sabrina, and returned to her seat.

Elaine placed the plate in front of Sabrina, and Fred placed Lorenz' meal in front of him. They both looked at what was served. Elaine then spoke as if she was the head waiter, "You have the house specialty, macaroni and cheese, fresh fish sticks, and tossed salad with Italian dressing. Please enjoy." She walked away, turned back and said "What do you expect from 12 year olds?" as she shrugged her shoulders.

"Looks fine to me," said Lorenz.

"Really nice to me too," smiled Sabrina.

In an instance they both enjoyed the meal. The choir started another song and this time the crowd went to Lorenz' building to hear them. In a few minutes there were nearly twenty people on the roof top listening to the kids' angelic voices. Lorenz and Sabrina continued to consume their meal and never noticed the crowd as they gazed at each other and held a silent conversation. Neither one spoke a word but held continued focus on one another. When Elaine returned, they looked at her as she poured sparkling grape juice in their cups. "They practiced for a couple days for you two. I knew they sounded good, but I never expected them to get so many folks interested in their singing," Elaine commented.

"I never knew they could sing like this. Who helped them put it together?"

"No one helped; it just happened to work out this way. Don't they sound great?"

"They sound wonderful, really wonderful" Sabrina and Lorenz replied in unison.

Elaine walked to the other side of the roof top to stand in the crowd. The kids are singing the last song and really poured their hearts out with it. The last chorus the kids moved towards the table and formed a semi-circle around Sabrina and Lorenz. The song was so moving that many in the crowd had tears. And on the last note, a thundering applaud burst as if a storm appeared out of nowhere. The crowd clapped and asked for an encore. The kids turned from the table and walked towards the stair well. "That's it for tonight folks, no more songs. We'll announce our concert in a few days. Thank you for your support," spoke the maestro. The kids bowed and waved as each filed down the stairs and the crowd still clapped.

Fred went over to the table and said, "When you're finished, please let Elaine know and she'll bring out dessert. Take your time we don't have to be in until 9:00 tonight." He waved at Elaine and turned on his way out. Down stairs the singers grouped together and reflected on their performance. Then they disbanded going their separate ways. The crowd disappeared off the roof tops and in moments Lorenz and Sabrina were alone with one young lady waiting to bring dessert out. Lorenz waved his hand towards Elaine and said, "You don't have to wait on us; we have it from here ok."

"Okay, but I want to bring out your dessert anyway. I'll go get it and be right back."

"Sabrina, what do you think?"

"I have never had anything so lovely in my life as this date."

"Me either. I never thought the kids would do such a thing for us."

"And they did wonderful. I'll have to tell them thank you one by one."

"We can do it together. I'm sure they would love to see us do it as a couple, don't you?"

"After what they put together for us, I'd have to say yes they would."

"Then let's not disappoint them. We can tell them at the next community center meeting next Tuesday."

"Maybe we should do something special for them as they did for us."

"That's a nice idea. We can do something special but right now let's focus on us. If we don't it's a possibility there isn't going to be a we."

Elaine returned with the dessert. Two chocolate covered Twinkies. "Dessert is served," she said.

"Thank you Elaine," Lorenz said as he looked at Sabrina.

"Thank you Elaine," Sabrina said.

They both looked at the Twinkies and started laughing. "What do you expect from pre teenagers?" asked Lorenz.

"I think it's great," responded Sabrina, and in a wave of the hand she took one Twinkie and bit it. "Just as I remembered when I was a kid; still great."

"Yes they are. But I thought the dessert would be something more the way they kept forcing the serving."

"They just wanted to complete the meal, you know kids. They have to do it all and it's not a bad thing."

"Sabrina, it seems you know something about kids. That is a wonderful thing. Are you planning to have a family one day?"

"Well, it has been on my mind but not in the near future. I have to find the right partner first. I mean, the right partner not a sperm donor."

"Oh, I hear that all the time; Sperm donors that is. I understand what you mean by partner. It is very important for two people to see life as partners and not just mates. Not that I don't like mating or dating for that matter. But partners, is having someone at a different emotional level."

"I agree. It is having someone at a different level that can work things through and keep the family vision."

"Vision?"

"Yes, vision on what makes the family a family. A vision on what love is and how to maintain it, you know the importance of roles and the responsibilities of each person. It's the importance of nurturing and developing children, the focus on the relationship, and having a partnership pushing to greater success levels."

"You mean really be in tune and maintain general focus on each other and the family. Maintaining the unit as the gift from god."

"Exactly, the family is a gift and I want my man to be that partner in life."

"I see, you have a great philosophy on family. I like it."

Music played from the radio as they talked about anything and everything from child bearing to modeling. In no time darkness overwhelmed the candles. Lorenz looked at Sabrina and said, "Would you like to continue our conversation at my place?"

"Sure, I thought you'd never ask."

They both made head way to the door. Lorenz first picked up the paper plates, bottle, and left the blown out candles on the table. He thought to return in the morning to finish cleaning the mess. Sabrina looked at the city again and gave a once around the lovely view and remembered how the evening started. "You couldn't ask for a better first date," she thought before stepping into the stairwell. Lorenz followed with the exact thought and stepped lightly behind Sabrina.

***

Rodney stood as Simone returned to the table. "Is everything ok?" he asked with   concern in his voice.

"Sure it is. Why would you think anything is wrong?"

"You took off so abruptly. I thought I said something heart breaking."

"No way. Everything you've done and said so far has been great. You are very good and the best gentleman."

"Sounds like an exit statement."

"Don't be silly, I'm going nowhere."

"Well, then, where did I leave off?"

"Let's just say love at first sight."

"You were listening."

"Of course I was listening. Are you going to finish or move into a different direction?"

"I'm finishing, really finishing. Dessert looks great doesn't it?"

"Yes it does. Looks kind of familiar, what is it?"

"You don't recognize it?"

"No, not at all."

"Taste it and I'm sure you'll remember."

"Okay" and with a stroke of the fork, she tastes a little, smiles and looks at Rodney with a smile. "You made this the night I ate at your house. How did you get it here?"

"I come here so often that the owners and I are quite friendly with each other. Once I told them about you, they allowed me to bring in dessert and keep it here for us."

"You went to that extreme to impress me?"

"Of course, remember the love at first sight comment earlier? Well, you impressed me so much that I wanted tonight to be perfect and impressive for you. And I wish that my actions are received as being genuine."

"Oh, they are genuine alright. I don't think anyone would do so much for a first date as you've done. The only thing you haven't done is feed me as a child."

"It isn't that I hadn't thought about it, I have to have something to look forward too."

"Oh you thought about feeding me. I'm glad you didn't; at least there is something I get to look to do some other time. How nice."

"Simone tonight is just the beginning of us, it is the spark to our everlasting flame of affection, and each interaction from now on is our fuel to burn stronger with desire. Every time the fire grows, so will our love get stronger, our minds meet as one, and our will to move closer to a union becomes our focal point. I am sure you know what I mean because you have the desire to be with me as I for you. I would like this first step to be something everlasting."

Simone was taken back to how serious Rodney's emotions were towards her. She thought of his pouring was more of an outcry for sex and not genuine enough for a woman to believe. *If he thinks I'll fall for this, he has another think coming. What a line of crap he's telling me*, she thoughts before responding. "Rodney, I don't quite know how to respond. I mean it's nice for someone to feel the way you do. I am enchanted but not quite to the extent as you. Intrigued with thought of tomorrow having love and commitment; what woman doesn't have that thought. But for now it's just a thought. Don't get me wrong, I like you and want to find out more, but build a life together from one date, fall in love from interest, it isn't me. So I don't want to lead you down a path I'm not willing to travel."

"I said earlier, I didn't expect you to be here with me. It would be nice if you were, and that would make my effort of showing you my emotions easier, but I wanted you to know my feelings. As uncommon as they are, I wanted to make an early stand and profess my feelings. I know it scares you, and it scares the heck out of me. This is a first on my part, especially since I've dated quite a bit. So bear with me please and let's just enjoy the rest of tonight. I vow not to bring it up anymore."

"I'll bear with you for a while. It isn't that I don't enjoy the attention or the company. I do like you Rodney that's why I'm here."

Tom sent the waiter with six roses to Rodney's table and presented them to Simone. Just as he bowed a violinist appeared and played a love ballad. Rodney reached for Simone's hand and winked at her with a glisten in his eye.

"Rodney, you're going way out for this first date."

"As I said earlier, it's not just a first date, it's an investment of what's to come. Well, not in those exact words, but you get the jest."

"Yes, but, again, it's a little much for me" Simone replies and pulls her hand back to her side of the table. "I'll think about it, really give it some thought."

Pouring the last of the wine, Rodney raises his glass towards Simone. "Here's to you having an open mind and heart." Simone reluctantly raised her glass and tapped Rodney's before taking a drink. They drank the last of the wine   and the waiter appeared. "Did you enjoy the dessert?" he asked.

"Yes I did, what about you Simone?" replied Rodney.

"Oh, yes the dessert was fantastic. Thanks for asking."

The waiter took the plates and silver ware from the table. Rodney waived for the check and sat in silence for a moment. *Should I ask her where she'd like to go or did I blow the evening professing my emotions so early*? he contemplated. *The park should be fine and whatever happens, I'll bounce back with the next date*, he decided. Rodney looked at Simone and spoke as she said, "What's next? I'm anxious to see what you have planned?"

"Oh, I was just going to tell you. I think a carriage is waiting for us that will take us to a nice jazz spot."

"Really, you're kidding right."

"No, I'm not kidding. Remember I wanted it to be right for the first date. Besides, it is a perfect night for a ride. Are you ready?" Just as he asked, the waiter returned with the check and Rodney signed the receipt. He stood and moved over to Simone to pull her chair out as she rose from her seat. "Please," he said, as he led the way with his arm extended towards the front exit. He retrieved their coat and sweater from the coat rack and placed her sweater around her shoulders just as they exited the door. In front was a horse drawn carriage. The horses were dark and tall, the driver waved at Rodney. Rodney returned the wave and took Simone's hand as a gesture to come along. The driver approached the carriage and pulled down steps so Simone could safely step into the carriage. He assisted her and she found a comforting spot near the middle of the seat. Rodney walked to the other side and entered. "Hi John, thanks for waiting."

"No problem. Still heading for the same place?" he asks.

"Yes, the same place and take your time; I'm sure the lady wishes to see it all."

"You've got it." he replied and in one snap of the leather strapped, the horses started moving.

The night sky was clear with stars scattered about, the air was cool but not so cold to caused them to bundle for warmth. The air was fresh and the park street was filled with on lookers as they passed each block. The buggy took them to old town where buildings displayed candles in the windows. "This is lovely Rodney. I've never done this before." said Simone.

"It is lovely and very nice," he took her hand and held it affectionately. "Yes, wait until you see my favorite spot in the city."

"Your favorite spot?"

"Yes, my favorite. It's a building with this fantastic tower, big bells, and the architecture is geometric from the Renaissance era. It is sort of Gothic but cathedral. It has its charm and every time I see its beauty, I feel the architect had ideas way before its time. The building isn't quite like the ones today, the workmanship is awesome."

"It sounds lovely, are we near it yet?"

"Not quite, but there are other things I'd like to show you."

The horse drawn buggy continued the journey through old town, traveling the winding road around the town's center. There is a park in the old town that has a band gazebo and tonight there's a concert and dancing. The closer they arrived to the location, the louder the music. They got there just as the band in the gazebo stopped for a break. "Whoa Missy, Mick, whoa," the driver yelled to the horses as he pulled the reins towards him. The horses stopped and the buggy became stable. Rodney jumped out, went around the carriage, and took out the stairs. He assisted Simone's exit off the buggy. "We'll stay here for a short time then finish our buggy tour a little later."

"How nice, a concert at the park."

"Yes, it just so happens to coordinate well with my plans for tonight. I hope you like live music and cozy dancing."

"Of course I like it. I love to dance, not that I am the greatest, but dancing is fun."

"Then let's find a seat before the band returns."

They walked along the path to the table area and found two available seats. "Are you interested in a drink?"

"No not now thank you, maybe later," Simone replied.

The couple sat close to each other, Rodney placed his arm around Simone as they observed others in the music area. People of all ages are walked, talked, and sat in the area seemed to enjoy the event.

"Nice evening to be out at a park concert. It is something I've never attended even though I've heard about it for years," said Simone.

"Yes, it's been active in concerts every year and the performing groups are more popular. I mean they are mainstream jazz groups and show up for either free or a fraction of their usual cost. You can't beat the entertainment the city provides."

"It is nice. Do you know who's playing tonight?"

"Sure, it's a band from Philadelphia called," in unison they say "Pieces of A Dream."

"How awesome! This is free for the general public. Are you kidding? You mean a mainstream group like Pieces of A Dream is here and the park isn't crowded?"

"That's just it. The park isn't overly populated because the marketing for the music isn't a city focal point. No funds for marketing which I guess they use the money to pay the bands instead."

"Oh my, and I am like the average city dweller and not know anything like it. My Aunt Marge used to invite me out here all the time. I never attended, not even once did I entertain the thought."

"I'm sure your Aunt caught a number of great acts. One year there were Santana, Bobby Womack, Isley Brothers, Bob Dillan, and others at that level. And the kicker was they were all free. The city picked up the cost."

"No way, those are awesome entertainers. As a matter of fact, I paid $85 for my ticket to see the Isley Brothers back in the day."

"Free!"

"Free and sponsored by the city."

"Yes, sponsored by the city and it's every summer."

"We need to get the word out."

"No, let's keep it quaint. The city will increase its marketing or publicity project soon. So let's keep this one to our immediate friends before they start charging."

"I see your point."

The band returned from their short break. The music started and Simone enjoyed the show. Song after song and without skipping a beat, Simone tapped her foot, applauded at every change, and stood for the soloist when she clapped in appreciation. She smiled at each glance of Rodney from time to time. Rodney returned the smile and observed the beauty he admired in Simone. *She has a mind, a great figure, and a wonderful personality. No wonder I'm crazy about her*, he thought.

The concert was nearly over; the band is played its last song for the night. Simone looked at Rodney and said, "What's next. I'm enjoying everything tonight. I can't believe you showed me so much for one evening."

"We have to complete the carriage ride." Rodney reached for Simone's hand as an invitation as her guide. He led her back to the carriage, but walked by her side. "The carriage is right over there and the last part of the ride is only 15 minutes. There is one more thing I'd like to share with you. It's my favorite building in the city."

"I'm learning more about you Rodney, so lead the way. I bet it's wonderful."

Rodney assisted Sabrina into the carriage and   sat really close to her. He placed his arm around her and pulled her closer to him. The ride was slowly moved   as horses paced themselves traveling block to block.

"Tell me about this building you want me to see Rodney," said Simone.

"The building was designed in the late 1800s. The architect was not very popular as his work was a fluke that's never been repeated. This is the only building of its kind even though its Gothic in style. But the architect made this work for him and the owner. A family lived there for generations. And as they sold pieces of the estate, the property became enclosed with neighbor after neighbor. Now the house is on the national historical list. The family donated it to the city which uses it to centralize special offices. This way the house is public property and can never be destroyed.

"You should see the interior. The stairs are hardwood, with hand carved rails. The chandelier is crystal, authentically designed and one of a kind. The walls are made of solid oak, and the door trim is carved with symbols of wealth which is decorative in nature. Over the years, the owners added something important that represented their generation. Each oldest child of the first born on their 18th birthday had to design something that they felt represented the family and his generation. Throughout out the house, you'll see multiple pictures, hand carved sculptures, family symbols, jewelry with wood carvings, and the likes. Don't think the house is cluttered, because it isn't. Some of these items are small, and some really stand out. However, that was a genuine tradition."

"What happened to the original owners? Why did they give it to the city?"

"Well, the family out grew themselves. They became modern and moved from old town. It's kind of like they became suburban

Americans. Except for one member of the family, he stayed in the house and continued the family's tradition. When he passed, the family decided to create an endowment for future generations and expand the house's beauty for the general public. The family now lives across the world and annually returns for their reunion. To this day, each extension of the family brings one artistic item to add the décor. They bring art and sculptures from new and old eras to decorate each room giving it a dynamic theme."

"It is really different from what I see. It seems like a place from Europe than from America. From what you've described, it sounds quite lovely."

"I wish it was open tonight so I can give you a tour."

"We can do it the next time."

"I'm already excited about it. It sounds so well put together from the way you describe it. Now that I know its history, it seems like a different place."

The carriage strolled closer to the house as the hoof beat sound of horses stepped on the pavement. Each building in the neighborhood depicted a different era and architectural style. There were Georgian style houses most of the East side of the street and Victorian style houses were next with some accented with French windows and doors. As the carriage approached the next corner there was this overshadowing house, bricked home, gothic in style and Rodney's eyes sparkled as his enthusiasm showed. The house was exactly as he described earlier in the evening. Pulling Simone closer, Rodney whispered, "Can you feel the strength of the house the closer you get to it?"

"I guess so. I feel something over shadowing."

"Yes, it's over shadowing, because it's the house influence and the neighborhood."

"It is over powering and seems almost as it should be in a scary movie."

"Scary movie, you really think so?"

"Yes. It's kind of eerie, but somewhat intriguing."

The full view of the house appeared as the moon light struck the house with its glowing rays, and shadows of the gargoyles stood firm against the building's steeples. The shadow of gargoyles made it seem as if someone stood on the roof and watched everyone's movement. The rose colored glass at the top of the foyer reflected the sparkle of moonlight and gave a spectacular show to any on looker. And from a distance the glittering light gave a harmonic dance like a child's kaleidoscope reflected the sunlight. The front door was those of a castle, thick and large, handles of iron rings, and doubled to swing outward from the center. The porch was tiered concrete, with pillars that rose to the second floor and met the roof's overhang. The round pillar design was like the Roman architecture at the forum and made of solid rock. The porch rose from the ground, with six stairs, as if it led to the entrance of a great monument.

"I wonder what gave the builders an idea to build such a place?" asked Simone.

"It was love for something unique and a reminder of home," answered Rodney, with a smirk on his face.

"It seems like you know so much about it. And it is different especially for this part of the country. I never knew the building was here."

"It's my favorite. One day when it's open we'll have to take a tour of the inside. Then you'll see why I love it so much."

"That might be a day in the near future."

"Yes, in the near future." Rodney said with a smile.

The carriage ride rounded the lake, while it reflected a glittery glow from the wading water, as if it were a path leading to the opposite shore. "Beautiful ride and tonight is so lovely. I like our first date," said Simone.

"You made it great, no whimsical mysterious side of you came out and I too enjoyed our time together."

"These were unusual events for a first date, the most different ever. And you are such the gentleman. What a breath of fresh air you are to me."

"And you are the breath I await to take whenever I'm in your presence."

"There is nothing more than having time with a wonderful man. It's early to be so impressed. But I am definitely impressed."

The carriage stopped at the restaurant; the valet opened the door and reached for Simone's hand. Rodney stepped around to Simone from the opposite side of the carriage and arrived to her side to reach for her hand as they walked to the car. He smiled as his eyes gazed upon her as he observed she moved like an angel. Simone seemed glow of contentment which accompanied her in the night; she looked of pleasure and happy from a wonderful event. He thought of a future of, *Us* and motivation to open the door. *What should I do next?* he pondered.

Simone loved the evening. She admired all activities which included the ride back to her place. He was silent played a touch of soft jazz on the radio as he drove the car to her home. *It was awesome not to be asked a million and one questions about our date. How was I feeling, or am I feeling great as a temperature check for his success? He did the impressive to allow me to soak in the moment and enjoy the silent conversation.* Simone thought about it, *He is impressive and such a lovely man. He knows exactly what I want and seems to provide it without effort. Or at least I think he does."*

Rodney broke silence as they neared her place. He asked, "Will you allow me to call you tomorrow or do you prefer giving us time to let things settle?"

"It would be nice hearing from you tomorrow. I don't mind being shown a little interest," she smiled with her answer.

"Great, I will call you and probably make an afternoon of it."

"I'd wait to see what my schedule is like before making plans. I normally do many things on the weekend."

"At least I'll get to hear your voice if nothing else. But keep your door open with a little time for me. I'd love seeing you again."

Rodney stopped the car, stepped around to open her door. He provided assistance to Simone. She took his hand, exited the car right into his arms for a quick embrace. Her move surprised Rodney. He responded and capitalized on the hug he'd received.

"Thank you for a lovely evening Rodney," said Simone.

"You are more than welcome. It was my pleasure to spend time with you on our first date." He looked into her eyes, tilted his head for a cheek kiss, and waited for a response. She faced the other direction not to accept a kiss on the lips. Not yet in her mind. She stepped back, grabbed his hand and led him to her front door. And the entire way she smiled with joy and heartfelt emotions to open a greater door to Rodney. But, doubt prevailed as being too soon for a second base maneuver. A kiss good night will have had to do.

***

Sabrina moved closer to Lorenz for a quick embrace. Lorenz lifted one arm over Sabrina's head to grasp her shoulders and showed the strength of his hug. A quick peck on the lips, a sigh of passion and an in depth kiss followed. No spoken words. Just the physical nature after an enjoyable conversation of mind blowing connections took both a step closer to joined pleasure. No sooner than the deep kiss ended, they both stripped their clothes. Another kiss on the cheek, a nibble at her breast, and tender kisses down her neck, Lorenz followed a sensual ritual. Sabrina replied with a bunch of sighs and stronger grasps for him to get closer and do more. The more she wanted and Lorenz obliged. They sat on the couch and she pulled him closer to certain body spots where the strongest nerve sensations were aggravated. Shudders flowed through her body as Lorenz kissed her g-spot ever so gently. Without pause, Lorenz moved closer and closer to her lips for seductive kisses. He followed the line mid drift as following a yellow road. From her stomach navel to her lips, Lorenz stopped inches apart after each kiss. She lay on her back and embraced Lorenz at every opportunity, with a sigh and ah. He thought her responses were a reflection of her desire for more.

Lorenz stood and pulled her up from the couch headed for the bed. Sabrina followed, hesitated for only a moment, and without reluctance gave him a push towards the bed. He stepped clumsily and fell face first on the bed. She burst into laughter and right on his back as if she's riding a pony for the first time. Quickly he maneuvers under her ending face to face with her still on top. Hugging her with a great move, kissing her lips with conviction and desire pouring from his entire body, he entices her to respond as if every muscle in her body relaxes to his every wish. He strokes her hair, gently touching her face, and with the other hand keeps the pressure of body closeness.

With excitement and passion combining for a great union, the two stopped to finish stripping their clothes. A moment later they both paused to view each other's body. "What a fine man," Sabrina thought. "Lorenz, you are so beautiful."

"And you are a queen of any man's dream Sabrina."

Both moved around on the bed and without hesitation involved themselves in a body embrace. Intertwined, caressing, kissing, and heated. Lorenz explored her body with his empowering limb, and just before further exploration, he stopped and reached for the protection of life. He downs the cover in seconds and without delay he rolled on the top of Sabrina, to fully indulge himself to their first union. Slowly he penetrated the cavity and in no hurry he concentrated on one spot, kissing her, she responded in sighs and small moans and circular hip motions, spreading her legs for more entry. He continued to penetrate for a spot of passion and founds a spot on her neck that sends chills down her body.

Feeling the results of her body, he made one thrust to full engulfment of affection. A screech of passion comes from Sabrina and she grabbed Lorenz with her legs and arms, still shaking from her chills and this time increased body movement. With goose bumps all over her body, she held him tight as if she didn't want him to move. He continually moved his body in rhythm and in a moment stood on his feet holding her up without disconnecting. With his strength, he moved her body up and down upon his masculine prowess. Moments later, their bodies start to shake from pleasure and in a controlled movement; they both fall onto the bed while still deeply embraced.

No words were spoken between the two for minutes later. No release of passion as they continued to hold each other close, as if a comfort zone both overwhelmed them with relaxation as if this was a routine moment after years of involvement. Hours pass with them holding each other, Lorenz moved to take a full view of the beautiful woman lying in his arms. He stared as she continued to relax with her eyes closed. *She is so lovely, a beautiful spirit, and seductive to the eye as well as the mind. I haven't seen a woman of this caliber since my first year in college. And not knowing the quality of women then as I know now, I'm sure of my past exposure to The Total Woman. Making love to her is a gift, the icing on the cake, the strawberry dipped in chocolate, and the greater fuel to my desire for more. I need more of her to satisfy my need for love and affection. She is the one, I know it, and tonight confirmed it for sure.*

Sabrina woke with Lorenz staring at her. She automatically thought something was amiss with her. "What's wrong?" she asked.

"Nothing is wrong. I'm admiring your beauty, your mind, and the way you make me feel," responded Lorenz.

"Oh really? You have so much going on yourself and after tonight, I am so sure you're the one I've never met before. I never thought anyone could be so passionate the first time sharing their bodies sexually. It is such a wonderful experience. This may sound silly but are you like this with everyone you have sex with?"

"I can't say I have. I know there is something more with you that I've never experienced. However, you know the first thought is always an honest response and without a doubt, you are special."

"Special?"

"Really special and I don't want to sound childish, but you're one of a kind. I'm sure to many others it's the same with them. No woman has ever made me drive to explore such great pleasures, especially from the first encounter. Special, yes, you are extremely unique and an angel to my spirit."

Smiling and blushing, "You're such a lovely man."

"I'm glad you think so. And you haven't seen the best of me yet. Would you like anything for breakfast?"

"Just a glass of juice would be nice. I have to get going pretty soon. I hate to love and run, but its business and nothing against you." Sabrina moved to gather her clothing and directed her walk to the bathroom. She looked in the mirror over the sink and started dressing. She pulled her bra around, snapped it and twisted the bra to position. She slid her panties on before running water in the sink. She splashed water over her face, grabbed a towel and dried. She finished dressing and stood in the mirror. She noticed how blushed she seemed to look. In no time, she created   polished look with no tools but her hand and water. She fixed her hair just enough to manage a very attractive image. She pulled and turned to leave the bathroom and Lorenz appeared. "My god, you're a fine piece of work. I'm sure you hear this all the time," Lorenz commented.

"Believe it or not, in my profession, you hear just the opposite. You get more professional rejections than you do work; especially when you're a struggling model."

"You're struggling?"

"Yes, no doubt I'm struggling."

"Oh, then what on earth can we offer each other?"

"That's something we need to discuss when there's time. Right now I have to head out to a shoot." Taking the orange juice Lorenz offered, she took a couple of sips and passed the glass back. "Thanks. Can I call you later?"

"Well, I hope you do. If not, I'll call you."

Chapter 8

Marge's Relapse

"Aunt Marge, are you feeling better today?" asked Simone. It's early morning and Simone dropped by Aunt Marge's house for a quick check on her favorite aunt. "Is there anything you need from the store? Is there anything you'd like to have?"

"I'm doing fine. I can't think of anything at the moment. I haven't had a feeling or desire for anything special lately. I don't seem to be the same as before."

"Don't worry; you're fine according to the doctors. It's why they released you and sent you home."

"Well, let me tell you the same as I told them. I don't have the greatest feeling about myself   , but my soup isn't cooked yet."

"We'd hate you leaving us before your time. Please pay attention to the doctors, Aunt Marge."

"I take all the drugs like a good patient. But nothing seems to get me feeling as before. It's like there's this drop in energy. I suppose those vitamins the doctor prescribed should help me there."

"What about the other prescriptions?"

"Oh, I follow directions. I just want more soup these days."

"Huh?" Simone asked thinking, *that's a strange statement.* Simone walked into the kitchen and noticed the stove fire hadn't been on for some time, and the soup was in the pot. "No wonder you don't have soup yet; the fire isn't on. How long have you been waiting for your soup?"

"Not long before you came in. I started it nearly thirty minutes ago. I went to check on it and the pot seemed slow at getting warm. So I let the burner warm up slowly."

Surprised at her answer, Simone said, "Real slow for sure," then carefully lit the burner and set the flame high for a quick response.

"Aunt Marge, you need to pay attention to your cooking. You didn't turn the burner on. That's why it's taking so long to warm up. You should have it in a few minutes. Is there anything else you'd like besides soup?"

"Soups all for now baby."

Simone left the kitchen and wandered to other rooms of the house. She walked into the bathroom and took a look around. She found nothing out of the ordinary and continued her walk through. Each room she tried to find something out of the norm or any indicator of Aunt Marge being different. So far each room there was nothing to be alarmed. There were a few things out of place on the hutch, which was normal for a lived in look and nothing to take great interest. Simone returned to the kitchen, she founds the soup boiling and reduced the heat. "Aunt Marge, soups done. Do you want it in the kitchen or the dining room?"

"Dining room and I'll be right there," replied Marge. Marge slowly moved from the den to the dining room. She stopped for a moment to catch her breath, stood next to a chair as if the back supported her, and moved to the seat on the east side of the table. The east chair faced the window to the street and provided a fantastic view of house activities. It's like she sat on the porch in summer or spring. And it gave Aunt Marge a sense of company when no one was around.

"Here you go Aunt Marge. I hope it's cool enough for you to enjoy right away. Since you've waited so long for the soup, there's no doubt you're hungry. Is there anything else you'd like with the soup?"

"No dear, the soup should be just enough. Thank you." Aunt Marge took her first sip after cooling the soup with a blow from her mouth. She repeated and Simone was observant and attentive. "What did you do last evening Simone?" asked Aunt Marge.

"I had a date Aunt Marge. It was lovely. This was the first date with a guy who has a lot of class. I bet you'd like him."

"Oh, you think I'd like him. Is he anything like the one I was supposed to like before who had lots of class?" she giggled while she asked.

"No, nothing like that guy at all. He was a jerk and I didn't realize it. This one seems   different. He has true style, is a gentleman, and seems   really patient. He knows a lot of people, comes from a great family, and smart. I mean, he's unique and I know this from our first date."

"He sounds lovely. But you haven't said one thing. Is he handsome?"

"Aunt Marge, no doubt. He is one handsome guy. He has a build that's awesome. You know, like the model guys, nice complexion, good muscle tone, and has a smile that will light up Texas."

Aunt Marge took another sip of her soup while she listened, and realized Simone hadn't spoken of a guy with such enthusiasm for nearly two years. The last guy turned out to be a real jerk; very selfish and self-centered on everything around himself; even   their relationship. That girl cried many of nights for that guy to change. It's nice she gave dating another chance. "Are you making him out to be something great so you can bounce back from the last guy?"

"No way, he's really a great guy. And as a matter of fact we did something you would have loved. It was just like the dates you use to tell me about with Uncle Arthur. He took me dancing in the park to the big band. It was under the stars, in the moonlight, and there were other couples from giggly teens to sixty something." Simone ballerina around the floor in the dining room while she explained; "He is something for sure. Yes, you're going to like him."

"All of this from one date. He really impressed you and I'm so happy to see you in great spirits. It's a good change."

"Oh, yes, it is. I know it's been one date, but this one has promise."

The doorbell rang, twice as if there were someone in a panic to enter. Ding dong, again it sounded louder than the first two rings. "I'll get it Aunt Marge," said Simone. Simone walked to the door, peeped through the peep hole, pulled the door open and said, "Why are you ringing the door like that, Sabrina?"

"Oh you're here. I thought Aunt Marge was alone. I didn't know you were here."

"You always ring the doorbell like that?"

"No, of course not, but this time of day Aunt Marge is normally asleep. How long have you been here?"

"Just long enough to feed Aunt Marge and check the house over. Things seem normal," she exclaimed as they walked into the dining room.

"Well, that's nice to hear. Everything normal," said Sabrina, "Except one thing."

"What's that?" answered Simone.

"The date last evening was awesome. And I'd have to admit this one is a keeper. He's so humble and giving; handsome, witty, has great work ethics, and spiritual."

"Yours turned out great too. I kind of knew it would when you forgot to call me. I didn't think it would be the best ever though. What did you do?"

"Nothing much except have dinner on the roof top of his apartment building. And get this, he had his youth choir serenade us and serve us. I mean it was a different dinner, you know, kids made it, and it was good. But the events were awesome. The kids sang so well that crowds of people around the building started to applaud after each of their songs. It was an amazing date," She turned and spoke, "Hi Aunt Marge."

141

Simone and Sabrina walked into the dining room, took seats at the North and South ends of the table, then watched Aunt Marge eat her soup. "Hi child," said Aunt Marge.

"Are you doing ok Aunt Marge?" Sabrina asked.

"Just fine! I think being home helps with my recovery."

"Recovery?"

"Yes, recovery from those symptoms those doctors identified as the cause of my sickness."

"You aren't sick; you're as healthy as an ox."

"No I don't think so. I know something's wrong but I can't place a finger on it," said Simone.

"If you don't have indicators to something then we can't make assumptions."

"No, there isn't anything that would cause you to think there is a problem. Is there?" replied Simone.

"Nothing other than a gut feeling, and sometimes those feelings are right on point. I can't seem to put my finger on it. Since I left the hospital, I've been feeling really weird. I'm sure it's nothing to alarm you over. I'll be fine and of course with more rest and good diet, things will get better."

"Okay," Simone and Sabrina replied in harmony.

"Finished the soup?" asked Simone.

"Yes, I have. But I'm like hearing about your dates. Share more. Tell me everything, and leave nothing out, even the nasty parts."

"Aunt Marge," they both giggled in reply.

Aunt Marge's physician called for her to have a session with a couple of specialist; a neurologist and cardiologist. They gathered in an office just large enough for three people. On the wall was an X-ray reader, it displayed Marge's x-rays and in the hand of the cardiologist was the test results from her tests the other day. In the other doctor's

hand was   results from neurology. Each doctor sat and reviewed the
tests. In their analysis, there was nothing different for a woman of
Marge's age. As a matter of fact, she seemed to be a great health, and
that's why the physician called f or special opinions. Each doctor
reviewed in depth and openly discussed what the evidence showed.
They brought up scenarios and historical events making them wonder
the root cause of Marge's fainting the morning she was found. Why
didn't she get to a level of illness that showed why or something that
highlighted a prognosis while she was in the hospital. Her normality
was   interesting   for a woman of her age. But there was   something
which caused her faint spells.

Doctors would not find what sparked her condition. Marge's charts
indicated everyday symptoms of a cold or early signs of a foreign
virus her body feverishly fought.   Doctors were baffled and
conversed intermittently that nothing seemed to jump out at either one
as a cause of her fainting and high fever.

Doctor Lorenz Maynard was called into one of the conversations
on Marge. He wasn't aware of a specific patient, he adamantly
listened to the multiple case discussions. He took notes and
graphically identified each area of medicine in reference. Later he
went to an office and pulled reference books off of different shelves.
He searched for symptoms within the group of notes he recorded. He
then circled a trend of events those specialists identified, but nothing
jumped out as a definite probability. Last, he contemplated contacting
the patient for a follow-up visit. Before getting up from the desk, he
made notes of questions to ask the patient. Within no time, he's listed
items that would give him clarity.

Lorenz contacted the leading physician and inquired to meeting or
visiting the patient.   The doctor directed him to patient services to
locate the patient and provided Lorenz with his permission to find out

as much information as necessary. When Lorenz went to patient affairs, he made his routine rounds with patients on the way, he reviewed charts and provided the attention and focus to them in a usual fashion. When he finished his last patient, he stopped at the nurses' station and called Sabrina.

"Hi Sabrina, I was thinking about you and decided to call."

"Hi Lorenz," she smiled during her reply, "It's nice hearing your voice. I hope your day is going well. I'm with my aunt and sister so I can't talk long."

"Ok, I wanted to know if you were available tonight. I'd love to see you."

"Well, I have a few errands, but tonight sound interesting enough. What do you say about 7? Will this work for you?"

"Seven it is, let's call if things change."

"Sure. See you then, your place."

"Bye lovely woman."

"Bye," Sabrina disconnected the call and turned to Simone with a smile. She explained, "That was Lorenz. He's ready to see me again and it hasn't been 24 hours."

"And did you expect anything different from him?" asked Simone.

"No, nothing different, except that he's not my normal type."

"That's what gets you hurt. Those men in your life before shouldn't be your norm. I'm glad you've changed your taste in men. Hopefully you won't cry on my shoulder this time." Aunt Marge added.

"Oh Aunt Marge, you're so dramatic. I didn't cry on your shoulder. I asked for advice, and then I cried."

All three ladies laughed at the comment. It was a flash of older times when the young ladies sought advice and comfort from their favorite aunt. Marge understood those emotional challenges a young lady would go through. Since their mother passed, Aunt Marge was a great substitute and was hip enough for the times. She gave great insight to many things. And it seemed that her advice protected them from the harsh pains of relationships; that is, when they followed her it.

Aunt Marge lifted her left hand and placed it on her forehead before she said, "I'm feeling a little warm. Is the heat up today?"

"No Aunt Marge, the heat is off. The air conditioner is off; the weather is perfect as this is a weird summer's day. It's nice out; you could mistake it for fall or spring. I suspect you don't want to go outside on the porch, if you aren't feeling very well," said Simone. "Are you feeling differently than before? We wanted to make sure you were feeling better. After your soup, we'd hope you were up for a ride to a park or up for a walk through the mall. We know how you like to window shop. Do you think you're up to it?"

"I may want to sit on the porch. It would make me feel better. I'd like the way the sun makes me feel and I'd like it, as I think of it."

"Good. Let's get your sweater just in case it's a little cool." Simone retrieved the lacy pink sweater from a dresser drawer that Aunt Marge wore on special occasions. It was the same sweater she wore to Simone's graduation, and in pictures on Thanksgiving at grandmother's house. She wore that same sweater to any event calling for a picture. Simone pondered, it's *the only sweater you'll find on any picture. She loves this sweater. I'll take this one and see if she wants it.*

In the front of the house, she held the pink laced sweater in her right hand while she waked through the hallway. Simone looked on the wall for pictures that reflected her aunt in the sweater. She stopped for a moment and looked at one picture in particular. It's was a picture of Aunt Marge and Uncle Arthur during a time when she seemed happy and content. *I remember the day they took this picture. As a matter of fact, my mother took the picture and she laughed so*

145

hard about it being professionally done. Just think, an eye from my mom being professional, no way. It is a nice picture and Uncle Arthur is so handsome. I hope to find a loving man like him. He was awesome. She moved into the den, Simone called out to Aunt Marge, "Will this sweater do?"

Aunt Marge turned, looked at the sweater and answered, "Yes that one is nice. Are you two girls ready?"

"I think we are. I am not going to stay too long because of a scheduled shoot. But I will be along for a short period of time. I hope that doesn't bother you." answered Sabrina.

"No it doesn't bother me one bit. I know you're a professional lady, and you have to work. As a matter of fact, I'm proud you do what you do. Says much for today's woman; I wish we had opportunities you enjoy back in my day. Life for me would surely be different."

They picked up their purses and headed to the car. Aunt Marge with her pink sweater didn't mention the fact that it was for dressier occasions. Unlike her normal focus, she never evaded to the point that a walk in the park during the afternoon would have been successful. Her agreement for the park was her favorite despite how she knew the girls loved the mall. She would usually insist on the mall because the girls loved the mall, but this time she felt the need for fresh air.

"Let's not move too hasty and fall over the stairs Aunt Marge," Said Simone. "I think we can get to the park in enough time. I 'd rather we get there safely than have an accident along the way."

"Okay", replied Aunt Marge. "Which car are we taking?"

"I can't drive you all because I'll have to leave for a shoot," answered Sabrina.

"That makes it your car Simone. Let's get going. The sun will be down before long and you know I hate driving while it's dark."

"Who said you were driving?" They chuckled while settling in the car. Sabrina whipped her car right along the street behind Simone. While she waited for things to get moving, Sabrina turned on the radio at a popular hip-hop station. She started dancing to the music and thought of Lorenz. *Oh, I'd love to get him dancing. The way that man moves, it's remarkable. I feel him now*, she thought. Simone finally settles in the car and placed the key in the car's ignition. The car started while she checked Aunt Marge once more to ensure her seatbelt was connected. She turned on the radio and the sound was loud. "Can't you turn it down a little baby?" asked Aunt Marge, "It's a little too loud for me and you know I'm not a fan of this supposed to be music."

"Not a problem. I don't mind listening to something else." Sabrina turned the radio to an oldies station she asks, "How about this station? Will it do?"

"Yes, child, that's fine."

Simone signaled and eased into traffic. Sabrina followed so there were no cars in between them. They headed north, through neighborhoods full of life on a major roadway. "You know," said Simone, "I can remember this road being empty and never any having traffic."

"Yep, things sure do change. And sometimes change is not for the better."

"What does that supposed to mean?"

"Not that all changes are good. It's different these days. Just something I noticed as I get older; and supposedly wiser. You know the saying, wiser with age.'

Snickering Simone replies, "Yes, wiser for sure but with age, come on Aunt Marge, you're no older than 50. How can you say older with age?"

"Child I wish I were 50. I'd have a new man in my life, go dancing all night, and have that man yelling early in the morning. I'd whip it on him."

"What?" exclaimed Simone, "I don't think I've ever heard you talk that way."

"I am a woman you know. I may be old in age, but I can still think about those great days."

They arrived at the park's parking lot, Simone signaled Sabrina to park next to her. Simone jumped out of the car and smiled at Sabrina making a gesture, *You're not going to believe what I heard.*

Simone walked to Aunt Marge's side of the car, she saw the passenger door open and one leg and foot on the ground. Immediately she reached for Aunt Marge's arm to assist her in getting out of the car. She spoke as she exited the car, "I know this is slowing you down, but thank you for being patient with me. I love the park. Can you feel the fresh breeze?"

"Yes, I feel it. I love bringing you here. It's the same park you brought us to when Sabrina and I were kids." Sabrina said while she closed the car door, "I remember when we came to the park; you were the only adult with us. I mean all of us. It had to be 13 kids with you. Today I look back and wonder how did you keep us in line and behaved so well?"

"It was easy those days. You all behaved. The fear in you was I'd tell your uncle or parents. The repercussions were devastating to you then. And besides, you all were so good. I had no problem with either of you. I loved you all so much, and you were all like my kids back then. Even when your folks would drop you off, you didn't even say good-bye to them and you jumped at starting your visit with me. I had all of you eating out of the palm of my hand. Literally," she laughed.

They walked along a paved walkway and sat on a bench near the small lake. The trees were tall and full of green leaves, colorful with bristling sounds as the winds gently touch each leaf. The sun was beaming and caused a lot of heat. The warmth of the day was like spring or fall. Aunt Marge sat on the bench and hummed an oldies song she recently heard on the radio. It was just like the days of Simone and Sabrina's child hood. "Old habits die hard," said Sabrina. "I remember that same song when we played kick ball over there."

"Yeah, I remember. It's been sometime since we came to this park. We use to come here so much. Hey, let's look over near the pond where we use to play."

"Okay"

"Aunt Marge, will you be ok for a minute or two?"

"I'm fine. You go ahead. I'm sure no one will bother me," answered Aunt Marge.

"We'll be right back," said Simone, as her and Sabrina walked towards the old playing field. "Girl, something's up with Aunt Marge," she told Sabrina. "I don't think everything is fine in her mind."

"Yeah, she's gotten old but I'd never think something is wrong. I guess she will be ok if she   rests more often."

"No, I think there's a lot more going on than what's showing. She talked about missing sex on the way here. Can you believe that? She never talked about having sex. Even when we used to ask her everything our parents wouldn't answer."

"You know, that's right. She never mentioned her sex life to us. It was always Simone and Sabrina answered in unison, "those fast girls who got their dues. Not my pretty nieces." But she'd answer our questions, no matter what we asked."

"She answered them all right. I remember when I thought babies were brought by a big bird and she showed me where a baby came from. It scared me to death just thinking a baby would get through that part of my body. A baby was so big and my vagina was so small.

I asked her how and she told me that they'd stretch me so far that I wouldn't snap back to normal. I think I was 12 years old at the time."

"That would scare anyone." Simone laughed with her hand over her mouth.

They arrived at the pond and saw small boats, ducks, and a concrete ramp. Nothing like the solitude of years before. Immediately the girls turned back towards Aunt Marge. They saw her sitting without moving; just sitting   in peace and harmony with the surroundings. Quickly the girls turned back to face the pond. "Wow it's changed. I guess no one thought this city would ever turn let people boat in the pond. At least kids are using it for miniature sail boats. At least it's not a super market parking lot."

"That's a great thing right?" asked Sabrina.

"I think so" said Simone. "Let's get back to Aunt Marge. We should be sitting with her before you leave."

"Yeah, let's do that." They   headed back for the bench. Aunt Marge was sitting motionless. She sat silently for the first time in days. She hadn't moved one muscle from the last time they looked at her. She didn't rock nor moved her head. "Is she asleep you think?" asked Sabrina.

"No, I bet she's t meditating or something like that."

"Probably so, she hadn't' been out in the park for quite some time now and the sound of the birds is probably helping her relax."

They arrived to the bench where Aunt Marge and took a seat. "Aunt Marge," called Sabrina, "Are you ok?"

"Mmm, huh," Marge responded.

"Good. You know I'll have to leave in a few."

"Mmm huh," she didn't motion a change in position.

"I'll let you know when the time comes. What are you doing?"

"Listening to someone calling my name."

"I don't hear anything," said Sabrina.

"Neither do I," said Simone.

"Hush, I hear it loud and clear."

The girls sat in silence as Aunt Marge closed her eyes and started snoring with her head leaning forward and her chin down. "How can she sleep like that?" asked Sabrina.

"I don't know. But as long as she's content it doesn't matter. It's got to be comfortable for her."

Minutes passed and Sabrina looked at Simone to indicate her time to leave for her next shoot. Sabrina stood from the bench and touched Aunt Marge to say good-bye and noticed no response. She didn't see Aunt Marge's body move nor hear her snoring. "Simone," Sabrina softly spoke, "Simone, do you think she's still asleep?" Simone looked for signs of breathing and noticed there's a moist spot on the grass, and started to panic.

"Aunt Marge," she yelled in a loud voice. "Aunt Marge wake up," she repeated in a higher tone. Still there wasn't a response or noticeable movement from their elderly aunt; nothing at all, no movement or breathing, and the moist spot weren't from rain or running water. Sabrina got on her phone and called for an ambulance. Simone touched Aunt Marge's wrist in search of a pulse.

"I found a pulse but it's weak." said Simone as she continued to hold Marge's wrist.

"Try to wake her; I'll get the ambulance here," Sabrina instructed.

"Aunt Marge, come on. Wake up. Please wake up." Nothing; no response or movement from Aunt Marge as Simone held her close and tried to wake her. She didn't respond but Simone felt her faint breath.

"The ambulance will be here shortly. They said in five minutes," barked Sabrina.

"Good," replied Simone. "Come on Aunt Marge, wake up."

Faint siren sounds became louder as the ambulance approached. "Good, that's the ambulance. It didn't seem like it will ever get here."

"Three minutes. Can you hear a siren? I don't understand why it's taking so long for them to arrive."

"Three minutes, seems like forever. Come on or it'll be an hour before they arrive. Come on!" pressured Simone.

In two minutes the ambulance arrived with the EMT specialist running to Aunt Marge's position. Immediately they place Aunt Marge on a gurney and look for vitals; blood pressure, heart beat, and body image. The EMT asked Simone questions. "What's her name?" he asked Simone.

"Marge," she replied.

"Ms. Marge, can you hear me?" He asked while he raised Marge's eye lid and flashed a light in her eye for a pupil response. Again, Marge didn't respond and her pupils barely moved. The EMT checked vital signs a second time, he realized there was little sign of life. He called to his EMT partner. "Let's get her in the ambulance and head for East Side hospital. Everything's faint. I'll start an IV on the way."

"Okay, let's go. Ready lift," the EMT specialist replied. They lifted Marge onto the ambulance and called for either of the girls to go along. "Which one of you is coming with her?"

"Sabrina you go in the ambulance, I'll follow." said Simone. "We'll come back for your car later."

"I have to call the shoot for a reschedule." Sabrina shouted.

"Okay."

The EMTs moved with urgency. Without looking back, they did exactly as planned and headed to the hospital. Sabrina held Aunt Marge's hand and dialed to cancel her photo shoot. She spoke to her photographer with a sense of fear. "I'm sorry the shoot can't happen today. I'm with my Aunt Marge on the way to the hospital. We'll have to reschedule. I'll call you later." Immediately ends the call."

Simone, drove her vehicle, called her office and exclaimed she followed the ambulance to the hospital. She told the director of her mishap and was reminded that she wasn't to come in today and if she needed more time, the director wanted a notification.

The ambulance maneuvered about traffic and arrived at the hospital within 10 minutes. The driver pulled the ambulance up to the dock. When the ambulance doors opened and an Emergency Room Nurse was waiting for the situation report from the paramedics. The nurse grabbed Sabrina by the hand to assist her exit and then moved her to the right of the vehicle. The paramedics jumped with extreme caution to ease Aunt Marge down with the roller gurney and get her into the emergency room. Through the double doors, there were multiple beds, people moaning, stations with people of harsh wounds, and   open spots with medical equipment in the ready. Doctors, nurses, and technicians   moved briskly about as if each patient was on their last leg.

Simone parked her car in the emergency lot, whisked towards the hospital doors as if she'd ran the hundred-yard dash. She nearly missed an oncoming car, she moved like the wind to reach Aunt Marge. Side stepped the counter, she blazed through the double doors of the emergency entrance and   looked for Sabrina. Moving from curtain to curtain, she glances quickly to see where her aunt landed. Running behind her was a clerk who attempted to stop her from entry into the area.

"Miss, Miss," the clerk yelled.

Simone, without turning shouted back, "I'm looking for my aunt and sister. They arrived just before I did in the ambulance outdoor."

"Miss, Miss," the clerk exclaimed, "If you'd come back to the counter I can tell you where she is."

Just as Simone stopped, Sabrina called out, "Simone, over here." Simone stopped and turned towards Sabrina, and in two steps she was next to Sabrina and Aunt Marge. The clerk stopped and asked if either had time to check Aunt Marge in as soon as possible; both Sabrina and Simone turned and in unison answered, "Yes" and turned back to Aunt Marge. Sabrina saddened from her fear and left Aunt Marge for the administration room.

Doctors checked Marge and noticeably Lorenz started shouting directions.

"Status on this patient," Dr. Maynard asked the paramedic.

"Not sure exactly, her vitals are BP 90 over 55, dizzy, in coherent, and her lungs full of congestion, and she seems weak. We think she's having a slight heart attack. We arrived on the scene and her condition hasn't changed. It's your job to know why. We transported her here and kept her stable. Our job is done. Let's go partner."

"Thanks guys. I'll take it from here. Nurse let's get her into 24. Retake her vitals while I give her a once over." Lorenz started checks for   symptoms. He scanned her pupils, checked her heart beat, and breathing. He took notes of her condition under Simone's observation. "Simone, right?" Before she acknowledged her name, he continued, "Can you tell me what she did   before coming here?"

"Sure, she had a bowl of soup, talked a little, went to the park and she fell into a deep sleep. She didn't respond to us. That's when we called the ambulance to bring her here."

"Did you notice if she took some type of medications?"

"No, nothing that I know about, other than the prescription she had from the last time being here."

"We don't have an idea what's causing her condition. I'm going to review her record and see what type of meds she's on. She's stable for the time being." Lorenz turned and headed for the nurses' desk. "Nurse, can you get me the records on Marge Blaine please? Call me when you have them." He walked to another emergency bed.

***

Simone looked for Sabrina and dialed her cellular phone. "Hey, where on earth are you?"

Just as Sabrina walked through the waiting room, headed to admissions clerk and answered her cellular, "Hey, I'm near the admission desk."

"Oh, okay. Aunt Marge is stable right now and Dr. Maynard is reviewing her medical record. He couldn't find anything immediate as an indicator to what's happening to her."

"Did you say Lorenz Maynard?"

"Yes, he's on call. I guess you aren't worried about Aunt Marge since you're asking about Lorenz."

"Yes I am worried about Aunt Marge. Just surprised to see Lorenz on duty; are you coming out? Or should I come in?"

"I'm heading out. Take a seat and I'll be right there."

Simone ended the call, snapped her cell phone, and went to the waiting room. She noticed Lorenz at a different bed where they performed emergency medical care. Blood spurted all over the bed area while nurses and Dr. Maynard attempted to stop the bleeding. It was only for a moment that Simone looked, but it was long enough for a queasy feeling to fall over her. In a dash, she jumped through the double doors to the waiting room. "Sabrina," she called, "You're not going to believe what I just saw." And before saying anything, she caught herself not to announce her thoughts because people looked at her. She calmed her voice and said, "The usual thing and nothing more."

"I can only imagine," said Sabrina. "Well, what's the verdict?"

155

"Nothing yet, the doctor has to review her record before doing something. He's got to know what's going on before he can do anything. He's in his prognosis and response phase. I'm sure he'll let us know something as soon as he finds out. Let's find a seat and wait."

Minutes rolled   to 45 past the hour. Not one sign of any doctor coming out to explain to them. Sabrina walked to the nurses' counter and asked about her aunt. The nurse looked for someone, hesitated, placed a pad down on the counter, turned around as if searching for someone. She walked   to the ER section. Sabrina looked at Simone and shook her head from side to side and displayed disgust with her facial expression. Sabrina waited at the counter, for 7 minutes. A nurse appeared from the back and asked, "Can I help you?"

"No," Sabrina replied and explained, "Another nurse is checking on my aunt. I'm waiting for an answer."

"You can have a seat and I'm sure she'll call you when she returns."

"Thanks but no thanks. I want to be here when she arrives."

Two minutes passed and the original nurse Sabrina asked returned to the counter. She looks at Sabrina and said, "The doctor will be here shortly."

"You can't tell me what's going on with my aunt?"

"No I can't. I was directed to tell you the doctor will be here shortly. Please have a seat."

Sabrina took a seat and saw the doors to the ER open. A doctor walked out for someone in the waiting room and called for Williams. The sound   being so close to Whittingham touched the girls' nerve. They watched people leave their seats to gather around the doctor for an update. Within a minutes three people around the doctor began to cry. One of them whaled loud enough to send streaking pain down one's spine. "Oh, god no!" she cried. They embraced each other and sat near the exit doors, the doctor returned into the ER to continue his work. Sabrina and Simone observed the three people and sympathy for them invaded people in the room. No one attempted to console them. Minutes later a different doctor walked out and calls for "Ms. Blaine." No one responded to his call. The doctor repeated "Mr. or Ms. Blaine." Again, no response within a minute, the doctor returns through the doors looking at the chart. Sabrina jumped up to the nurses' counter and asked, "When am I going to find out the conditions on patient Marge Blaine?"

"The doctor was just calling for Ms. Blaine."

"Oh my goodness, we were listening for Whittingham. Please get that doctor back."

"I think I can manage. Have a seat and I'll get him back."

"Thank you," said Sabrina.

The doctor returned to the doors and calls for Whittingham. Both Sabrina and Simone walked over to hear the doctor's explanations.

"Ms. Whittingham." the doctor checked.

"Yes," both Sabrina and Simone answered.

"There's good news about Ms. Blaine and of course there's troubling news. Ms. Blaine suffered a stroke and that's the bad news. The good news is that is wasn't bad enough to paralyze her. So, you'll have to watch her diet, help with meds, and a daily regime of exercise to continue her muscle use. And from her chart, I noticed she was here before. I asked for a few more test to ensure there is nothing else on the horizon. Let's keep her here for two days."

"Oh, sure thing doctor, we'll have her back in two days," said Simone. "Is there an appointment set up for her?"

"No, Ms. Willingham, I'd like to observe her for two days," said the doctor.

"Oh, she was just here for a few days with multiple tests. I think you can see her record and besides she'd like to be home." explained Simone.

"Well, I know the case well," answered the doctor as Lorenz approached. "We need to test her to make sure of our diagnosis," he said as he smiled at Sabrina.

"Well, it's your call and I think it's a good idea since you know the history," replied Sabrina.

"We can't let her stay here," said Simone.

"We can," replied Sabrina. "Let's let the doctors be doctors. It'll be ok for two days."

"Good, then its settled," replied the ER doctor. "The nurse has the information. I'll pass it on to her primary provider. She will let you know the test schedule. I think it's the best thing to do. And you two can see her as soon as we're done here. She's being transferred to a room as we speak. I wish I can tell you what room, but I haven't the slightest. I'm sure the nurse has the room assignment."

"Thank you doctor," Simone and Sabrina replied in unison while they observed Lorenz and the attending physician leave The girls turned to the nurses' counter. "We're looking for Marge Blaine's room," said Simone.

"Just a moment" the nurse replies and looks at the computer screen. "She's in room 671, 6th floor."

"Thanks."

Sabrina and Simone walked to the elevators, pushed the up button and silently waited for the elevator's arrival. "Simone," Sabrina addressed.

"Yes,"

"What are we going to do to help Aunt Marge? Should we place her in a senior citizen home?"

"You know I hate doing that. And the reality is our schedules are hectic and there's no way we can support her day in and day out. Maybe we can get a live-in helper."

"I don't know about that the live in. I think a live-in is dangerous; unless it's a family member that wouldn't mind."

"You never know about family unless you ask. There's so much having her placed in a home or having someone come. We have to really look at this for a minute. We were lucky to be with her this time. Imagine if we'd visit and she was still at home with no one around and then her having a stroke. Would we be as lucky?"

"You have a point. I think we should put her in a home where there's 24-hour observation."

"She's going to hate that idea. You know she likes to be independent. I bet she'd rather have a live in."

"But the live in is no guarantee for 24-hour observation."

"Neither is a home. But at least there's a greater chance someone is around to help if need be."

"Yes, you're right. We should look into it." The elevator arrived and they entered. Sabrina pressed the 6th floor button and stepped to the center of the elevator.

"Hello Sabrina," a voice from the rear of the elevator. Sabrina turned and locked eyes with Lorenz.

"Oh, hi Lorenz, I didn't think I'd see you here; I mean at least right now," responded Sabrina

"Oh you're not here for me?"

"I wish it were for you. Not that I don't like seeing you, it's my aunt."

"I wish it were instead of your situation. Did the attending explain what happened to your Aunt?"

"Mild stroke. She's had a mild stroke. I think it's a second time."

"I'm sure your Aunt's doctor has a plan for her. You must be heading to her room." The elevator stopped at the 4th floor. "This is my stop. Please call me later. I'd love seeing you again." Lorenz left the elevator and walked without turning around. Simone saw that he didn't turn around as the doors closed. "You blew that one didn't you?"

"Oh heck no. Didn't you hear him say he wants to see me soon? He's going to; it's just at my leisure."

"There you go in control again. He seems really nice so don't be too controlling."

"I got this one sis, don't worry, he's a doll of a man and definitely on my radar."

Chapter 9

Quality of Life

The Elevator doors opened on the 6th floor. Simone and Sabrina walked to room 671 and entered without knocking. There were six people in the double bed room; two nurses on each side of Aunt Marge. The other patient was very quiet and sound asleep. Those nurses set up the last IV, and comforted Aunt Marge the best they could. Aunt Marge was out of it, as her eyes were barely open. But here condition was an improvement since they arrived hours ago.

***

Rodney jumped with excitement as he told Dan of his wonderful date with Simone while they sat in his apartment. "I'm telling you it was great. No better than great, it was awesome."

"Sure it was the best. It had to be. I've never seen you so energetic after a date."

"It's that noticeable?"

"No doubt, it's noticeable alright. Another step and I'll figure a way to package your energy and sell it as kinetic fuel for cars."

"No man, you don't understand. She was amazing, beautiful, classy, and beautiful. Did I say beautiful?"

"Yes, I think you said it three times. That woman really has you doesn't she?"

"No, well, maybe, I guess so."

"She has you alright. Have you called her since the date?"

"No," replied Rodney, "I haven't called her yet. As a matter of fact, I'm waiting for her to call me."

"Now why on earth would you do that?"

"It's a classic way to ensure she had a wonderful time during the date. Plus, it doesn't make me look to aggressive or desperate."

"If the date was so great, why would you think you're being aggressive?"

"It's just classy to wait."

"You're much better than that Rodney. You do your thing man, call the woman and talk to her about the next time you get together. It should be easy to set   the next date. Not that you'd have to do more than the first. Setting your standards so high during the very first date was crazy, but it's done now. So what do you think would work for an encore?"

"Okay, I'll call her. And let me think, the date should be something simple and yet elegant."

"Yes, elegant and simple."

"I got it, a picnic in the park on a Sunday afternoon."

"That sounds nice, but did your first date have a ride in the park?"

"Oh, yeah, but it was a good experience. And if dating in the park seems a little much for a second date, then I'm just showing her I like wilderness."

"Ha, ha, ha, that's funny," Dan laughed "Wilderness? Don't you mean nature?"

"So you get the picture."

"Man this woman has you out of mind and character."

"You know she is awesome, just awesome."

Rodney walked in the bedroom of his apartment, picked up his cell phone and dialed   six of the seven digits. Just before he pressed the last number, he looked in the mirror and saw his image with a   glow. *Yes, I'm glowing in the middle of the day and it's all because of Simone. Wow! Man I look so different. It's a wonder I recognize myself. I haven't felt this happy since, a long time ago.* Rodney placed the phone back on the dresser, and decided to get dressed first. He looked into the closet and selected a nice pair of black slacks, a light color blue shirt, and matched his shoes and belt. He dressed as if headed to the office or meet a friend for coffee. For his taste, he wasn't too impressive but very neat. His clothes gave him the appearance of a neat person, with style and class. He took one last look in the mirror, nodded with approval, and walked out to the living room of the apartment.

"You cleaned up quite well. If I have to say so," said Dan.

"Thanks man, I try to look nice when I have too."

"Did you call?"

"Snap, no I didn't. I started to but had a different thought. I'll surprise her with flowers and take her a picnic lunch. That way she'll think I'm spontaneous."

"Nice touch. He's back on track." Dan laughed.

Dan and Rodney left the apartment in different cars, waved at each other and drove off. Rodney called Simone on his cellular phone. Simone answered on the fourth ring, "Hello."

"Hi Simone, its Rodney."

"Hi, I'm at the hospital. Can we talk later?"

"Hospital. What happened?"

"Something's wrong with my aunt. We were at the park and it seemed as if all hell broke loose. Well not exactly all hell, but something unexpected."

"Is she doing ok?"

"Best to be expected at the moment, but we're not sure what the problem is."

"Are they running tests?"

"Yes and will run more tomorrow. Right now she's under observation for changes in her condition. I know they'll find something this time."

"Let's hope so. I hope things get better. Are you doing ok?" asked Rodney.

"Yes, so far. I'm just worried about Aunt Marge. I want you to know how much fun I had on our date. I hope we get a chance to do it again."

"That's what I called about. We should start dating exclusively. I'd like to take the chance on us without going through so much of the norm. I have a great feeling about you, us, and our future. I feel like nothing before when meeting a lady, and it's got to be because of you."

"Exclusive? I don't know about being exclusive so quickly. I hardly know you and how you are in multiple situations. I have to know how you'll respond to different places, things, and conditions."

"You mean, you're a woman who wants to see more of the person and not just looking to beat the ticking clock?"

"Why shouldn't I be more aware of you as an entire package and not pass judgment from one date?"

Rodney took a deep breath and sighed. He responded with doubt in his voice. "I had hoped for a better response than take our time and build."

"Not your normal answer from a woman. Not too shocking is it?"

"No not shocking, just surprising."

"Surprises are good."

"Not this type of surprise. You see, multiple women dream of a day when a good guy comes into their lives and offer quality in a relationship. I understand your doubt in my character in some point. What I don't understand is our multiple encounters that show you how interested I am to take this relationship to a higher level. I thought you'd want us to move on."

"In my heart yes but in my mind its best to move slowly and see how we fit overall."

"Fit over all. I thought you knew this and it's why we started dating."

"Dating is it. Not moving in together and making plans for the future."

"Oh, I see, you think this is making plans for the future. As I said earlier, we would be exclusive. Are you seeing someone else?"

"No, no time for it. Between work and my aunt there isn't much time for anything else."

"Did you enjoy our first date?"

"Yes."

"How about the dinner at my place with your cousin, was I wrong to assume you were into me?"

"No, as a matter of fact, I'm quite glad you've shown interest. And of course I am interested in you. But I'm not ready for a commitment."

"Very well, I see your point. Does this mean we can't go on any more dates?"

"Of course not, I'd love going on dates with you. Remember, I said let's build this relationship and not rush into it."

"Okay. Caution is the operative word to building. Well, I hope your aunt gets better. Call me when you can. I'd love to talk to you more."

"Is that it? You're ready to leave the conversation?"

"No, not really, but I thought you had something else going on that requires your attention."

"Yes I do, but you are my focus at the moment. I want us to do something soon."

"That would be great. But since you're busy, it has to be your call when. I'll take care of the where and what."

"It's a deal. I'll call you soon."

"Talk to you then."

"Bye Rodney."

"Later, Simone."

Rodney snapped the cellular and placed it in the carrying case. *Man was I wrong or just too damn interested in this woman?* he thought. He arrived at his building complex, parked his car and headed to his apartment. Rodney walked into the family room of his apartment and picked up the phone book with business and associate contacts. He flipped pages in search for a name that struck him with interest. Before he realized what happened to him, this contact information jumped from the page. "Oh man oh man, what a woman, and I pushed her away when I met Simone. Should I call or just sit for a moment?" he said aloud.

"You should sit for a moment," Dan said as he entered the apartment.

"Man I didn't realize you were here. So you heard the conversation between Simone and I?"

"No, I didn't hear your part, but it isn't difficult to figure out the other comments. She is just being cautious. So don't go do something foolish."

"Coming from you that's some serious advice."

"Yes, but remember that was before I heard how serious you are with Simone. I mean, serious enough to impress me that she's the one."

"Yeah, my thoughts exactly, she's the one."

"So be patient and let things work out. Focus on being there for her without being annoying."

"Annoying?"

"Come on Rodney, We've been with friends for years. Don't you know I understand you and how driven you can be with women?"

"It's not annoying to show your feelings to a woman on a daily basis."

"It is when they aren't open to it just yet."

"Okay, no spontaneous gifts, visits, and multiple calls throughout the day with this one. I'll be patient as much as possible."

"Let's hold you to this. Oh, and give me the name and number of the woman you're about to call. I can use a date tonight."

"Yeah, ah, no, you'll have to find your own. This is my stash for emergencies."

"What? You're going to do me this way! Just remember, when I get on the wagon of fun, there won't be much for me to share."

"When Simone comes around, I'll have a wagon of my own. I know it."

***

Simone finished the call and attempted to contact Sabrina. She dialed her number and waited for an answer. Again, the voice mail answered asks for a message. "Hey Sis, give me a call when you can. I think I may have pushed Rodney away too soon. Call me." After Simone folded the cellular phone, she moved towards Aunt Marge, looked at her peaceful slumber, and allowed a tear to fall down her face as she spoke softly, "I sure wish you were available to talk right now Aunt Marge. I could use your point of view if I'm cold, or if I'm waiting for a prince charming that isn't coming. I could be pushing the prince charming away right now. I practically threw myself on Rodney weeks ago at his apartment. I can't believe my fear or why I want to be so careful. This could be the one. Or, is he? I did have a wonderful time on our date. It was charming, romantic, and full of that special great feeling factor. It was too good to be true for a first date; no flaws and he were the gentlemen of men. Did it all scare me? Am I afraid of the quality he brings? I haven't had a man with so much to offer, the right touch per say. Is this what life has for me? Moving too fast for a sure thing to last; I practically told him to back off."

"Simone is that you," asked Aunt Marge. Looking at Aunt Marge, Simone replied, "Yes ma'am, it's me. I'm here. How are you feeling?"

"Like a mule kicked me in my chest."

"Should I call a doctor? Is the pain unbearable?"

"It's really painful, but I don't want any drug because I want to talk to you. I heard you talking about Rodney."

"Oh?" said Simone. "How did you know his name?"

"You called it out just loud enough for me to hear. I thought I was dreaming for a moment. You know how drugs can make you think you hear things and not respond."

"Aunt Marge, we shouldn't think about my situation with a man. We need to focus on you and how we can get you better."

"Oh hush young lady. I know what I want to do. I want you to listen to me." Simone sat in the chair next to Aunt Marge's bed. Simone gave her total attention to the elderly lady whom she adored in her life time. She attentively sat and leaned forward in her chair, touched Aunt Marge on her arm and without a spoke to her through her eyes and ears. Simone commented in a tender voice, "I'm all yours Aunt Marge, tell me what's on your mind."

"Child, you've done the things in life only many have dreamed to do. You deserve someone kind and intelligent. You can close doors that open wide and regret the time you have now and the gift presented to you. You don't know what God has for you and remember people come to you in light of what you think. It is a reason for someone to be so into you from little to nothing. Those relationships last a life time. Take your uncle and me for example. We dated for a short period and I knew he was my gift. I thought just as you and my mother said the exact same things to me as I'm telling you now. Take the gift of life being offered to you. Don't run away from it and make excuses with uncertainty. It's time for your quality of life. Go live it."

"Aunt Marge, that's the first time I heard how you and Uncle Arthur started. I had no idea you two dated for a short period before getting married."

"Yes, it was two dates and we walked down the aisle. He was the best thing that ever came into my life. Look at the blessing his love brought me. That includes you and Sabrina. And don't forget the others I love so much. Go child, get your man and open your mind, spirit, and heart to him. He'll do right by you and be right for you. I'm getting tired and the pain is awful. Call the nurse for me baby."

"Yes Ma-am," Simone answered and ran out of the room for the nurse's station. "My aunt is in serious pain and she needs you right now," shouted Simone with anxiety, "SHE'S IN PAIN DAMN IT. One of you had better move this instant." As her last word flashed out of her mouth, Sabrina returned to Aunt Marge's room and immediately took to her side. "I'm here for you Aunt Marge. Hang in there, the nurse will be her in a minute. I think one sent for the doctor."

"Thank you baby, I know this is hard on you, but it's not as painful as losing your uncle. I can handle this baby. I can handle the pain."

Two nurses walked briskly into the room, grabbed her chart, and give Aunt Marge a few pills and a shot the doctor ordered for reported pain. In minutes Marge's pain subsided and she returned to an incoherent state. She fell into a sound sleep. It was moments like this that made life seem like a battle. In Aunt Marge's mind, she dreamed of days where laughter and fun filled days of love and affection from her loving husband. There were flowers in bloom, even when those days seemed gloomy from a winter's storm. There was comfort in her home, when the kids would visit and showed their school accomplishments from the earlier week. There was her favorite dish she loved to cook, and cook, and cook. *My goodness, I'm missing all of the important things I use to have.*

Aunt Marge saw herself as a young woman who walked on a sandy beach during summer. It was the same beach she loved to visit on the California coast, light colored sand, and waves crashed against rocks/. The beach was secluded from the general public and of course gave a chance of romance. *We are a romantic couple. "Come dear sweet man; walk with me on the beach next to the waves.* Aunt Marge was dressed in a white sun dress she loved to wear over her bathing suit. She kept her girlish figure over the hears and never lost her ability to dress seductively in simple out fits. The wind blew her hair through the straw hat and the breeze made her laugh with the seagulls.

Earlier years she remembered the children attended middle school, how proud she was about all of her niece and nephews who graduated and moved to higher learning. *"I attended each child's first day at college. Especially Michael, he was truly ecstatic about his first day. Michael had us running all over campus and even shared his first college meal. We teased him about that day for years. Don't you remember honey?* she said to Arthur.

It seems like my years of living and those fond memories were fantastic. I enjoyed the exciting times of life, especially watching the children mature into lovely adults. Oh, and for them to have kids of their own, what a pleasant experience to share. Family makes a world of difference, and of course watching the next generation means everything. I'm so weak these days; I can't go to any of the kids' events. No baking for them, no college visits, no parks or playground, no picnics, and I can hardly stay focused on a movie or two from home. What kind of life am I living? Doesn't seem like the one I had, or not much to enjoy. I've lived well and done things most people dream of doing. I've out lived my siblings, in-laws of my generation, and all of my friends. I don't know how much longer I have to hang on living this life. I just don't know. God, if you take me now, I'm sad only for not living as I did in the past. I'm happy because there is a greater life with my generation of friends, love, and family. Whatever you have in for me lord, I'll gladly go.

Aunt Marge mumbled unheard of words to Simone. She said the darnedest things while asleep under heavy sedation. "How could she utter anything is beyond me?" asked Simone. *Aunt Marge seem pretty peaceful right now. I'd better call Sabrina.* Simone dialed the phone with one hand and looked out the window and observed anything worth looking over. It seemed like the sunset was in its transition as the sky dimed into darkness. Night fell and the reflection of this long day blasted Simone's thought. The harsh reality of Aunt Marge's sickness asserted into Simone's mind it was coming to an end. One ring, two rings, three rings, fourth ring and Sabrina didn't answer. Simone sat in the chair, read a magazine, watched television, and finally fell asleep. She woke after a couple hours and didn't see Sabrina. She decided to call and within one ring, Sabrina answered, "Hey Sis."

"Hey, how are things?"

"I can't tell for sure. It doesn't seem like things are pretty bad for her at the moment, she looks comfortable. She's been resting for a while now."

"That's good."

"When are you coming by?"

"On my way in now, I should be there within 20 minutes."

"Good. Can you bring a cappuccino, please?"

"What?"

"A cappuccino. It helps me sooth and settle my thoughts."

"I'll get one. I hope I find an open place this time of night."

"You will I'm sure."

"Increase that time to 30 minutes for the extra run."

"I'll see you when you get here."

"Keep the faith sis. Bye"

"See you soon, Bye."

God, if you're listening, please get Sabrina here safe. Help Aunt Marge get better, thought Simone.

Chapter 10

She's The One

"Dan she slammed me, rejected me, killed my ego from one phone call. I swore no woman would do this to me," said Rodney.

"Are you kidding? She didn't slam you; she probably meant you were moving too fast."

"No, she slammed the door in my face. I've never had a woman do this to me."

"It's true. As long as I've known you, rejection doesn't come your way too often. And besides, you don't get too excited over a woman who would think of rejecting you."

"Is this what rejection feels like?"

"Ah, yep, sure is."

"Man is this crazy. I shouldn't let a woman make me feel so crappy. I've got to do something."

"Something like what?"

"Go to the hospital and see her tonight. She won't slam me down in person. I know it. I can get her to take a chance. Man, I've got to try. I won't be able to sleep or function if I don't."

"Rodney I've never seen you this worked up over a woman. Even before she creamed your ego and well heart for this matter, it's a first."

Rodney paced the floor in thought of what to do. Tears swelled in his eyes, as each pondered flash of not having Simone in his life, entered the forefront of his emotions. Rodney stopped and looked into the dark of night through his apartment's bay window, he recalled other women in his life over the years. *None of my former girlfriends are like Simone, they can't compare. Her features are   real, angelic, and her body is that of a goddess. The woman is just fine, awesome, and truly compatible. I know this from one date,* he thought.

"Hey man, I'm heading out. You ok?" asked Dan.

"Yeah, I'm ok," replied Rodney.

"Tell me what you did with Simone tomorrow. I know you're up to something. I know oh so well. Just remember, it isn't a conquest this time. It's real because I see it in you."

"You don't have to worry about me being stupid. I want this woman for the rest of my life. I know it."

"Good luck."

"Don't need it but thanks. It's fate. The rest of my life starts right here."

Rodney returned to pacing the floor and walked from one room to the other. Periodically he stopped at the bay window and stared into the night as if there was a message coming to him. Like his childhood days when he felt there was a letter on its way from a family member, his instinct graveled him into a gust of emotions. He knew it would come and in anticipation he looked out the window for the mailman. Rodney turned towards the front room of his apartment and then it hit him. It was an idea of a life time and it had to happen tonight. *If I can't get to her direct, I'll do it through her aunt. NO, that isn't a good idea, the woman is ill, not a good thought. How bad do you want this woman? Drastic measures call for drastic actions.*

Rodney rushed out of the apartment and headed to an all-night convenient store. He jumped in his car and drove to the hospital, and looked for an open convenient store in route. He saw a gas station convenient store opened He turned in and parked his car at the front door. He entered the store and it was nearly empty except for the clerk and two customers. The store had multiple items Rodney could choose for an impression. From candy, drinks, wine and beer, to day old flowers; all are items were something he could present to Simone. Especially give her something at a time where her spirit needed lifting. *A small gift may do the trick.* Rodney selected a couple of day old flowers. Two pink roses barely held on to dear life; not quite wilted, but still projected their sweet aroma. *These will do just fine*, he thought. Rodney turned around from the refrigerated flowers, checked for another item as a soft drink for himself. He looked intently to make the right drink selection as he lost himself in thought and anxiety to see Simone. *Am I doing the right thing forcing myself in her life at a time like this? No class at all. I should just go home and wait it out.*

***

Sabina pulled into a convenience store near the hospital and parked her car right near the front door. She checked her purse for money, made sure she had enough for Simone's cappuccino and for her smoothie. *I've just enough without going to the ATM*, she thought. When she walked into the store, she immediately headed towards the coffee counter grabbed a cup and started the cappuccino. While it's poured, she looked at the cups for the smoothie and as she as she moved towards the machine, she saw Rodney in her line of sight. She didn't stop the start of her smoothie before she noticed a gentleman walking around lost in the store. "Hey, whatever it is has to be hard to find." Sabrina spoke to the gentleman.

"Yes, sort of, I'm confused to surprise my girl with a flower or something to munch on since she's been at the hospital sitting with her relative."

"That's sweet, taking her something. I bet she'll be happy to see you," responded Sabrina.

Rodney walked to the cashier and looked back at Sabrina. He recognized features of Simone, the nose, eyes, and build. When Sabrina approached the cashier, Rodney stepped to the side and asked, "Do you have a sister named Simone?"

"Yes, I do." Sabrina looked at Rodney and asked, "You wouldn't happen to be the guy she went out with the other night would you?"

Rodney smiled and answered, "If it were the other night and she mentioned a hot guy that she admired. I hope I'm the one," he laughed. "Nice meeting you…"

"…Sabrina," she answered as she extended her hand to shake his.

"How's your aunt?" asked Rodney.

"Not sure, Simone said she isn't doing too bad, but not well either. I guess she's in a middle state. You know how some people are when they've aged."

"No, I haven't a clue to that. I guess she's fighting to hang on and get better. You know, she sounds like a great lady."

"Oh, for sure she's the best."

Sabrina noticed the roses Rodney held. "Oh, those are sweet. Are they for me?" Smiled as she knew the answer.

"Well, I can get you one, but these are for Simone. I wanted to bring a couple for your aunt but the selection is awful. You can't find a good flower, especially this time of night. The last of the good ones are holding onto dear life. Besides, I didn't think your aunt would embrace dyeing flowers. Not good."

"Good point."

After they paid the cashier, they headed to their cars. "I'll follow you on the way Sabrina. Don't tell Simone I'm coming ok. Please. I might change my mind about visiting this time of night."

"Don't turn back. I'm sure she'd like to see you. Trust me on this."

"I can trust you on it. I don't want to push my luck."

"Get in the car and let's go. Follow me and don't let me down. I know she wants to see you."

"Okay, I'll follow you to the hospital. Wait for me so we can walk in together."

"Sure, no problem."

Sabrina backed up first and pulled into the road. Rodney followed directly behind her. They left the convenient store with multiple things in mind. Sabrina thought, I *think Simone will love to have a companion with a strong shoulder*. Rodney pondered, *I hope Simone takes me in her mind and allow me to open her up to a wonderful life. If she doesn't, I' don't know what to do.* Both drove into the parking lot. Sabrina found a parking space close to the double doors and Rodney parked on the next row immediately behind her.

"You found a nice space Sabrina," said Rodney.

"Like the lot is entirely full, how can I not find one?" responded Sabrina.

"That was obvious huh?"

"Are you nervous about something?"

"Yes I am to be honest, I want Simone happy I came tonight. I'm not so sure about this."

"Will you trust me? I know how much she likes you. I know she had a great time on your date. I know she needs someone like you in her life. Trust me on this."

"Ok, again, I'm trusting you."

They walked into the hospital straight into the lobby. They meet a security officer, nurse, and janitor talking in a group. The security officer scanned them as they walk closer to the elevators. "Can I help you?" asked the officer.

"We are headed to the seventh floor. Going to see my Aunt, Marge Blaine in room 671," responded Sabrina.

"Please be careful with your step, I just waxed the floor," said the janitor.

"No problem," both Rodney and Sabrina replied.

Rodney and Sabrina took notice as if they were being watched for family resemblance. No way can either of them inquire to the relationship link. And without inquiry, they successfully passed and entered the elevator. "I thought for sure one of those guys would ask us for proof of relationship," said Rodney.

"No way, today the family nucleus changed. You'd suspect they too were family."

"Good point."

"What floor are we heading too? I want to get there before the flowers die."

"Sixth floor."

Rodney pushed the button for the sixth floor. The elevator doors close and silence fell between them until Rodney spoke, "I hope Simone accepts these wilted flowers."

"She will. Stop worrying. I know my sister and how important you are to her."

"I'm important?"

"Sure, why do you think I told you to come along? I don't think she'd be anything g but excited to see you."

"I sure hope you're right on this."

"I am."

They exited the elevator as soon as the doors opened. Sabrina walked first and led Rodney to the room. Without a second thought, they walk directly to the room. Just before Rodney entered, Sabrina tells Rodney, "You should wait out here. Let me get Simone to come out for a moment. You two can then go to the waiting room down the hall on the other side of the wing. It will give you some privacy. And it gives me time with Aunt Marge. You know, that quality just the two of us time. I need it."

"Ok, I'll wait until she comes out. Don't tell her about the flowers. I need the surprise effect in addition to me being here."

"Sure thing," replied Sabrina as she entered the room. She Closed the door behind her, Simone hugged Sabrina as if it was over for Aunt Marge. With a tear she looked at Aunt Marge who was sleeping. "She hasn't moved since taking pain medication. That was when you called earlier," said Sabrina.

"She looks peaceful. When will she get back to being herself?" Sabrina asked.

"I don't quite know. She had a really different conversation earlier. She overheard me talking to Rodney and as usual gave me her opinion."

"Oh, Rodney is outside the door waiting to see you."

"I can't believe it. Out of all the times to visit, why couldn't he wait? Now is not good for me."

"Go easy on him sis. I told him you'd be glad to see him tonight. I thought you wouldn't mind."

"He's a nice guy, but this is trifling. He could at least wait until Aunt Marge's condition is better. I don't like the idea of him thinking I should just fall into his arms. I don't like it."

"It wasn't quite my idea he comes, but I thought you'd be happy with it. He's really a sweet guy who adores you to death. Who else would come out here in the middle of the night trying to really show his feelings?"

"Impressive or not, I am not feeling it. He has to move on. It's like I'm not in the right state of mind to respond to this. I need him to go home. I should send you out to tell him I'm not interested anymore."

"What, not interested?"

"Exactly, not interested."

"You should tell him yourself and be done with it if you feel so strongly against him. Don't lead him on; just tell him how you feel about his antics. I still think it's nice of him to be concerned about you and your feelings for Aunt Marge."

"Nice, but no thanks. I can find comfort from a dog that would be better soothing. I'll tell him to go home and don't call me ever again.

I think he's trying to take advantage of me at a vulnerable time. How low class is that?"

"Then you'd better tell him. I thought for sure you'd feel different. I encouraged him to come here tonight. I saw him while getting your cappuccino," said Sabrina.

"It's nothing like having to tell off a man in the middle of the night when your aunt is fighting for her life. Just so damn inconsiderate of him making me angry, ugh I'm so pissed. I am going out there right now."

"You better before you cool down and rethink how nice he is for being here."

"Come on Sabrina, you're pushing Rodney hard on me aren't you?"

"No, just reminding you about him being such a nice guy. Go, go and tell him what's on your mind. I'll be here with Aunt Marge. Go."

"I'm glad to lay into him."

***

Rodney, stood outside the room door and heard Simone's last comment, "I'm glad to lay into him." Rodney turned   for the waiting room where he now wished he'd stayed. *If I act as if I don't know about her disgust, I'd be better off. As a matter of fact, heck I'd better leave and let her just be. I can leave the flowers with the nurse and place a note on it.* Without a second thought, Rodney went directly to the nurses' counter and looked for something to write with. *A sticky and a pen will do the trick*, he thought. He saw Simone walk out of the room headed in his direction. Rodney turned left and walked to the opposite side of the nurses' station. He did his best to avoid Simone at the moment. He became stealth in his mind and ducked into a near office. The room was empty by chance and there was no one to ask if it were ok to be in there. He took advantage of the

180

concealment. Simone stepped to the empty room where Rodney was supposed to be. "Not here. He should be glad he isn't here. I'm in the mood to kick him away from me and without even starting on the inconsiderate behavior he showed me tonight. If he's so inconsiderate I'm glad to see it now and not later. How fortunate am I?" Simone returned to Aunt Marge's room. One of the monitoring machines loud alarm sounded indicating a problem. Again, Aunt Marge wasn't doing so well. Her heart was fabulous thought Simone. "I can't live without her."

Sabrina ran out of the room trying not to be loud as others were rest. She ran to the nurses' desk and looked for assistance. Simone, stood near the nurses' station and saw Sabrina's look of disgust and ran without a word back into Aunt Marge's room to check and see what's up. Sabrina walked behind the nurses' counter and looked into the immediate office, no one was around. She walked to the next office and found Rodney, "Are you serious?" she commented on Rodney hiding from Simone. "Aunt Marge isn't breathing, have you seen a nurse or doctor?"

"Yes I have, as a matter of fact. There is one in this cot. I was just about to wake him."

"Excuse me. Hey doctor" she shouted while she approached to the cot.

Lorenz rose from a deep sleep, he'd been there for 36 hours and it was the first time he'd gotten a chance to get a little shut eye. When he fully woke, , he looked directly at Sabrina and asked, "When did you get here? I didn't expect to see you until Saturday night."

"Wake up, there's an emergency. My aunt isn't breathing any more. I didn't see her chest rise or fall, and her body seemed cold to my touch." Responding to Sabrina's comment, Lorenz got up and dashed towards the door. "What room?" he asked while he pushed the door. He repeated, "What room Sabrina?"

"671, she's at the far end near the window." She briskly replied and walked behind.

Rodney decided to hang around just in case Simone wanted a little support. He waited near the nurses' station. He intently listened for any information on how their aunt responded to Lorenz.

Lorenz entered the room and saw Simone leaning over Aunt Marge. Simone was crying, and Sabrina then whaled in tears. Lorenz pulled Simone back as he spoke, "Let me tend to her. Move back so I can examine her." Simone grabbed Sabrina and moved into the hall way.

"Sabrina, she's gone. I know it."

"No, let Lorenz see if it's true. I can't believe she's gone. I know she isn't, not yet."

"I didn't feel a heartbeat and she's really cold."

"I know that, it's why I came out for help. I thought she was sleeping when I decided to check on her. When I felt how cold she is, it's when I ran to the nurses' station."

"You know she's gone."

A nurse came dashing by as the two girls huddled together in consolation. She ran right into Aunt Marge's room, responded to Lorenz as if it were a code red. The girls heard Lorenz and the nurse calling out symptoms and instructions as if the two were well practiced partners played a routine sport. "Blow, 2-3-4-5, blow, 2-3-4-5, blow, 2-3-4-5-6-7 blow, and repeated for nearly three minutes. Nothing." Lorenz said, "We need to shock her heart." And the door flew open for two additional nurses to enter the room. "Stand by- all clear," buzz goes the electrical shocker. Her heart didn't take it. "I guess it wasn't meant to be," said Lorenz.

While bigger tears fell down Simone's face, Lorenz exited the room. He touched Simone on the shoulder and said, "I'm sorry girls, she's gone. There wasn't a heartbeat nor was she breathing. We tried to resuscitate her but she didn't respond. It was peaceful to go as she did. At least she had you with her during her last minutes. I'm sure she knew her time was up."

"Oh, no, no way, no way is she gone. I was just with her and I saw her breathe," said Sabrina.

Lorenz pulled for Sabrina to console her with his embrace. The three of them stood together while Sabrina cried her heart out for the loss of her favorite aunt. Rodney observed Lorenz' move and looked for Simone when she earlier broke the embrace and walked into Aunt Marge's hospital room to look at items reminding her of the woman who meant so much to her. *I can't believe it*, she thought, *I just can't believe it, my favorite aunt is gone."*

"Hey Simone, are you ok?" asked Rodney as he entered the room.

"I thought you were gone."

"No, I hung around hoping to see you and have a talk. I never expected your aunt to pass on," Rodney said as he approached Simone in hopes of consoling her.

"No, who expects such a thing," replied Simone.

Within an arm's reach, Rodney stepped closer with open arms and Simone   allowed an embrace. Tears fell from her as she got closer to Rodney. She cried on his shoulder, and Rodney whispered, "She's in a much better place. Just think of her not having pain anymore. Nothing on this earth to interfere with her happiness; she's with you now and forever. Her love will never die, it's in your heart and memory. You have similar loving qualities of a great woman. She left you her legacy and dynamic character. She is in you Simone. You'll never be without her."

"But she didn't have to leave. Not yet."

"If not now, when? It was her time and she knew it."

"Still, it wasn't supposed to happen like this. I wanted to shower her with family love first. The family was getting together soon. It's still a plan but for a different reason now".

"Well, don't change your objective, just change the cause. You should celebrate her life."

"All the generations of children will want to be here for her," Simone spoke while still sobbed, "She was our matriarch."

"And you shall celebrate her life and love as a family. Don't worry about that at this moment; just find peace for yourself. I'm here for you."

Rodney's last four words struck a nerve. It was earlier anxiety where Simone headed to find him with a purpose. Anger struck and in a flash, Simone's body language and face reflected her emotion. She pushed away from Rodney, moved across the room and in a flash her anger returned. Simone spoke in anger, "You are one dumb man. You must think I'm some desperate filly who needs a man for comforting. And you have the nerve to be here with some dead ass roses. What kind of man comes to a hospital and tries to get a woman on his good side? Do you think I'm so desperate or a fool?"

"Which question do you want me to answer first?"

"Oh a smart ass too; not only are you dumb, but a silly man at that."

"No, I came here to show you my love."

"Love? How dare you play on words like love and support?"

"Look Simone, do you want me to leave?"

"Yes, but after I finish telling you a few things; hell, for that matter it's a waste of breath on you. Damn it, go, get away from me!"

"I'm gone. But call me if you ever decide this was a bad decision."

"Sure, I'll call, never."

Rodney left the room in angst. He was mad as heck over Simone's outburst where she claimed he did not have honest emotions for her.

Her loss damn it, he thought and then mumbled, "I can have any woman on this side of Jordan. I got all emotional for a crazy lunatic. What kind of crap is this at a time where she needs support? Only a crazy woman would say such bull."

Outside the hospital room, Lorenz and Sabrina were still together. Lorenz, stepped back as Rodney mumbled his thoughts. "Hey, is she ok?" he asked.

"The crazy woman is ok," Rodney replied.

"Crazy woman; I don't understand. What happened in there?"

"Simone is crazy, I tried to console her and she lashed out at me for being an opportunist."

"I'll go in there and talk to her," said Sabrina, as she walked towards the room.

"No, don't go for me. Go for her and yourself. I think she needs someone but not me. Not now. Not ever."

"Don't give up on her just yet. It's a hard time; she's just lost her aunt," Said Lorenz.

"Give up? You can't give up on something you don't have. It was fun while it lasted. Hey doc, I'm heading home. I should have stayed there instead of coming here. I'd be better off had I not come."

"Maybe a good point," Lorenz agreed, "But at least she knows you are serious for her and there if she needs you."

"Not any more. That boat sailed. See you around," said Rodney as he walked briskly to the elevators.

"Sure thing, I have faith on seeing you again."

Chapter 11

Celebration of Life

Family members were notified of Marge's death. They traveled from each coast of the United States, from the West coast of Africa, and from Western Europe, Asia, and the far Pacific Rim. There were family members who Simone and Sabrina didn't know of no recognized in the thousands of pictures in Aunt Marge's photo albums   of her life. "I didn't know Aunt Marge had so many relatives. I knew she was originally from the west coast, but my goodness, she didn't tell much about her upbringing," said Sabrina.

"She kept her past to herself. I can only imagine why," replied Simone.

"I'm sure we'll find out about her child hood from some of these people."

"What about the cousins we know? Have you called them?"

"Yes, I called them and that's how the word got out so fast. We have to get things together before many of them arrive. I'd hate for the family to criticize us for not having things in order."

"You're right about being organized. She kept a folder of important papers in the bedroom closet. I'll get it," Simone said.

Simone left the kitchen headed for the master bedroom. She stopped along the way and admired a number of hall pictures. Pictures were displayed on both sides of the hall walls and many of them were of Aunt Marge accompanied with friends and family. One was a perfect portrait of Marge during her prime. Simone always loved that portrait because it was something she wanted to do as a child. *I wish there were pictures of my mother*, thought Simone.

The largest picture was of their Aunt Marge and Uncle Arthur, posed in an embraced as forever in love. *There's one with her and me, and another of Sabrina and Aunt Marge. Separate but fair in*

attention; Aunt Marge was good at ensuring us she had no favorite
between the two of us. I'll always admire that of her. No favorites.
Simone selected one of the many pictures for the funeral program. *I'll*
suggest her portrait in the living room instead of any of these along
the hallway. When she arrived at the master bedroom, she took a
single look around and a tear rolled down her face. Many things
reminded Simone of her aunt; the brush, jewelry, the empty bed and
the house coat she last saw her wear. *My goodness, will I ever stop*
crying, she thought, *The files; focus on the files.*

She walked around the bed room and found a box at the end of the
dresser next to the far wall. The square box was a two drawer
cardboard file cabinet. One drawer had photos and the other marked
important papers. *Aunt Marge was definitely organized.* Simone
opened the bottom drawer to multiple folders with specific titles;
insurance, house hold policies and repairs, legal documents, will,
warranties, and others. Fortunately, those drawers were not locked, as
some items were of value.

Simone took out the legal document folder and read about multiple
items of value. She saw stocks documents, bonds, and the house deed;
These documents are worth a pretty penny. The next folder she
selected had the will. Another tear rolled down her face, as she
opened the folder and pulled out the folded document. Before reading
it, she returned to the kitchen so Sabrina can read the with her.
"Sabrina, I have it." Simone called out as she arrived at the kitchen.
"You do? Did you read it?" Sabrina answered.
"No, I thought we'd read it together."
"Good point. What else did you find in her folders?"
"Aunt Marge has stocks, bonds, and other valuable documents.
She also has a bank deposit drawer."

"What? A bank deposit drawer is where most people keep valuable things. If her will was in the folder, then I wonder what's in the deposit drawer."

"I don't know because most of what I think of being as valuable is here in this folder."

"There's only one way to find out. Let's start with the will."

"Yes, lets."

Both Simone and Sabrina sat at the kitchen table next to each other. They both had one hand on each side of the folder where their view was equally on it. Like a scene from years ago when the two were in preteen years and Aunt Marge sat across from them, they sat beside each other leaving the open chair for Aunt Marge. They remembered those nights when Aunt Marge scheduled many summer events that she presented the girls with flyers to better explain what they were going to do. The two young ladies read flyers together exactly as they read the will.

"There's a letter in the folder. Should we read it first?" asked Simone.

"Sure, it might explain something not written on the will," replied Sabrina.

Simone opened the envelope and retrieved a letter. Unfolding the letter, a little piece of metal clattered to the table. It was a key. The letter read:

Dear Simone & Sabrina,

If you are reading this, either I've passed on to a better place, or my mind is no longer sharp. Whichever the condition, please remember how important you girls are and how you two were the center of my life. Even though you never knew I had favorites, you girls were the ideal nieces. Please believe me, it's hard having favorites, but you two were easy to enjoy out of all the others.

Life gives special conditions all the time, and of those conditions you were the guiding light through it all. I love you as my own and always considered you as such. When your parents died, they entrusted me to support you through your trials and tribulations of life. I loved doing it. You two are my girls, my daughters, my children; even though I loved your cousins too, you two were my sparkle. Please remember how much I love you and enjoyed you in my life.

You know, I never told you about my life. It isn't a secret, nor is it something I'm ashamed of. It just never came up. I realize over the years we've always focused on your immediate family and your uncle's side of the family. Since I didn't have children of my own, it was never a focus to tell you more of myself. Not from my family but now is as a better time than before. Not from my family but now... I don't understand this line

My family was from beyond meager means, living a life style much greater than the one I settled for. No, I didn't leave for independence, and it was not to run away from that type of lifestyle, I honestly loved your uncle. My family roots started back from Ellis Island, mostly European as my grandfather was the true immigrant. Fortunately for him, he came here with a needed skill. A vision for business and a direction for market development, he created market research methods and commercials. Yes, even in those days, there were commercials. Most were street merchants, talking about their items, so Grandfather created a script and sold it to street merchants. This was before copy writing, so he changed it quite often for the typical product. His name became known throughout the city and to all merchants. He started placing advertisements in papers as they became popular. He grew to a marketing conglomerate.

My mother came into the world as the first American. She was
beautiful. Long flowing hair and eyes of coal, her features were
Middle Eastern. Even though she was European by ancestry, she
picked up all the genetics of the Mid East. She met my father,
another marketing mogul. He too was of European decent and
dark. Not quite the normal dark complexion of a Greek, but that
of a Moroccan. He stood tall and lean, with a remarkable bone
structure. Quite the handsome man if I have to say so.

I was the youngest of four children. My siblings were all well-
educated just as I but the standards of living we grew up to know
did not make me who I am. When in school I ventured into the
city and found a true love. I discovered a love of people. I opened
myself to befriend any person within the city block. I ventured
into to all sorts of areas. Most of them were forbidden to a person
like me. Yet, I managed to get in there without a problem and was
treated kind at every corner.

My new found love did not sit well with my family. I didn't do
as planned according to my father. I went where my heart led me,
and saw people as they were. No color, race or ethnicity; just
good people without accepting some misguided history. I explored
on my own and found out who I am and what my true desires
were. This is when I met your uncle. I knew then he was my love
for life. I knew from his first hello, he was my heart and I his.
Nothing could tell us differently, nor hold us back from being one
in life.

My parents were quite upset with my decision to love a poor
struggling man. Yes, your uncle was struggling in the world. He
had grand ideas and a strong work ethic. He did all and
everything with a focus to achieve in any business. And of course,
you know of your uncle. He did what made him successful and
achieved being the envy of so many. I'm quite proud of him and

loved him for it. Though my parents didn't accept him from the beginning, he won their hearts later in years.

You should contact my lawyer, after you read this letter. He will guide you through the rest of my instructions. The will in the drawer is only partial in content. There is a reason you'll understand after your visit. And, be advised, there will be a large number of family coming if it is due to my passing. I know them, the word of my passing on will travel fast and they'll come from around the world. Believe me, they mean well and will do whatever it takes to support your decisions concerning me, so love them as you loved me.

Please remember that I love you with all my heart. Tell the rest of your cousins I loved them as well. Keep the faith as life continues to show you truth and love. Understand your journey and <u>please</u> listen faithfully to your heart. All in love will prevail as life trains you for greatness. Simone, you stay on your path to greatness. It's in your gene pool and be smart about your personal decisions. Sabrina, my rose pedals of the world; show them how lovely you are and stay focused on your gift. You have the chance to impact change and redefine beauty.

Without thought, you were my girls, my daughters of the world.

Love always,

Aunt Marge

Simone and Sabrina had tears in their eyes. The letter gave them a message of love and history. It made them reminisce to when she was living and spoke while sitting in the den having coffee. It was a routine the three of   shared time and time again. The message was clear to visit the lawyer in the will. Not understanding why, the girls both allowed their imagination to run. "Simone, It has to be money or an endowment she left us." Sabrina thought before saying, "It's a very important item of history that maybe her family left; the reason she didn't talk much about them until now as something she wanted us to know." Both girls sat silently for a moment before leaving the kitchen table. Sabrina stood first and said, "You know, this letter gives us a little explanation to her past. I wonder if there are many family members left."

"I bet there is. We have to find them. I think the answer is in the part with the lawyer," replied Simone.

"You're probably right. What about the will? Shouldn't we read it first?"

Without hesitation, Simone took out the will and unfolded the legal document to its full length. Sabrina returned to her seat after retrieving a glass of water. "Are you ready?" asked Simone.

"Yes, let's find out what she wants us to know."

Last Will and testament: Being of sound body and mind when constructing this, all of my worldly possessions are to be distributed as such;

First bank account, I leave to Nephew Henry for his children's college trust fund.

This house, 608 Wilshire Ave, I leave to Niece Diane to solely possess.

All furnishings, left untaken by my nephews and nieces, may be sold and proceeds will be divided amongst great nieces and nephews.

Additional properties and funds are under separate instructions at Berkley and Associates, PC 753 Holgorn Ave. 030-893-0213 (Attorney Philip Berkley III).

I request cremation and my ashes spread at sea during my farewell cruise. The funeral cruise is prepaid and prearranged. However, I leave the program development to Simone and Sabrina. Contact the Mosley Funeral Home and inform them of my death. They will know what to do. I leave additional coordination to your devise for the final touch. I'm confident you'll send me home with a nice farewell.

In addition to my wish, Sabrina and Simone are to equally share executor responsibilities of this will and testament.

Given full length of my testament on __25th__day of _May, in the year of our Lord 2002 _____

"Yada, yada, yada, legal stuff", said Simone.

"I can't believe she didn't leave us anything around here." Sabrina said.

"Of course not, she saw us as independent, proud, and strong women. She told us that all the time."

"I'm just a little surprised at her not leaving the house to us."

"You know Aunt Marge, she wanted the neediest to have an opportunity of living a good life."

"What about the bank account. Are you on her account as joint owner?"

"No, but I'm sure we will both have access after probate. We have to see the lawyer."

"Why don't we call him and see if they are still around. I've never heard of this firm. Have you?"

"No, neither have I."

Simone picked up the phone and dialed the number on the will. A receptionist answered, "Berkley and Associates, can I help you?"

"Yes, you may. May I speak to Phil Berkley the third please?"

"May I ask who's calling?"

"Simone Whittingham, niece of Marge Blaine."

"I'm so sorry to hear of your loss. Mrs. Blaine was a great and loving lady. I'll patch you in right away."

Surprised to the response, Simone gazed at Sabrina in amazement. Covering the mouthpiece of the phone, she says "Wow," to Sabrina.

"Huh?"

"You should have heard the response when I told the receptionist it was for Aunt Marge."

"Ms. Whittingham, this is Phil Berkley. I'm sorry for the loss of your aunt. What time would you like to come in and review the documents?"

"Thank you for the condolence. I, ah, we would like to come in tomorrow morning. Will this be okay?"

"How about 9:30 am. I'll have some coffee ready when you arrive. Do you like flavored cream with your coffee? Your aunt sure did. She spoke highly of you two and quite often. I finally get to meet you."

"9:30 is fine. Cream?" Simone held the mouth piece again, while she asked Sabrina "What flavor cream do you want at the lawyer's office?"

"Cream flavor? I don't know; Amaretto." Sabrina said while shrugging her shoulders.

"Phil, I think we'd like Amaretto. We'll be there tomorrow morning."

***

Rodney arrived at his apartment. He changed into his training clothes. He looked out the window to see if the weather allowed him to wear shorts and a t-shirt. Happy with his answer, Rodney left the apartment and ran one of his running routes. *Three miles, a short run will do the trick and give me time to be in the office early.* thought Rodney. . He lurked back and forth between cars as he crossed streets striding for the sidewalk. He tracked down a path near a dumpster, and circled at the park entrance. On the return, he passed the corner where he gave assistance to an elderly lady one morning. Another bend and I'm back in the apartment.

"Three miles in 23 minutes; I'm happy with this. It's not world speed, but it's good enough for me."

Rodney returned inside the apartment and saw the answer machine light indicator flashed. *I missed a call. I hope it isn't important.* He pushed the play button, and the answer machine rewound the call and played;

"Hey man, it's me. This is a reminder of our meeting, it's is highly important for the future of the firm. Don't get side tracked with your thoughts of Simone today. I need you, we need you, and the entire firm needs you. Come with your best game today. Please. I'll see you at the office." Message ends.

Talk about pressure. I must be driving my folks crazy with disgust. I don't know what to do with Simone. I want to give up, but she's the one. She is the one; think of her after this meeting. Think of what I can do to win her over. Come on brain, what should I do?

Knock, knock, knock on the front door. "Hey, it's me coming in, don't shoot?"

"Hey Dan, if I had a gun I'd put myself out of this pain."

"What pain? You, running like a jack rabbit all the time?"

"No, Simone. Man I think I've lost her."

"Don't you have a big presentation this morning?"

"Sure, but that shouldn't stop me from thinking about her. I have the presentation under my belt. I know what to say and do. The job is easy; it's Simone I want to impress. She's the one dude. She is the one."

"Then think of her after the presentation. I'll help you set things up. But right now, it's got to be business. We have an hour to get downtown."

"I'll be ready in 20 minutes."

"Tick, tick, tick, times flying and you'd better get moving." Dan pressed. "You've no time to mess around and look in the mirror. Skip that part and let's go."

Rodney replied from his bedroom, "Headed to the shower now. I'll be out in a few minutes. I'll shave in the shower to save time."

"Too much information; just get moving," Dan responded while he turned the television on to the news.

Rodney jumped from the shower, dried, and dashed into the closet for his lucky suit. "Hey, Dan, can you call Berkley Associates and confirm us setting up the conference room in 30 minutes?"

"Sure. Do you have the number?"

"It's on the counter, on top of my brief case. It's the number on the cover of the brief."

"Got it. I'll make the call. You don't have much time. Get going."

"Right on it coach."

Dan made the call from his cell phone. He dialed the number and calculated how long the drive would take to arrive in the midst of traffic. "Hello, Berkley Associates?"

A recording answered the phone call with a message, "Good day, and thank you for calling Berkley Associates. I'm sorry but the office is currently closed. Our office hours are 8:30 am to 6:00 pm daily Monday through Friday. Please leave a message after the tone and a representative will contact you as soon as possible. Thank you again for calling Berkley Associates where the attorney is a family extension......beep."

Dan left a message, "Please call Rodney Witherspoon of Hillman and Kraft Marketing to confirm his early arrival to prepare your conference room for the 10:00 meeting. His cell number is 220-555-1212. Thanks and he's looking for your call."

Dan ended the call and shouted for Rodney "Hey, are you ready yet?"

"Almost there partner. I'll be out in a second."

"Times wasting, we have traffic to fight. We've got to get going. Hurry up."

Rodney finished tying his tie, grabbed his coat, and headed for the front room. "Ready dude; grab the briefcase and let's go."

"Are you driving or am I?"

"Your car is ready. Since you know the way best, you drive. I can review the presentation once more."

Both men exited the apartment and walked to the car. Dan unlocks the door with his remote while walking down the side walk. started the engine and pulled off. "Hey did you forget anything?" asked Dan.

"Don't you think it's a little early?" asked Rodney.

"No, you forget, we have to take the interstate for the quickest route. And let's face it, during this time of morning it isn't so quick."

"You're right. I thought about taking the main street but that would be much slower. Oh, I didn't forget a thing."

"Why didn't you schedule them to come at our office?"

"The owner said he had a very important meeting with a client. It's one of his larger accounts."

"That makes sense. Did he say how long it would take?"

"About 30 minutes. He has time right after that and the next available opportunity to meet will be during the next quarter."

"A law firm is that busy. Wow!"

"Yes, that's why they want us to market them for growth while the tempo is high."

"Isn't it a weird time to look for growth when you're busy as ever."

"Actually it isn't. The timing is great. Think about it."

"I'll have to give that some thought," replied Dan.

Dan turned onto the interstate, and traffic seemed to be moving right along. Dan clicked on the radio for a traffic report. "We have 40 minutes to get there," commented Danl.

"We'll make it. If traffic keeps moving like this, there's time for a coffee stop." said Rodney.

"Let's not get too out front yet. Traffic is slowing to a standstill."

***

Simone was ready and called Sabrina. "Hey its time; we have 40 minutes to arrive at the lawyers. You know how they hate us being late."

"Yeah, but it's a lot of time."

"No, remember we have to get on the other side of town."

"I'm ready, just finished my coffee."

"Come on then. Grab that folder on the kitchen counter and bring it with you."

"Got it."

Simone and Sabrina headed out of Aunt Marge's house and jumped into Sabrina's car. Sabrina started the car while Simone turns on the radio. She found a channel giving the traffic report. "This is WKRK with the latest traffic. It seems like a snail's pace for the interstate this morning. There is a stalled car at exit 282. Even though the car is on the side of the road, there's considerable rubber necking. If you're heading into town before mile market 282, take exit 288 and head North on Turnip. Turn East on Kinzie and hit the interstate just past the stalled vehicle," the announcer informed.

Sabrina took the announcer's advice. She pulled out into traffic and headed out of the neighborhood streets. At the major intersection she turned north and headed for downtown. Music blared from the radio as Simone looked out of the window. Not a word was spoken from either   as the car got closer to a major intersection. Simone

198

looked at the buildings and said, "You know, I've always wondered who owns those office buildings on this street. Did you ever notice they are always   full? I mean, the buildings are awesome in decoration as well as presentations. The entire two blocks accent the skyline of the city."

"Yes, I've wondered over the year. You never see space ads for these buildings. I guess the businesses own the building," replied Sabrina.

"Maybe so; if the businesses didn't own them, could you imagine the revenue it brings per year?"

"It has to be quite a penny."

Sabrina turned the car west to the next block to avoid the slow traffic. One block and she headed north again. "How are we doing on time?" asked Sabrina.

"Not bad. If I keep moving like this, we'll be there in five minutes or so. If not, I'll have to call the office and tell them we'll be a little late."

"I hope we find a parking space. You know how the city can get with parking."

"I thought the office has visitor's parking."

"It wasn't on the flyer and it's not common for that area."

"Isn't this a high power law firm?"

"Yes, but they probably didn't negotiate parking for customers. But you never know."

"We'll find out when we get there."

Rodney and Dan were two miles behind Simone and Sabrina on the interstate.

"Dan, take this exit," said Rodney.

"What?"

"Take this exit. I know another way to the office. I should have thought about it from the time we got on the interstate. It'll save us time out of this mess."

"Ok, which way after the exit?"

"Turn left. This will take us on Turnip. Once we get to Turnip, we'll turn north; right if you've forgotten which way is north."

"I know north. Just tell me which street."

"I'll remind you when we get to Turnip."

"Ok, good. I hope like hell you get us there within the next 15 minutes."

"If traffic keeps moving, we'll make it in 10."

"It seems to move   at the moment. We need to get there and set up before the meeting."

"Keep driving, we'll get there. Leave the navigation to me and just follow my directions. Here's Turnip, now turn left."

"I didn't expect Turnip to come so quickly."

"Remember, we aren't too far from the office buildings. Just keep moving if traffic allows."

"Right, I'll keep going with the flow."

Sabrina and Simone arrived at the office building. Sabrina maneuvers the car under the building to the parking garage. They found a parking space, exited the car and walked to the elevators. As they entered the elevator Sabrina asked, "What floor"?

"I think the 5th floor," answered Simone.

"Aren't you sure?"

"No, I didn't get the exact address. Why don't we go to the first floor and find the business listing?"

"Good idea."

***

Rodney and Dan finally arrived to the office building. Dan found a parking space on the street right in front of the building. He placed an old parking ticket on the window he left in his glove box from days before. "This will keep new parking tickets off in case we take too much time. Can you remind me to check on the car after we set up?"

"No problem. Just remember we may take most of the morning and I'm not sure if your old ticket will do the trick."

"If it doesn't I'll call in an old favor. Besides, this account is worth every penny to win."

"Then you're on your A-Game right?"

"A-Game, heck I'm on the top of the Pyramid."

"Oh, you're on the A-Game, but you aren't funny; it's time to get in there and set up the conference room. We can save the jokes for after the presentation."

"Man, you have to kill my motivation by being so serious. Okay, it's on. Let's go."

Dan and Rodney took the equipment and handouts out of the back seat of the car. "Do we have everything?" asked Rodney.

"Sure. I checked your apartment before leaving and the office last night. We have everything as planned," replied Dan.

"Great," Rodney answered as he approached the door. He held the door for Dan, and looked back at his approach. Rodney barely missed Sabrina and Simone's entry into the elevators.

"Okay, we are nearly there. I'm kind of nervous Simone."

"Why would you be nervous? I'm sure whatever Aunt Marge left us will be fine. I never expected anything anyway. I would love for her to be here now and we didn't have to go through this."

"Yes, you're right. Having her here is better. But I'm curious to know for what reason or why did we have to come here."

"You know the why Sabrina, it's the what we're after."

The elevator arrived at the 12th floor, opened, and in front of the office entrance. Large letters on the glass door **Berkley Associates** in gold print with black edging. There was a receptionist behind an oak quarter moon like desk. Behind her was a beautiful picture of a sunrise over the ocean, as if you were standing on a beach with white sand, green palm trees, and scattered brush, and two hammocks under the trees. The receptionist was a nice young man. *Not quite what I expected*, thought Sabrina. Simone led the way into the office and spoke to the receptionist. "Hi, we are …"

"The Whittingham sisters," said the receptionist. "Please come this way, Mr. Berkley is expecting you. Can I get you anything to drink while you wait in the office?"

"Oh, no thank you," replied Simone

"Sure, a cup of coffee will do for me. Use that Amoretto cream if you don't mind."

"No, not at all." the receptionist replied as he led them to the first office on the right. "Please take a seat and I'll be right back with your coffee." The receptionist left without closing the office door all the way.

"What an office," said Sabrina, "Quality decorating."

"Yes, my kind of office. One day I'll have such a place," replied Simone.

"You know, Aunt Marge always thought you'd have one."

"I remember her saying so."

Phil Berkley arrived in the office. "Good morning ladies. I hope you didn't have a bad drive coming here so early."

"No, we didn't," replied Simone.

"I want to give my condolences again. I'm sorry about your aunt passing so unexpectedly."

"Thank you," replied Simone and Sabrina in unison.

"Well, it's time we get to business. I want you both to be very comfortable as I read the rest of your aunt's will."

The receptionist returned with the coffee for Sabrina. "Thank you," she says to the receptionist.

"That will be all," said Phil. The receptionist left as Phil continued. "Ladies, the last will and testament of your aunt includes a large piece of history. Let me tell you this story before moving on to the document. Our families have done business for nearly 75 years. Yes, 75 years. Your great uncle and my father were partners in the early 19th century. Our family ties go back to billionaires of the early century."

"Billionaires?" asked Sabrina

"Yes, billionaires!" answered Phil. "It's no secret and I'm surprised you didn't know of your family history."

"Well, Aunt Marge had no children and we never knew of her family history or any of her relatives other than those of our father," responded Sabrina.

"This I know. She considered you two as her own. Though she may not have shown it, but you were her two girls. Anyway, her family was very well off for years. Until her father's death, many didn't know of her existence. Her father left her over twenty-five million dollars in assets, and two companies with an average annual revenue of two hundred million."

Rodney knocked on Phil's office door because the receptionist wasn't at his desk. Rodney and Dan took it upon themselves to find the conference room. He opened one of the double doors without hesitation for a reply, and stepped in. They didn't hear Phil's voice as it was during a shuffle of folders that the office was silent. Rodney's head was faced down on the equipment he carried. Simone immediately stood from her chair and turned in angst as she recognized Rodney. She immediately said, "I cannot believe you."

"Excuse me gentlemen," Phil said with intent.

"Oh, wrong turn I'm sorry. Hello Sir, not a good first impression," Rodney exclaimed.

"Not to worry, many people mistake the double doors for the conference room. It's down the hall on the left."

"Oh no, he's not here for the conference room. He's here being nosey and infringing on my privacy," Simone said and added as she looked towards Rodney, "I didn't want to ever see you again, can't you understand."

"Forgive my intrusion. I had no idea you would be here Simone. I have a presentation with Mr. Berkley in a half hour. Again, I'm so sorry for the intrusion Mr. Berkley," Rodney replied.

"No problem. Since you reminded me about the presentation, please move on, we have to finish here," said Phil.

"Sure thing sir; again my apologies."

"And you honestly think I'm buying that excuse," frowned Simone. "You just automatically end up here at the same office, on the morning we learn of my aunt's will. And you expect me to think of it as a coincidence? You must be out of your mind if you think you're going to get away with this intrusion."

"No Simone, it is totally a coincidence," Rodney spoke as he moved towards the door, "Totally a coincidence; Mr. Berkley and I have a meeting, a business meeting in now 25 minutes. If you'll excuse me I have to set up." Rodney moved outside the door and walked into the hall.

"Oh, we aren't over, and I mean I'm not through with your sneaky and whimsical ass," Simone continued as Rodney's back disappeared as the door closed.

"Please, take your seat," said Phil, "he's telling the truth. We have a business meeting and I have to keep my schedule. Please allow me to finish your background."

"Oh sure," said Sabrina. "Sit Simone."

Simone took her seat and intently listened to Phil. "Where was I, oh yes, the companies include two buildings. Yes Office buildings. My office manages the businesses as a long term agreement with your aunt. We've kept her as a silent partner for years. With the revenue we make as a team, it's something I'd like to continue. But before I throw my business pitch, its time I read the will."

Phil reached on the center of the desk, picked up two documents, and passed one to each of the girls. "Please follow with me as I guide you through Marge's last will and testament. Since we're pressed for time, let me direct you to the third paragraph.

'Leaving to Simone Whittingham and Sabrina Whittingham to share and share alike, the sixty percent of controlling stocks in both companies. I leave ownership in the Wrangler buildings on Turnip with operational control of the management organization, which is currently run by the Berkley firm. All assets mentioned are for each to share in one hundred percent of the decisions. Neither one of you can dispose of their assets unless it is to one of the other, or an immediate family descendent.'

"You mean Aunt Marge was a Wrangler?" asked Sabrina.

"No, not a Wrangler, but a Riesman."

"The billionaire Riesman family?"

"That's the family. As I said before, your aunt was the love child of Riesman and the only one to inherit both companies independent of the general family. The secret came out after his illness and there was a fight for the property. When your aunt married your uncle, she had no idea of her father, other than he was a nice man who always brought good presents. Her mother later told her of her father's position in the world just after she married your uncle. The family blew a fuse when she married a financially struggling man. But the love of your aunt made the family understand and especially got Mr. Riesman to accept him. Now fair warning for you, there are a number of Riesman descendants willing to challenge this will. Especially since you aren't of direct blood, and your connection to your aunt is through marriage."

"So this is why so many people are traveling here from around the world and they knew of Aunt Marge's death long before the news?" asked Simone.

"Exactly correct Simone. I've been notified by multiple lawyers and law firms to make a deal for the control of stock and those buildings. My loyalty lies with Marge's wish. You had a wonderful aunt whom I admired with all my heart. She was like a big sister to me, a sister that was much better than my own. She never asked for anything or didn't create a hardship on the family or firm. And, she was the best partner, business partner, a man could ever ask for."

"And that's why you wanted to maintain your management perspective on the property and companies?" asked Sabrina.

"As a matter of fact, yes, I'd like the firm to continue with the current agreement. It's working so well and of course there are equal benefits to the agreement. You get to receive rewards and profits, as I do, and you get to be a silent partner. Remember, your aunt never flashed her assets to the public and lived a quiet life."

"We were very close to Aunt Marge, and we had no idea."

"Exactly correct, and she did use her assets very smartly," Phil looked at Simone and said, "As in your scholarship to college." He then added, "She was the main contributor to your personal scholarship. Sabrina, she was the one who helped you get well from your illness when you were very young. I doubt you remember."

"I remember her being in the hospital all the time. I had no idea."

"And, she helped the family a lot with her money. Those cookies to every kid in school and being able to help in a moment's notice; I'm surprised you all never took advantage; especially you two girls. She loved you two so much, because you brought fulfilled her desire to be a mother that she treated you   as   her own. She talked about you two all the time." Phil stood and walked around the desk headed for the door. "I hate to run, but I'm now three minutes late for my business meeting. Please forgive me. I need your answers for my proposal as soon as possible. Oh, by the way, she wanted to be buried at sea."

"At sea? Yes we know," admitted Sabrina

"Good because I need the guest list of 300 people for a commercial cruise line. Her life will be the theme and I think it's appropriate to celebrate such a great woman. It's the last paragraph in her will." Phil left the office headed to the conference room.

"A cruise, that's our aunt going out with style," said Simone.

Chapter 12

It's Business

"Can you believe that woman?" asked Rodney.

"Boy, she has it out for you. There is no way you can ever get next to her. It's not in the future my friend," consulted Dan.

"I don't care, she's the one and I know it. I'll have to think of another way."

"Well, you do that some other time. Right now we need your best game forward. This account means a lot to the firm."

"I know its business first. It's always how it plays out. Business first."

"Did you place the handouts at every chair?"

"Only if you plugged the laptop and projector into the outlet."

"I guess we're done. Let's test the program."

The laptop booted and the projector warmed as Rodney and Dan looked on. They intently reviewed the power point slide show, added a few notes, allowed it to play on the large screen, and rehearsed answers to questions. All was set for the presentation and equipment checked out.

Dan walked out of the conference room in search of a coffee maker. Rodney stood near a large window overlooking the city. *How can she think such a thing?* thought Rodney about the recent incident. *"How can she accuse me of infringing on her privacy and following her? She has to be traumatized with the death of her aunt. I've done nothing but make an attempt to show her my emotions.*

"Right. Now can you get this out of your mind and let's focus on the meeting?" Dan commented as he knew Rodney's focal point on Simone.

"Yeah, sure can. Business first! I have to remember business first," Rodney admitted.

"Good, because it's nearly time. Let's stand by the door and welcome everyone as they enter."

They moved into positions by the door, stood side by side, firm and presentable to the entering staff. "Good morning," they said in unison as each member arrived. Without hesitation, each member took a seat at the conference table. Some started fanning through the handout, others looked at individual folders or schedulers as they reviewed or adjust their day.

"We're waiting for one more person," said Peter, an executive with the firm. "Phil will be right with us."

"Sure thing, we can wait as long as needed," replied Dan.

Within the minute, Phil entered the conference room and took position at the head of the table. "Are we ready?" Phil inquired.

"Yes we are sir," Rodney replied. "First, allow me to introduce us. This is Dan our lead designer for the firm. I am Rodney a lead Marketing Executive. We are here to present our company and win your business for your next marketing campaign. Please feel free to stop me at any time for questions during my presentation of the firm."

On cue, Dan started the laptop presentation, three 20 second films of business and product commercials showed on screen. Those films ran in sequence, one right after the other, without introduction. The film completed and Rodney ran right into the presentation. "As you just watched, the firm has major clients, creates dynamic customer reactions, and introduce products and services with quality. Our approach is creating material that meets the demands of both the company and the consumer. We have a niche in creativity which places your ideas to life. In your handout, you'll see a number of our clients, ranging from the top 500 to the lower 12 for any type of product or service. We pride ourselves with the opportunity to produce results in any market. This makes us extremely competitive and competent to capture the ideas and prestige you wish to present and attract the customer base to increase your business."

The laptop slide show began with page two of the handout. "We create your campaign with your partnership," said Dan. "We jointly brainstorm as an extension of your staff, study the market base of your focus, and create test pilots for immediate feedback as we develop a winning strategy and marketing brand."

"How do you ensure the right person is part of our team?" asked one executive.

"We send our best and brightest, whom we've recruited from top-notch schools around the country. We also place those with product and business interest as a match so the motivation is there. We pride ourselves with a group of consultants who are savvy in multiple areas of business, so one can assist you in your market as well as help you capture or expand your opportunity," answered Rodney.

"How long does a campaign take to develop?" the executive inquired.

"With the partnership and objectives of your firm, it's up the time scale of your efforts. Depending on the feedback we receive from the market, on average it takes three to six months. Sometimes sooner if the decisions are made fast," responded Dan.

The conference continued smoothly and lasted longer than scheduled. The firm's interest grew as the indicator was the depth questions the staff asked; which was a great sign for winning the project and contract. Rodney and Dan   packed their items to return to the firm. Phil stood by and observed the team work the two performed. "I'd think you two were salesmen if I didn't know better."

"Phil, we are in a sense. We take pride in our firm. We love our work," answered Rodney

"Oh, that's quite obvious. I'm glad my staff liked your presentation. It's going to be an easy decision for us. We have to talk numbers. Can you get back to me with more specific cost and not these generic numbers in the handout?"

"Not a problem. I will need to meet with you and get a better idea of the campaign you'd like to launch. I know we can do this as soon as you're available."

"How about this evening over dinner?"

"Dinner meeting sounds interesting. I can have everything in order by then."

"Good, my secretary will call you with the detail."

Rodney stood closer to Phil, and reached his right hand out towards Phil for a hand shake. "I'll be there and thank you for the opportunity to present our firm to your organization."

"You're welcome." Phil replied as he released Rodney's hand and exited the conference room.

"We did it. I have the numbers in my head now so it's going to be a nice dinner. Have any plans?" asked Rodney.

"No, but I don't think I'll need to attend. You can do this for us. I have faith in you. But, where on earth will we find consultants you described?"

"Let's not talk about that here, I have a plan. I have a really good plan."

"I hope so."

Sabrina and Simone, arrived at Aunt Marge's house. They entered the living room, where there were a number of new flower arrangements, cards, and two people who sat on the couch. The two Solemnly looked gentleman stood as Simone entered. "Good afternoon ladies," the tall handsome man spoke.

"Good afternoon." Simone replied without surprise and asked, "What can I do for you, and who let you in the home?"

"One of your relatives allowed us to wait here for you. Sorry to frighten you as we mean no harm. We are here to help you with your aunt's cruise line funeral request."

"We knew she wanted this and I'm glad you're here. How did you know?"

"We received the call from the law firm. And since all things are planned, our first set of instructions is to inform you. Please allow us to show you what your aunt had in mind."

"Okay. Can you let us get something to drink first? Would you gentlemen like a drink? Coffee, tea, or alcohol?"

"Coffee will be fine, thank you."

"Sure thing, Sabrina and I will be right back."

The gentlemen sat on the couch and opened a book of pictures. Sabrina and Simone entered the kitchen and brewed coffee. Like clockwork, the sisters put things together and grabbed four cups. Simone picked up the tray to carry the cups to the living room. Sabrina took the sugar dish and creamer and placed them on the tray. They both stood in the kitchen and looked at each other for a minute without saying a word until Sabrina asked, . . "How are we going to handle this?"

"I'm not sure just yet. Let's see what these guys are talking about first before we start thinking independent."

"Yes, let's hear them out."

You want to get the crump cakes from the refrigerator?"

"No, let's just go with the coffee."

The girls left the kitchen for the living room. Again, as they entered the living room, the two gentlemen stood. "Can we help you?"

"No thanks, it's not a problem. Cream and sugar are on the tray."

"Thank you," the guys said in unison. Now can we get to the plan? I'd like to start with your aunt's decoration idea. She wanted us to grab her youth photos and create a pattern of her development on the main deck. We plan to decorate the passage ways with her pictures. She also wanted one large portrait of herself in the center of the main deck area, where everyone on board is reminded why they're aboard. Take a look at the ship's layout and tell me where you'd like to place those portraits and what years."

"I have an idea," said Sabrina.

"You're the creative one between us, so go right ahead," replied Simone.

"Well, your aunt made a number of decisions early. So you don't have to be too creative, just the little things we ask will be sufficient."

"Good. This makes it easy to take care of the family invitations. They have to know when and where."

"We have the announcements ready for print. All we need from you is which one you'd like us to send. She limited it to these two and asked you to pick one. We will need an updated list. She had three hundred in mind to attend the funeral cruise."

"Three hundred?"

"Yes, three hundred; she included her family members who she suspected that will still be around, especially her father's kids."

"We learned of them this morning. I guess we can give you an updated list from the people we know," said Simone.

"The firm has a list of her siblings. You can invite fifty others as you seem fit. The fifty can be in thirty cabins. Just let us know how you want to arrange the cabin assignment. The others are all taken care of."

"We'll have your list in a couple days. I need to call a few people."

"No problem. Remember to call us if you need assistance. We want to leave the dock on Thursday evening and return Sunday morning. This way only one work day is missed by all. I'm sure the family will like the ceremony. Oh, we'll need your input for that as well. She set up a simple program, however allowed room for you to add an event or speaker. Let us know the modifications by tomorrow evening. This way the printing schedule will be completed on time."

"Again, no problem, we'll have everything done by Wednesday afternoon. The list of people will be available, and the program information will be there by tomorrow. I have to call everyone today as soon as we're done here. What time should all be at the pier for boarding?"

"The schedule says all aboard between 4-7pm. We leave dock at 8pm sharp."

"Great."

"What about the body and other arrangements?"

"All done, she wanted to be cremated and the ashes thrown over the ocean while underway. It's all in the program."

"Wow, Aunt Marge thought of everything. This makes it easy for us sis," said Sabrina.

"She did, and I think a little too well. We have other things to discuss too. Like what to do with, well, we'll wait until the time comes to discuss business."

"Yes, we will," replied Sabrina.

The gentlemen stood and extended their right hands to the girls. They shook hands together, "Again our condolences for your loss," the Gentlemen said.

"Thank you and you'll hear from us soon. Oh, what number can we reach you?"

"It's on the card and call us as soon as you need or get those things completed."

"Sure thing," replied Simone.

After the gentlemen left the house, Simone and Sabrina sat for a spell, in silence while looking at Aunt Marge's arrangements. "Wow," Simone broke silence, "she thought of everything."

"Yes, she did," answered Sabrina.

"First we have to get everyone on the ship. Let's start calling some of our people. We can get them to e-mail their list to the ship's purser."

"That's a faster way to get the lists updated. Hopefully, enough will show to fill the thirty cabins."

"I'm sure they will. It's a cruise too. Why wouldn't they?"

"Going home with a bang, Aunt Marge does it again."

"As usual."

Sabrina called Aunt Marge's friends and all the relatives she knew. Sabrina called Phil's office for Rodney's number. She dialed Rodney, and unfortunately got no answer. She left a message, "Rodney its Sabrina. You know, Sabrina Whittingham. I want to apologize for Simone's behavior today at the office. She jumped to conclusion a lot these days. It's not because of you, its losing our aunt that's driving her out of her mind. And I apologize for the misunderstanding at the hospital. Please forgive me for advising you to go the other night. I thought my sister would have been ecstatic to see you. Actually, I still think she would. So, I'm asking, or inviting you to Aunt Marge's funeral cruise. I'll send you an invitation for two. Talk to Diane about it. She knows the details. Please consider coming."

Sabrina then called Lorenz to give him details for the funeral cruise. "Lorenz, my Aunt Marge is having a funeral cruise. I want you by my side as I need you, just to stay strong for my family. We leave on Thursday evening and return Sunday morning. Can you please plan on being there? I need you and it will be a great experience."

"A great experience? I've never heard of someone having a funeral cruise. It's definitely a unique experience." said Lorenz.

"Does this mean you're coming?"

"I'll have to reorganize a few things, but for you I'll be there."

"Great, if something comes up don't hesitate to tell me. I'm counting on you being by my side the entire cruise."

"I'll be there. It's for my girl right?"

"Your girl? I'm considered your girl! Then you'd best be there for sure giving your girl that needed support."

"My girl, I'll be there."

"I like being your girl" Sabrina sniggled and explained the details for boarding, the location of the pier, and meeting to board the ship together. She then ended her call by saying, "Bye my man."

"Talk to you soon."

Sabrina continued to call her list of relatives and neighbors. She contacted most of them and as planned for the family reunion, she told everyone about adding a song from the family on the funeral program. Without a doubt and quick to accompany the suggestion, many family members agreed to sing. No one suggested a particular song, but they agreed.

Simone called Phil's office for an update to invitations going out to Aunt Marge's siblings and their family. She commented on being informed of who they were and how they are related. She insisted on meeting each and every one of them. As well, she wanted to know if Phil would speak at the funeral. Unfortunately, the secretary took a message for Phil as he wasn't available.

***

Dan stepped out of the car after he parked in front of the office. "It was awesome. We did a great job. I know we landed that account."

"Sure we landed the account. Did you have any doubt that we wouldn't?" replied Rodney.

"No. Well, there was a little doubt. It's because you haven't been on your game lately. You have Simone in your head and your total motivation focused on being with her."

"Yes I do have her on my mind. But it never stops me from business or performing."

"Oh really, I beg to differ. Aren't you forgetting who's been with you for years? I can recall a Tiffany who took your heart, and you lost three accounts."

"That was my younger infatuated experience."

"So what makes this time so different?"

"I know from within I'm different. I am sure because it's an emotion and desire I've never experienced. Simone Whittingham, a dream girl of dreams."

"You have it bad, really bad."

"How long do you think this is going to last?"

"Forever Dan. Forever."

"I hope so. I've never seen you so intent on being with one woman. Just think, you haven't been with her intimately yet. Isn't that the motivation? You know, taking the challenge to taste her body and get her in bed."

"Nothing like it at all. I'm really in it deep with this woman. No Joke!!"

"I believe you, really I do. It's hard seeing you so different. Yet, I know you're serious. More serious now than a man can realize."

"Serious, I am dead serious. I really have to get her in my world, and I'll do whatever it takes to win her love."

"Your chance is coming. I can feel it. Just because you normally get what you want."

"That's not quite how it happens, but I'll believe it."

"Let's go into the office and get the troopers ready for this new contract."

The guys entered the building and went straight into the office. Not a word was spoken as they met the receptionist, glanced at the message list on the counter, smiled, and in unison stepped down the hall way to their perspective office. No one ran into their office or called for the results of the presentation.

***

Simone left a message for Phil with the receptionist. "Please call me when you get a chance. Since you were close to Aunt Marge, I'd like you to speak at her funeral. As well, you know the family members I haven't met and have no idea who they are. Please call as soon as you can. Thanks and I hope to take me up on speaking at her funeral." She ended the call and placed the phone on the receiver. *I hope he calls and says yes to my request. It should be easy for him to introduce me to my extended family. It's nice to know he has interest in the companies we recently inherited,* she thought.

Sabrina left the den and moved into the kitchen. She retrieved a glass from the cupboard, reached for the closet wine bottle, and placed it on the counter. She t picked up a cork screw from one of the many kitchen drawers. Sabrina opened the wine bottle and poured herself a glass of wine, took a sip and called for Simone and asked, "I opened a bottle of wine, would you like a glass?"

"Sure, I need one," Simone responded while she walked into the kitchen.

"It's been an exciting day, but weirder than anything else. I can't say how weird, but our newly acquired wealth hasn't sunk in yet."

"I know right. It's a lot to swallow, especially at a time like this."

"I know, and Aunt Marge had such foresight to coordinate her own funeral. How amazing is that? It's as if she knew something was going to happen."

"She knew. We all know about ourselves, it's just a matter of time. And Aunt Marge was the type of woman who took initiative."

"Can you believe her being a love child? Wow, I thought she'd tell us that story?"

"Especially about being a love child from a wealthy man; now that's the amazing part."

"Equally surprising is the amount she left us. I can't get over it."

"We might as well get over it because it's like we have to learn how to deal with it. I don't want it to go to our heads and we make rash decisions."

"You're right and I'm still thinking about how we learn to adjust to a large sum of money. But before we get to business we have to get the funeral over first. What should we do?"

"Let's notify the rest of the family. I know the lawyer sent the notice to the family members we don't know, but the members we know, we can contact them."

"It's time we start the call out."

"Diane knows. I called her right after contacting Lorenz.," admitted Sabrina.

"Good. Did she call anyone else?"

"I don't know, but I called Rodney too."

"No, you didn't!" Simone responded in a loud tone.

"Yes, Simone, I did. The guy is crazy about you and he's doing everything he can to get next to you. Even taking chances that I thought was so sweet."

"What? You mean stupid. And I can't believe you invited him to the hospital. That was really bad sis, really bad."

"Maybe to you, but not to me; I thought it was really sweet and with him being so concerned about Aunt Marge and you, showed me how serious he is for you. Who else would take a chance from true love?"

"Love. How dare you say he loves me? You don't know he loves me and I know he's after our inheritance."

"How the hell did he know of our inheritance? How do you figure he found out?"

"He was at the lawyer's office wasn't he?"

"And we didn't know until Phil read the will. How can you be so idiotic about this guy? Are you that afraid of loving someone?" asked Sabrina.

"Love? You use that word so freely. No, I am not afraid and it's not likely he's interested that way."

"He's coming to the funeral so you'd better be ready to see him. And this time don't freak out, just let him show his condolences."

"You kill me with this crazy inconsiderate act. I'll deal with it, but don't act as if it's a gift to me. I'll just deal with him being there."

"You do that, now we have others to invite," Sabrina said while she poured another glass of wine. "You want a refill?"

"No, I want to walk next door and invite Mr. Slocum to the funeral cruise."

"I'll call the others," said Sabrina.

Simone left the house and headed next door. She took each step with caution and thought, *How am I going to tell Mr. Slocum about Aunt Marge's death? Should I just give an invite to him and why am I worried about it. He and Aunt Marge have been neighbors for years. I'm sure he'll come and be honored to say a few things on the cruise.* Simone arrived at the house and stepped closer to the door, it opened without her knocking.

"Hi Simone, I'm so sorry for your loss. I know you'll do the right thing with your Aunt Marge's funeral. When is it by the way?" asked Mr. Slocum

"Thank you for the condolences. I came to invite you to her memorial cruise."

"A memorial cruise? I know your aunt planned it. It was her style. I know it had to be her."

"You knew my aunt very well."

"Yes, she mentioned something like that years ago. I thought she was just kidding about her dream final cruise. We laughed about it and I'll be darn if she didn't do it. After your uncle died, she said her time will go out with a bang. And my gosh, she's actually done it."

"I know she'd love you attending. So will you come? It's on Thursday."

"I wouldn't miss it for the world."

"Would you be kind and say a few things about her?"

"Well of course. She was the greatest neighbor ever." He stepped out of the door and gave Simone a document size envelope. "And this is for you kids. I tried to give this to her years ago and she wouldn't take it. I want you kids to have it."

Simone took the envelope and opened it. "Oh my, I can't accept this."

"Sure you can. Its payment for her assistance years ago; let me tell you about the time I went through challenges in life. My wife was deathly ill and your Aunt gave us her last penny to help me stay afloat. I got behind on my mortgage and other bills for seven months. I tried to get loans and assistance from every program. Unfortunately, I made too much money to qualify for any public assistance. I decided to stop working and focus on my wife during her illness. The job benefits were exhausted, and I had no one to turn too. My home mortgage only had a year left and just before going into foreclosure, your aunt paid it in full. I'm sure it was her last penny, especially since she was on a fixed income. I know your uncle left her with the home, but her everyday living had to be managed to closely, and I'm sure she watched every penny. I tried to give this back to her for years and she wouldn't take it. Now, I feel better repaying my debt to her family. It's the least I can do. I know, it's a little more than what she paid, but since she didn't accept it, I put the amount in mutual funds and it matured. So, every penny is your family's money. Every penny and I have no regrets."

"Sir, the check is more than I'm sure she'd accept. You should keep this and enjoy your retirement."

"You sound just like your aunt, so kind, but no. This is for you. I have my funds and I'm doing well. My retirement is fine. I made sure to never go through that hardship again. So, thank you but no thanks."

"If that's the case, I'll add this to the family's account for the future."

"You do that and I'll be at the memorial cruise. Just let me know my time to speak at her memorial."

"Sure sir. Have a wonderful day."

"Thanks, you do the same. I'll see you there."

Simone walked back to Aunt Marge's home in disbelief. *Another cashier's check for nearly two hundred thousand dollars; something else to share with the family. And another person with a greater level of respect for Aunt Marge. You think you know someone and it's nothing like you think at all. She was awesome.* As Simone entered Aunt Marge's home, she walked directly to Sabrina who stood in the kitchen on the phone. She looked at her in direct eye contact and handed Sabrina the envelope. "Look at this" she said. Sabrina took the envelope and reached in to pull out the paper content. "Oh my goodness!" she exclaimed, "I can't believe this."

"I know right. I can't believe it either. I don't know what to say about it, but it's for Aunt Marge."

"She gave that amount to him?"

"No, it was much smaller. He banked the amount in mutual funds and never gave it to her. He tried but she never accepted it. He wants us to have it."

"No, you can't take this much money from an old man."

"I tried to return it but, he insisted we keep it. It's ours."

"More money to add."

"Yes, it is. I think we should distribute this amount to the next generation for college."

"I think we should add it to the scholarship funds. That way it's for everyone and not divided or lost its earning power."

"That's a great idea. Did you call everyone?"

"Done, I've gotten in touch with key members. I'm sure they will pass word to the rest. You know how they communicate with everyone."

"Good, then it's up to us to get things ready for Thursday."

"Let's do it."

Rodney entered the apartment with intentions of just relaxing after a long day. He headed to the kitchen and pulled a glass from the cabinet. He also pulled a bottle of whiskey from the shelf, headed to the refrigerator, and retrieved ice and soda. After mixing a cocktail, he headed for his favorite spot on the couch. *It's been a long day. Even though the presentation hit the spot, the office group responded with action, and my mind is still on Simone and winning her over, it's good but finally over. My long day is over and mind tiring at the least,"* he pondered. Rodney sat in silence and listened to whatever sounds the apartment made. He heard a beep from the answering machine. *I use to jump to the sound of the answering machine to hear who's called. Now, it's different. I really don't care who called especially knowing it's not Simone.* Additional sounds were apparent. He heard running water in an adjacent apartment, the sound of cars roaming by on the near street, a humming sound from the ceiling fan,

223

and air flowing in the central air conditioning vents. All of those sounds became soothing notes to relax his mind.

He took another sip from his drink, looked around the room, and remembered his time line to do other things. He contemplated when to get started, *I'll start my chores after finishing my drink and after a change of clothes.* After his last sip of the cocktail, he returned the glass to the kitchen and pushed the play button on his answering machine. "Rodney, this is Sabrina. I'm calling to invite you to my Aunt's memorial cruise. It's Thursday and lasts two nights; the ship leaves the doc at 8:00 pm. boarding starts at 5:00 in the evening. Please come, I'd love having you and of course Simone wants you there. Even if she doesn't realize it, she needs you. So, call me with confirmation. Oh, you can bring one guess if you like. You have a cabin for two. Call me for further directions. Hope to hear from you soon." The machine beeped and announced, "end of messages." Without another minute passing, Rodney called Dan. "Hey, what are you doing Thursday to Saturday?"

"Working I guess. Why do you ask?" replied Dan.

"We've been invited to Simone's Aunt Marge's memorial cruise."

"A cruise? This is new to me."

"And new to me too, but it's my chance to see Simone once again. Even if she doesn't want me now, she'll remember me supporting her through seeing me on the cruise. I can bring a guest. Are you interested?"

"When is it again?"

"Thursday through Saturday, leaving at 8pm Thursday evening. I didn't get the details of where it's headed, however it would be a great experience. And you know cruises, there's going to be single women. You'll love the experience. Oh, it's no cost to us and the cabin reservation is for two."

"Maybe I shouldn't go. The chances you'd have with Simone may be blown."

"No, not even a thought of being with her thoroughly as such; but it would be a nice situation to face. I know it's not likely to happen. But are you coming or not. I need you there to support me and have fun. What do you say partner?"

"For you huh? Well, I'm there partner. I guess it'll be a different experience."

"Great, I'll call Sabrina and let her know we both are coming."

"Let me know the rest of the details. I've got to go. Call me later."

"Will do."

Chapter 13

The Celebration

Many family members and friends showed at the cruise ship. Groups of people   roamed the decks while fruit drinks were served to anyone who'd like one. The fruit drinks were many Aunt Marge enjoyed during her lifetime. The ship's decoration was themed of the many phases of Aunt Marge's travel. From her early childhood to the age of her death, each deck had something unique reminding passengers of the reason their aboard. Pictures of her life with many of the passengers were mounted near each elevator. They were much like the ship's map giving direction. Everything on the ship touched or interfaced in Aunt Marge's life.

In the dining rooms, the menus were full of Aunt Marge's favorites. Her best chicken recipe was one of the items on the main menu. And the greatest cookies ever made were on the dessert list. Though there was a variety of items to consume, many of them were a reminder of the sweetest woman that ever lived.

Table decorations didn't miss a step in the theme of things. Aunt Marge's floral arrangements, reflected in the many pictures she took, were scattered throughout the dining rooms. Her favorite colors helped accent the waiter's uniform. The classical music she once enjoyed filled the room. Not to overdo it, those items were a part of the cruise and not the only thing offered.

Cabins were all assigned and decks had family and friends situated in eras of interaction. Amazing to all, she coordinated the bunch very well. It was as if her expertise was that of an event planner. Aunt Marge knew exactly how she wanted to leave this earth. At the minimum, she knew how to put the family and friends in a pleasant situation.

Rodney and Dan arrived at the pier. They climbed out of their cars picked up their luggage, and headed for the boarding ramp. In stride they walked with the rolling carryon bags and without saying a word both men hastily maneuvered up the gangplank. "Hey is this going to be something else or what?" said Dan.

"I think it's going to be quite interesting myself," answered Rodney.

"You know; things will be fine during the cruise. You'll find Simone and spend some time selling you all over again."

"Not so sure about that. I think she'll be a little busy with the family."

"If you thought so, why did you come along? She wants you here."

"Have you forgotten? She didn't invite me. Her sister did."

"Oh, that's right; I forgot who gave you the invite."

Rodney and Dan arrived to their state room, and saw the cabin door slightly opened across from theirs. Cabin Sierra 78 had jazz music blaring from its television, water running in the head, and the window shades opened allowing the natural light to shine through. There wasn't a sign of the occupant so the guys turned to their cabin opened it and stepped in. They looked around and decided who would sleep where and placed their things accordingly.

While in the stateroom they heard an announcement over the ship's PA system. "Welcome Aboard the Princess Enchantment. Thank you from the family and friends of Marge Blaine for attending the most amazing memorial event ever taken. As you settle into your state room, you'll find the memorial schedule and guest list. The guide also provides instruction in dining, safety guide, and additional instruction for an enjoyable three days. Do not be afraid of using the staff for your assistance. As a reminder, the family would like you to remember, there's no cost to anything you wish to do aboard the ship.

227

So enjoy as much as you like and make it the best memorial experience in your life. Again, I wish you an enjoyable cruise."

After Rodney and Dan settled in to their state room, they decided to tour the ship. "Let's head to the main deck and see who's on board," suggested Dan.

"Let's, do that. I wonder if the crew is serving drinks? I could use one right about now." answered Rodney and looked in the mirror before saying, "Let me clean up a little before heading out. You never know who you might run into."

"You're hoping to run into Simone. I can understand. Take your time man, get it right. I may get lucky with one of their cousins."

Simone and Sabrina were in their cabin when they hear taps on the door. "Hello, just a minute," Sabrina answered, as she walked to the door. She looked through the peep hole and couldn't make out the guest. She opened the door, and stepped aside to look both directions of the passage way. She didn't see a person in the passage which had focus on their cabin. "I guess it was the wrong cabin," she told Simone.

"Oh really, look again," suggested Simone. When Sabrina returned to the door, she looked right and there stood Lorenz. "Hi, Sweetheart," greeted Lorenz.

Sabrina embraced Lorenz and kissed him as if she'd missed him for years. She hugged him with a death defying grip of her arms. Sabrina exuded pure happiness and said, "I am so glad to see you. I knew you'd make it."

"I am a man of my word; at least I try really hard to be."

"Let me show you to your cabin," replied Sabrina. "Simone, feel like exploring the ship?"

"Will I be a third wheel?"

"No, not at all," said Lorenz. "Please come along, it could be fun once I drop my bags and we will hit the main deck."

"I know you two hadn't had time together, so why not I take a rain check on the tour thing?"

"No way sis, come on. Lorenz and I have a lot of time ahead during the cruise."

"Are you sure? I hate being a third wheel."

"You shouldn't be alone now. Come on let's get moving. We have things to do when we get back to the cabin."

"Okay" she answered, as she walked towards the passage way. Sabrina reached for Lorenz' hand and led him down the passage way. Simone followed, as if she walked in the foot prints of a bigger brother. "You know, I still can't believe we're here for Aunt Marge," she shouted to Sabrina.

"Neither do I; it would have been a great trip if it were for a different reason. I'm sure Aunt Marge wanted us to enjoy this as much as any other cruise."

"Yeah, I think so, and let's not think of this as a memorial cruise. Let's make the best of it. Why not? It's paid for," she said with a giggle.

Dan and Rodney left their cabin just as Mr. Slocum, Marge's lifelong neighbor, bumped into them.

"Hello young man, it's nice seeing you here." Mr. Slocum greeted Rodney.

Lorenz, Sabrina, and Simone rode the elevator down two decks headed to cabin Sierra 47. They exited the elevator and headed right for the cabin. They passed the higher cabin numbers   and walked towards Lorenz' cabin in search of Lorenz's stateroom. While en-route they come across Rodney and Dan, listened to Mr. Slocum as he recalled his first encounter with Rodney, "If it weren't for you, we' probably been here sooner."

"What's that sir?"

"Yes, you found Marge on the street remember?"

"I did what?" replied Rodney.

"I can't be mistaken; it was you who knocked on my door to get an ambulance. I remember it well. And you stayed on her side until it arrived. I may be old and forgetful, but one thing I don't forget is a face. Plus, such a grave event as saving a life is one you don't let go. You saved her life. If it weren't for you, no one would have found her for hours. Which the EMT said, it was good that you called us in time."

"I saved her life? I remember seeing an elderly woman on the street and not moving. I stopped to give assistance. She didn't respond to my questions so I knocked on your door. I stayed with her until...I remember now."

"Yes, you did. I'm glad you were there." Mr. Slocum looked to his right there was Simone, standing in awe.

"Simone, have you met Rodney?" With a tear in her eye and struck from the new information, she held her hand to her mouth and without saying a word, ran back to her cabin.

"What's wrong with her?" asked Mr. Slocum.

"Star struck," answered Sabrina.

"I'd say he's a star. A good guy too."

"You know Mr. Slocum; I told her the same thing. It's why I invited him to the celebration."

"Glad you did. I'll see you around Rodney, Sabrina, and young men," referred to Dan and Lorenz. He turned towards the exit and moseyed along the way.

"See you soon, sir" replied Rodney.

Sabrina, held Lorenz' arm and said, "Rodney, you should go to Simone. She'd really understand your sincerity now."

"I don't think it's a good idea," replied Rodney.

"Why not?" asked Dan.

"It's not a good thing. Just think, when you hate someone, blame them for harassing them, and later you find out he isn't such a bad guy, it's confusing; for me, and not alone for her."

"I see your point," said Lorenz. "Think of it like this, you've been there through it all, shown your effort and persistence, and now the opportunity to make it come true is here. Why not take advantage of the opportunity? It's in your favor."

"You're a marketing guy; you know the saying, 'Get it while it's hot'," said Dan and then added,

"Besides, she's your dream girl. You've admitted it many times over."

"Okay, okay. I'll head to her cabin. Meet you on the deck later?"

"Yeah we'll be there," replied Dan.

"Right after we," Sabrina blinks at Lorenz, "catch up on lost time."

"I'll catch you on the deck. It's no telling what time we'll see these two."

Rodney knocked on Simone's cabin door, waited for an answer and thought, *I'll tell her I didn't know. I'm sorry for not knowing it was your aunt. The connection never dawned on me. No, that's not it. How about...*

"Oh it's you." Simone answered as she opened the door.

"Yes, it is. I'm sorry for not telling you about finding your aunt."

"You would forget something like that. You'll do anything to get next to me. And it's a big thing that you saved my aunt earlier in the year."

"You know, I can't believe you," Rodney explained while entering the cabin. "I didn't know the lady was your aunt. How could I? I was running and saw a lady on the street all curled up. I thought she may have fallen and needed some help. I had no idea it was your aunt. I had no idea."

"Oh, the hero excuse; you had no idea. It seems like you're all over my turf, in my life, nearly every corner; Its killing me seeing you so much when I don't want to."

"Okay Simone, that's it. I am crazy about you, willing to do anything in the world for you. I've dreamed of you being my woman. My focus has been centered on you and how to win you over. It's like a challenge that's crazed with passion. Now I see it's my fantasy and no chance of it becoming a reality. I've never had a woman so hard to crack. And I ask myself all the time why am I fighting so hard to be with you? Why is it you I want so much? My dreams are filled with you in them. Yet, every move I make, every comment reaching for you creates an opportunity for you to push me farther away."

"Push you away? You mean skillfully challenge you to believe there's no chance for us."

"No skill, just rude and harsh. I think I've gotten my fill and want no more." Rodney turned to exit the cabin. Just before leaving the cabin, he looked back to Simone and said, "You know, a man with admiration and affection for one woman can only take so much rejection. I've done nothing but show who and what I am. I see now, it wasn't enough."

"Enough it was. Close the door behind you on your way out."

Rodney left and gently closed the cabin door. He shook his head from side to side and walked towards the first hatch leading to the outside deck. *Man, was I stupid for wanting her so much?* He pushing the door open, a strong breeze hit him and a tear fell from his face. He leaned on the protective siding on the deck and stared into the water.

And I can't believe I'm nearly broken up for a woman I never had. How can it be? Is it love that I have for her or is it the loss of a fantasy? Whichever it is, I can't believe the pain it's caused.

Simone turned to the portal and looked at the ocean and sky as she pondered Rodney's words. *You know, there is no way he knew the woman was Aunt Marge. Why am I so ignorant to believe he didn't know? Why am I so afraid of him? He's right. I've never had a man do nearly as much for me. The romantic evening, we shared was awesome, having dinner together at his place was fun, and his brining flowers to the hospital so late at night were very thoughtful. And I push him away from me. Why?* Simone turned to leave the cabin still contemplated her thought. "*I better rethink this. A man with so many qualities doesn't come often. And he's interested in me without really knowing who I am. At every opportunity he's shown true qualities of a good man. He's thoughtful, helpful, a civic contributor, and quite responsible in business. Oh, and he's handsome.* She walked to the nearest exit to the upper deck, opened the door and saw Rodney by the rail. "Rodney!" she called

Rodney turned and greeted Simone with, "I can't take anymore," and walked toward the ship's aft.

"No, Rodney, don't leave." Simone said as she followed, "I need to share something with you."

"Sorry, I can't listen to you," he spoke as he continued walking.

"Hey, I'm not going to run behind you."

In a faint voice he answered, "As if you'd ever," and continues creating distance between them.

"I am so glad you're here," said Sabrina. "I want this time together to be very special, even under these circumstances."

"Special indeed," Lorenz replied as he took Sabrina in his arms. He gently kissed her on the base of her neck, tracked upwards to her lips, and kissed each inch. They fell onto the bunk as they deeply kissed and   scrambled to get undressed. Without hesitation and like an orchestrated ballerina, they found themselves intertwined in passion. "It's been too long since I've last had you," Lorenz said.

"Don't think we'll do that again."

"I need you, as I've never needed anyone in my life. I need you."

"I need you too Lorenz. I can't live a day without having you in my life. I dream of you, reach for you, and desire you at every moment of the day."

"Baby, is this love?"

"Yes, its love," she answered. They stopped moving and laid facing each other. Lorenz held his breath for a moment and Sabrina stared deeply into his eyes. And without any signal they both whispered "I Love You" to each other. In their eyes, a moment of time froze and there was silence.   They held that moment together and embraced with greater strength. The passion was so intense that their bodies breathed in unison, and their strokes were electric. They cringed from pure physical pleasure. Sabrina and Lorenz held onto each other as if it were for dear life, not letting go for anything or anyone. Lorenz broke silence just as he looked into her window of affection and admitted, "I really love you."

"You know babe, it's a new day for us."

"Yes, a new start and a different direction in life."

"I can't believe it. I am glad we shared this moment, and it's one day I'll never forget."

"Neither will I. It's the first time I've told a woman I love you."

"Oh Lorenz, you can't be serious. I don't mind being the second or third woman as long as you mean it."

"No Sabrina, you are the first and only. I'd like to keep it that way. Not saying it's the future, but I breathe better when I'm near you. I rise to the sky and soar with birds at every thought of you. Each moment I'm thinking of you. And my heart pounds fast in the sight of you."

"I see, it's slightly different for me. My heart doesn't pound as fast, but my mind wonders to our future. Our pregnancy, our apartment, our struggle; I see our future and it's vivid. I've never looked so deep in my soul to the meaning of my dreams. Each dream has you involved living next to me. Lorenz, I've never dreamed of a man so exact and involved with me. I love you."

"Hello my lady, my princess, my queen. Welcome to the castle of my heart."

"Hello fine sir, my prince, my king. I love being in your castle."

***

Dan found Rodney as he strolled on the ship's sun deck. "Rodney," he called.

"Yeah," he responded as he walks   barely turned toward Dan.

"No way, I can't believe she turned you down again." Dan walked to catch up with Rodney.

"That she did."

"How bad did she do it?"

"She will always be my dream girl. It's just not in her book. As a matter of fact, it's becoming my book all the time. I've got to let it go. Man, I've got too."

"Then let's make the best of the rest of this cruise. We'll start over and get back to my best friend who lived for himself."

"Sounds like a good idea."

***

Family and friends headed to the ship's main theater for Aunt Marge's memorial service. Her favorite songs played and multiple flowers, wreaths, and pictures spread across the stage. The podium was center stage and prepared with notes for each speaker. Programs were dispersed across the theater for each table. People settled in and the program began.

Simone stepped to the podium, and welcomed everyone to the service. "Thank you for coming to Aunt Marge's memorial service. She was a dynamic woman, sister, friend, cousin, and neighbor. Her life graced us with truth, happiness, energy, and most of all, love. She gave us the type of love biblically described and truly practiced in definition. She provided us with an awesome taste of quality in living. She gave us more of herself than any of us can ever imagine. I, for one, received so much of her, that I find myself understanding her as I know myself. Everyone here received some type of influence from Marge Blaine, and today we celebrate her life." Simone stepped from the podium and left the stage.

A young gentleman approached the stage and sung a wonderful ballad, solemn in delivery and very melodic in verse. It was a favorite song of Marge in her youth. Not religious in nature, but surely a song of emotions. "I am a nephew of Marge Blaine. She was my greatest support in music, and because of her I launched a career in entertainment. I'll always thank her for doing so. There is no greater love for someone, than providing encouragement to achieve your dream. She encouraged me through it all." He exited the stage.

Mr. Slocum waked to the podium and pulled a card from his pocket; notes for his speech most suspect. He placed the cards in the middle of the podium and cleared his voice. "Mrs. Marge Blaine gave her best for all and everyone. If you remember her, you'll know she contributed above and beyond whatever the expectation. I mean, she gave her all without ever expecting a return. I am her neighbor and friend for over 27 years. I am a recipient of her definition of quality of life. My family and I are a part of her, an extension of your family, and I as a matter of fact, I feel like a brother who's lost his sister. We shared laughter and tears over the years, my kids call her Aunt Marge, and the grandchildren addressed her as their special Great Aunt. I say farewell to a lovely woman, one of love, and one we can always cherish. Farewell to you Marge, my sister. I know you're flying with angels."

Simone approached the podium as Mr. Slocum stepped off the stage. "I'm introducing the last farewell speaker for Aunt Marge. This gentleman has been her greatest companion outside of Uncle Arthur. Not as a love interest mind you, but a close family friend and confidant. He's the reason Aunt Marge had the funds to afford her farewell cruise. I present Phil Berkley."

Phil took the stage and approached the podium. He looked into the audience and went straight to his mission. "Thank you Simone for the invitation to speak for Marge and the introduction," he cleared his throat before moving along, "I am Phil Berkley attorney and business partner to Marge Blaine. She was the best partner any business man could ask for. Was she shrewd? Yes, more so than most thought as I heard earlier. Was she kind in every way imaginable? From what I heard, it's a simple answer. Yes, she was. I often wondered how Marge Blaine did so much for so many. She alone kept my office busy, setting up accounts, scholarships, or contracts for her family. She didn't just give, no, she made it an agreement that you, had to work for her support. I found her attitude included me, about working to get her support. I didn't have the large firm as I do today. But with her help, we grew.

Today, I want to thank my best business partner in the world for helping me achieve my dream. Thank you Marge Blaine and may your wings be forever felt amongst us." Phil left the stage as Simone approached and spoke at the podium.

"We decided to keep the program short and sweet. You know Aunt Marge would have made sure we didn't fuss over her. So, in kind, we're going to do exactly that. Everything here on the cruise is a theme of Aunt Marge. She coordinated everything, even the program you hold in your hand. She wanted us to celebrate her life, and I for one intend to do so. In the spirit of Aunt Marge, we'd like you to indulge yourself in every aspect of this cruise. Yes, we'll miss Aunt Marge, yet she'll be with us forever." Simone stepped down from the stage. The ship's band played music while the curtains opened and the lights dimmed. A large portrait of Aunt Marge appeared as a stage backing. Dancers entered wearing multiple costumes which placed Marge in different eras of fashion and time. Every song the dancer responded to was one of Aunt Marge's favorites.

A gentleman appeared   the moment of the last dance ended. He moved to the center stage and stood with a microphone in his hand. The man started with a joke of childhood and the changes Aunt Marge made with all the kids. From their first blanket to the cookies sent to college campuses. And at every joke, the theater roared with laughter. For five minutes, the comedian told situational jokes from Aunt Marge's life. For each minute, there were roars of laughter.

When the comedian ended his session, another saxophonist took center stage. It was Aunt Marge's favorite instrument. The woman played a lovely piece of music, another of Aunt Marge's favorite.

The next event was another dance; a creative dance from Aunt Marge's most moving theatrical play.

Last event and a surprise to everyone was a message from Aunt Marge herself. A videotaped played on the dropped screen at the edge of the stage. Her image was youthful and her dress was astonishing; typical Marge Blaine when in public "This isn't my last will and testament, or the reading of life instructions. It is my farewell to you. To my family, friends, neighbors, and associates and everyone here, I give you a gift. My greatest gift to anyone and everyone is the gift of love. Please don't sit and memorialize me as a person passing on.

Think of me as a distant friend without the means to call. You know the limitations of technology; no phone available and if you think of sending a letter, you better know I may not get it because mail service is slower than a snail's pace. Think of it as, whatever means on this earth, isn't available to get to me, but I will be there. Yes, I'll be there for you.

I brought you here on this cruise to understand its continuing life that counts. You have to live and let live, reach for the fun in your heart. You have to take what I gave you and go for your dream. Stop trying to compete with society's standard of living and enjoy life. You only live once.

Last, because I want to keep this short, remember I love you. I love you all and will be here for you. So, in light of the situation, I will share with you one thing. I leave multiple funds to assist you when needed. There are tight stipulations you'll have to meet, but it's for you. Use it wisely and without being foolish. For more information, see Phil Barkley at his firm for specific standards and instructions to help. And for my last gift, you should receive envelopes in your cabin. It's a surprise.

Remember, this is my gift to you so I expect you to enjoy the rest of the cruise. I sure loved cruises. It's my farewell so stop crying and raise your glass for a toast." Waiters passed out chalets of grape cider. "To my family, friends, and acquaintances, I loved you all and please love each other for life. Your best years are yet to come. Share your knowledge, your will, and your skill. Now drink up and enjoy my gift to you." The tape video ended.

A tearful Simone walked onto the stage while the band softly played and said, "Let's follow Aunt Marge's advice. Enjoy our cruise gift. Everything we have planned for the next few days is on a printed schedule in your cabin. I'll have her ashes on the top deck to release into the wind at sunrise tomorrow morning."

The theater emptied of attendees while Sabrina and Lorenz sat at a table booth and chatted in surprise of Aunt Marge's message. "You ok, baby?" Lorenz asked.

"Yes, I'm ok. Wasn't she awesome?"

"Yes, she was awesome."

"I really miss her. I'd love to tell her about us. She would have been so excited about our new found love. It's because I'm the last she thought would touch those deep emotions; especially over a man."

"No, she wouldn't be excited about it, she'd tell you it was about time."

Sabrina punched Lorenz and responded, "Sure she would," and laughed.

Still in tears, Simone returned to her cabin, stood on the cabin's balcony and looked to the horizon. She cried and whispered her thought to Aunt Marge, "Farewell my second mother, best friend, and mentor. I'll never forget you. And thanks for a new future." She sat on a chair and watched the moonlight sparkle over foaming waves. She sat in silence for hours.

Chapter 14

A New Beginning

Lorenz returned to the cabin to study before he left for the hospital. He assumed there wasn't much left for him to finish with the internship. He sat on the balcony with a book in his hand overlooking the ocean. After he'd read a few hours, Sabrina entered his cabin and called, "Lorenz, are you here?"

"Yes, I am on the balcony."

"With all the things to do on this boat; you come here and read."

"It's an important thing in my preparation. You know, I'm not finished with my internship just yet. As soon as I feel comfortable with the program, I'll slow down."

"I know baby, but it's our time together. We don't have much of it so why not make the best of it? I have a lot of shoots next week and it's my turn to glow with our love."

"Yes, you're right. I only wanted to catch up and review a few things before returning to the hospital. So I thought you'd like to enjoy catching up with your family."

Sabrina replied while she pulled Lorenz's arm and encouraging him up to embrace her in the cabin, "That's nice of you to think of me, but you're important to me too. I don't want waste our time when there's an opportunity to get closer." She enticed Lorenz with a long luscious kiss, and she pushed him on the bed for a full body embrace.

The ship docked pier side and set up the debarkation process. The announcement over the intercom instructed passengers with debarkation events. Deck after deck, the announcer directed the passengers off the ship and onto the pier. Simone and Sabrina rolled their suitcases to the debarkation hatch, walked the gangway, and went to the parking lot. Without a word to each other along the way, they silently discussed the recent events. It was their way of communicating since they were kids. One look at Sabrina and Simone knew of her new found emotions for Lorenz. Sabrina, understood Simone's disgust, stayed clear of conversation about Rodney. Both ladies continued to load the car before they arrival and sat in the front seats. Sabrina, behind the driver's seat, started the engine while Simone stared into space. "Are you ok?" asked Sabrina.

"Yes, I'm ok," answered Simone.

"Good. We're starting a new life and it starts now."

"I realize this is a new beginning for us. New found wealth, a career decision to make, we have to develop a plan to continue Aunt Marge's work, and no time for a man."

"No time for a man?"

"No time at all for Rodney. I've decided to focus on our new beginning."

Sabrina drove out of the parking lot into traffic headed towards their home. She paused at an attempt to bring Rodney into the conversation. She considered a way for a response without causing anger. Sabrina asked, "You mean, you didn't open the door to Rodney when he went to the cabin to talk to you?"

"I opened the door and heard him out. I'm not ready for anything with him. He may be a good guy and all, but it's not a good time for me."

"So, if it isn't now, when is it a good time?"

"I can't answer that right now. I haven't an idea."

"You mean to tell me- you didn't give a quality man like Rodney a chance?"

"Sabrina, giving Rodney a chance isn't important. I think we have a lot to do in the near future. We have a heavy plate with what Aunt Marge left us."

"Sure, we have a large plate of change, but support is important. Especially from a smart intelligent man like Rodney. Did you ever think he'd be of assistance to you or us for that matter?"

"No, he'd be a nuisance. I'm sure of it and that's why I decided to focus on us and our inheritance for the time being. A man can come at a later time in my life. Right now isn't it or he isn't the right one."

"Your decision sounds final. I guess he's out and money is in. I never thought you'd push a quality guy away when he presented himself to you."

"I didn't see him as quality, and besides, we have other things to achieve now.

"I agree, we have other things to achieve, but I have Lorenz and he's part of my new objectives in life."

"Enjoy him while you can."

"What's that supposed to mean?"

"Just what I said; enjoy him while you can."

"That is so discouraging and I can't believe you aren't happy for me."

"Oh, I'm happy for you, just not sure he's there for you and not our inherited wealth."

"You know what Simone, he has no idea about what Aunt Marge left us and I'm in love with him."

"In love with him, are you sure?"

"Yes I'm sure. Have you ever heard me claim loving someone before?"

"Well, maybe when you were younger. You know, the teenage phase we all go through. But all in all, no I haven't."

"Then you know I'm really into Lorenz. He's it, I'm telling you. I had no idea this feeling would be so strong and it came unexpectedly. It was a sneak attack on my heart. When he told me…."

"Told you? You mean he told you first?"

"Yes, he told me in the most romantic way. It was awesome and the connection is out of this world."

"Oh, wow. My little sister is really in love. I just thought you were on your usual fling and having fun. This time you actually fell in love."

"And you rejected the same offer of affection. That man loves you and he did all the right things. I can't believe you rejected Rodney."

"That's my business. It's my objective to love who I see fit and at a time that's best for me. Never is it a time to love someone to please you nor him for that matter; and now is the time I choose and he isn't the one."

"You want my opinion?"

"Not really, but you're going to tell me anyway."

"You're passing up a wonderful man and they are hard to come by. You know, we aren't getting younger and the pool of great available guys is slimming. I honestly think he's one that got away."

"I appreciate your opinion, but he's not one that got away. As a matter of fact, he was thrown to the wolves for all I care."

Silence grew in the car. Both Sabrina and Simone decided not to say anything more on the matter. They both focused on internal thoughts as Sabrina drove to their perspective homes.

***

Lorenz arrived at his apartment from a cab. He exited the cab, grabbed his gear and headed to the apartment building. "Hey Lorenz," she exclaimed. Lorenz didn't see anyone in his direct sight, he looked around on the street for whoever called. "Hey," Lorenz answered.

"I haven't seen you for a few days. I know your shifts didn't change or did they?"

"No shift changes. I took a couple days off and went to a funeral. I mean a memorial service." Lorenz responds after he recognized the voice.

"Oh, really? I'm sorry someone passed on. Was it a relative of yours?" asked Robin as she looked out of her apartment window.

Lorenz replied as he looked up to Robin. "Not one of my relatives; it was my girlfriend Sabrina's aunt."

"Oh, your girlfriend; I hope all went well. I'll catch you later."

"Yes, maybe later."

Lorenz continued upstairs to his apartment and opened the door. Robin walked after him as he entered and handed him a postal envelope. "Before I forget, this came for you earlier this week. I called the hospital to get it too you, but no one would help me find you."

"Thanks, I appreciate you signing for the letter."

"Oh, no problem. Should we open it?"

"I will after I settle in. I need to put these things away first. Thanks again for holding and delivering the letter," he said while he escorted Robin out of the apartment.

"Will you let me know what it is? She said as she turned towards Lorenz. "Remember if it weren't for me, you'd not get the letter."

"I will. And thanks again. I appreciate it. I'll call you later right after I open it." Lorenz then closed the apartment door and placed the letter on the coffee table. Robin returned to her apartment and continually wondered the content of the letter.

Lorenz finally settled in from the cruise. He poured a drink from the refrigerator, sat on the couch, and go the letter. *It's from the hospital. I wonder why the hospital administration is sending me a letter*. Lorenz opened the letter and begins to read the content. "Oh my, I passed all exams and this is my official notice of completing my internship. I thought I had two more surgeries to perform. My last two months was preparing for a job someplace in the world. I've got to talk to Sabrina. She should have some kind of input to us and our next move. I can't leave her behind. I'd better call her." He dialed Sabrina's number. Just as the phone rang, there's a knock on the apartment door. He answered with the phone at his ear. "Hey, Robin, what's up?"

"Have you opened the letter?"

Lorenz held his hand up towards Robin signaling give me a minute. Sabrina's answering machine picked up , "….Leave me a message," allowing Lorenz to excitedly shout, "Hey, give me a call when you can. I have great news and need to talk to you. I love you." He ended his call

"Love you?" Robin asked and inquired, "You mean you're in love with that model woman! Are you sure its love?"

"Oh, its love, no doubt Robin. It's love all the way. I've never felt like this before, and you know, my type of women doesn't beat my door down. It's a gift and I'd like to cherish my gift while I can. And she's an angel, a lovely one at that."

"All this time, you never recognized me as a woman of caliber."

"Recognized you? Oh, you're a gold mine and a lovely person. I never thought of you in that manner. Was I supposed too?"

"Damn right you were supposed to. I am a quality woman and cared for you in ways you'd never known. I've wanted you to be with me from the time you started your internship. What's that, three years ago?"

"I never knew. I'm sorry about that. It's just I never focused on women until Sabrina. And I hadn't planned on seeing her then either. It just happened and I'm glad it has."

"Thanks a lot, Lorenz. You break my heart without knowing it. What a man you are." Robin turned in tears and ran across the hall to her apartment.

Lorenz stood at the apartment door for a moment as he watched Robin slam her door. *Wow, I knew she was kind of interested but, not my type. Why didn't I tell her years ago instead of being nice? Man, I blew that one.* Lorenz thought and then pondered, *Oh well, I didn't lead her on either.* Lorenz closed his door and started looking at multiple hospitals throughout the country. *I know there's someplace I can land a position on a staff or practice. There's one for me out there somewhere. I wonder where Sabrina would like to go. I know she's able to go anyplace with me.*

***

Sabrina arrived at her place and settled in for the evening. She picked up her phone and dialed her access number to retrieve messages. "You have three messages. To hear your messages…. Your first message is: Sabrina, your next scheduled shoot is Friday morning at the Waycross building. Be there at 9:00 am. Call me if you have questions." *It's the agent, he never leaves his name; as if I need it,* she thought. The answered machine announced the next message, "Hey, where have you been? You know I can never get my fix of being with you. I'm crazy about you. Why haven't you called me? It's been months now; is there something you want to share with me? Call me." It was James, her long time beau of excitement. He travels all over the world and usually Sabrina's main focus when he's back in the states…Next message. "Hey, give me a call when you can. I have great news and need to talk to you. I love you." Sabrina's heart fluttered at the sound of Lorenz' voice; she quickly dialed his number. Lorenz answered. "Hello."

"You called. What is it? It sounded urgent."

"Well, it's exciting news. I'm finished."

"Finished what?"

"School silly."

"Were you that close? I thought you had another year."

"No, this was my last year. I thought I had two more procedures to perform. My last was before the memorial cruise. I got my confirmation letter today."

"That's great news. Congratulations Doctor."

"Well, it calls for a celebration. And it calls for us to think of our future."

"Yes. I'm heading over to your place as soon as we hang up."

"I'll be waiting."

Sabrina dropped everything, picked up her purse, and went for the car. She drove to Lorenz' apartment twenty minutes. She walked to Lorenz' apartment and knocked on the door. "Who is it?" Lorenz asked.

"Hey, it's me." Sabrina answered.

Robin opened her door and yelled, "You're the one; the bitch who took my man!!"

"Excuse me?"

Lorenz opened the door and exclaimed the same as Sabrina. "What in the world are you talking about, Robin?"

"You know, it's true Lorenz. She stole you from me."

"How can you say such a thing when there's nothing between us?" said Lorenz

"You better get this woman out of our business, Lorenz. You know, I don't play with my emotions and will not allow you to do it either."

"She isn't a girlfriend of mine. She is my neighbor, I swear."

"Sure, Lorenz. Tell her of the time you spent many of nights over the past three years at my place. Tell her how I helped you study for your exams. Tell her."

"All those things are true. She fails to mention we were always friends and neighbors. It never went anywhere. I swear Sabrina, when

248

I told you I love you, it's from my heart and no games. Think about it, you've never questioned me before, why start now?"

"Robin," said Sabrina, "You're quite delusional. Lorenz and I are serious now, so whatever you thought you had, isn't anymore. He's got my heart now and I'm ensuring it stays that way."

Robin was in tears as she returned into her apartment, after shouting "You bastard!!"

***

"So, where were we?" asked Lorenz.

"You were going to talk about your letter and finishing school. What's the next step?"

"We have to decide what cities to submit my resume. You know, I can either stay here or move to another part of the world. I don't want to make that decision on my own. Especially since I see our future together, it's a decision we need to make."

"Really, you want my input to your career?"

"I want your input to our future. I'm not going any place far from you. I love you and I really mean I love you." Lorenz kissed Sabrina.

***

Simone elected to review all of those documents, deeds, and letters from the lawyer's office. She drafted a list of items to achieve for her transition. She made a plan how to accomplish each item on the list, which included   a new business and maintain those programs Aunt Marge managed. She looked at her own desires in life. The list she created while she sat on the balcony overlooking the ocean. Not one of her items included a relationship, though she'd like one, but not at the moment. *If I only had someone to bounce my ideas off of."* she thought and continued. *My ideas seem right in line with a solid future, a comfortable one, and sharing it…. well, it'll have to be shared with Sabrina.*

***

Lorenz returned to the hospital for his scheduled shift. "Hey, Doctor Lorenz Maynard," said the nurse.

"Hi Nurse, how are you?"

"I'm great. We missed you. I hear you're finished here. Are you ready to move on?"

"No, not really; I didn't expect to finish so soon."

"Soon? Don't you realize you've been here for three years plus?"

"I have, but it zoomed by so quickly."

"It's because you were so focused. I heard the hospital director wants to chat with you."

"Oh, is it something I failed to do?"

"It's nothing of the sort. As if you'd fail anything. Anyway, you should run up to his office when you get a chance. He's asked about you once this morning."

"Thanks and I'll catch up with him sometime this morning. I'd like to catch up with my patients first."

"As usual, welcome back."

"Thanks again and I'll chat with you soon," as Lorenz said as he walked down the hall and held one thumb up. The morning moved into afternoon in no time. Lorenz finished his time on the job after he focused on each patient. After his visits, he spoke to his patients and not one asked of his situation. During the last of his visits, he spoke to the patient on a personal matter. "Can you believe no one inquired to my getting engaged?" he said.

"Congratulations. When's the wedding?"

"Wedding" Lorenz replied. "What wedding?"

"Didn't you say you were just engaged?"

"No, I didn't say I am engaged, I meant I'm thinking of asking Sabrina to marry me."

"Oh. I misunderstood. I assumed you asked and she accepted."

"No, I haven't asked her just yet"

"Then why not? Let me tell you something while I can. Once you find someone special and your life seems better, you have to embrace the change. If you don't embrace the change and not capitalize on the opportunity, your life loses. Yes, you lose on a gift greater than you can imagine. If its love, as I see it is, then go and make the world a better place. You have to do it soon before it changes. Once you capture love, it gets better and better over time. Go tell the young woman how you feel and ask her. Hesitate no more; your life depends on it."

"I see. Did you get married?"

"Yes, but not at the moment I should have. I allowed conditions to change before asking. If I hadn't hesitated, the love you have now would be the same love I enjoyed in later years. Listen to me, don't let your beginning get away from you. You need the spark you have now as a reminder for hard times ahead."

"Yes, yes, you're right. I have to act now. Thanks. Oh, before I leave, can I get you anything? You have the right amount of pain killers, you're on track to recovery, and your tests were all negative. Is there anything I can do to help you feel better?"

"Yes, call my wife in. I've something to tell her."

"Sure, no problem; and thanks for the advice." Lorenz left the patient's room and signaled the patient's wife over. She approached while Lorenz stopped her en-route and said, "The wise man wants to see you. He's doing great so take good care of him," and smiled as he left the woman to her husband.

***

Sabrina telephoned Simone after her morning shoot. Simone answered "Hello."

"Hi Simone, I have lots to tell you. Are you busy?"

"No, not really, I'm reviewing a list of things I want to get done. It's a good thing you called."

"Yes, it's a great thing I called."

"Great? You're excited about something. What is it? Did you get a magazine cover deal? Did you land another major account? What is it?"

"I think Lorenz is going to ask me to marry him."

"There you go, fantasy world colliding with reality. What makes you think he's going to ask you?" inquired Simone.

"Why do you have to criticize my thoughts? Why?"

"I'm not criticizing your thoughts. I'm a realist and Lorenz isn't ready for marriage. Where'd you think he can get the time for you during his internship?"

"He finished. He's graduating soon and asked me to help him select a city to live. He wants me to go with him."

"And you think that's a marriage proposal?"

"I think it's a step in the right direction. I see myself going with him. Either as his wife or not, I'm going. Knowing Lorenz, he's going to ask. I can feel it."

"Then I wish it comes true for you. Don't set yourself up for disappointment. You know how men can disappoint you."

"There you go again. Why Simone? Why do you always find a negative point in my life and situation?"

"I'm not being negative; it's protection for your heart. Expect the worse and if chance you're right, then all is well. But if you're wrong, don't expect the pain to leave so quickly."

"Is that what happened to you and Rodney? Did he hurt you before he got a chance to show you love?"

"No, nothing got in our way, it was my decision. He wasn't right for me."

"I think he is. And a matter of fact, he's the best guy who's ever shown you the right type of interest."

"He's got you fooled. Whatever he did to impress you, didn't work on me."

"He's authentically a good guy. One day you'll understand."

"One day I just might." Simone replied as she abruptly disconnected the call.

Chapter 15

Three Years Returning

Rodney woke early morning for his routine run. He headed out of his condominium, passing his neighbor he greeted him, "Good Morning," as he walked past.

"Good morning." Rodney replied.

The neighborhood changed over the years. The vacant lot near the old apartments is now a major condominium complex. Fortunately, Rodney purchased the penthouse condo years ago. The marketing firm he started flew into profits within the first year. The new firm was amazingly profitable due to the multiple accounts it won throughout the state. The best thing was he didn't leave the neighborhood he loved so much. Practically all of his friends and relatives were close buy. His minimal life style change landed him into a superb comfort zone; perfect for bouncing back after a heart disappointment.

Rodney stepped on the sidewalk, performed his routine stretch and prepared for his morning run. He headed on his short track   with a strong pace. *I've got lots to do today*, he thought while he ran south on main street. Just like before during his morning run, the street livens with people and activities as the morning evolves.

A number of cars moved along the main street as he turned right at the next block near Marge Blaine's old home. As in every morning in the last two years, and like clockwork, Rodney made his run in 40 minutes. His route led him back to his home where he finished his workout and prepared for the business day ahead. His suits were immaculate, stylish, and tailored, and gave him a true executive image. He jumped into his Bentley Continental sports car, drove to the office and parked in his reserved space. On his way to the 12th floor, he stopped at the coffee shop picked up his favorite coffee flavor and caught the elevator. During the lift, he thought, *Without a doubt it's going to be a wonderful day.*

Dan called Rodney's cell phone with an urgent message from a client. Rodney answered the call "This is Rodney."

"It's the MaxMin account. The CEO didn't quite like the results of our test market. He thinks the numbers are too low as a result of our marketing strategy. He wants to talk to you this morning or he'll cancel our contract."

"Don't worry. Get Mark to catch the recent numbers for Pit Pot and Elab Men for a comparison graph. Meet me at the office and get Mr. Johnson to schedule a meeting at MaxMin this afternoon. We'll win his confidence back in no time.

"Okay, will do."

"What are you doing in town? I thought you were meeting a new client."

"I met him last night and it looks great. I can't see a reason why he won't contract with us for his next campaign."

"Great. I'll see you at the office."

Rodney arrived at his office, walked behind his desk and looked out of the big glass window. He spotted the park, the old house his family once owned, and the old office he worked. "Life is good" he thought, "Life is really good." He sipped his coffee, and looked at his desk. He felt it would have been better had he shared his success with a love of his life. He remembered, being a single chief executive/owner was often a lonely position. His mind went to imagining a photo of Simone on his desk and the memory of her took too his smile to a sigh. Rodney allowed himself to day dream and reminisces to a time of enjoyment with a woman he totally admired. *She was lovely and I missed out on a wonderful woman. Even though she didn't want anything to do with me, I still think she was the one. I see her smile, hear her laughter, and feel her in my arms as we dance. I can actually smell her perfume, and remember her touch on my arm as we walked to the carriage. My lovely woman in every way. I hate things didn't work out; life goes on."*

Twenty minutes passed and Rodney snapped out of his reminiscent thought. He looked at his watch, moved behind his desk, and sat in his leather chair. Rodney powered into super executive mode and has business rolling to his usual pace. After the second meeting, he set a path to catch up on the lost moments from this morning. He called for a brief update from key organization members. One by one they brought him up to speed on sales, marketing, and projects. By noon, he was one step ahead of his agenda. Rodney was back to himself and the day became another business success.

It's nearly 6:00 pm and the majority of Rodney's staff left for the day. Rodney, stayed in his office for additional reviews of client contracts. It was his routine, spending arduous hours ensuring the next campaign was greater than the one before. He swept every project with a fine tooth comb, with his detailed review. He took noted how to satisfy customer expectations, and listed opportunities for new business with each client. It was a skill he picked up over the years in marketing organizations. Early evening and his work day finally came to an end. Rodney found himself set to leave the office and noticed the traffic jam on the main street of his building. He decided to stroll down the street, as he did many times in the past, instead of fighting traffic. At the end of two blocks, he found himself at the art gallery he often visited. A walk through always gave him solitude and peace from the remarkable paintings. *Each painting holds a story*, he always thought.

***

Simone stepped lively at the exercise tape on her flat screen television. She followed the exercise routine religiously and used it as an additional workout to her physical trainer's visits. *I love the way exercising makes me feel*, she thought while she moved to the music. Simone stopped at the end of the tape and headed for her shower. She stepped into her elaborate amenities bathroom. Her mansion has magnificent bathrooms with her master bathroom being the favorite amongst four. This bathroom had a steam room and an individual shower. It's also provided access to a large wardrobe closet. As she entered the bathroom, she stepped on clothes and towels left behind by her husband. "Stefan is such a spoiled slob," she commented. "Why can't he put the towels and his dirty clothes in the hamper like normal people?" She threw those items in the hamper and stripped her sweaty clothes. Simone jumped in the shower.

Stefan walked into the kitchen and poured a cup for coffee. He moved over to the coffee pot and dislikes the odor of the fresh pot. He placed the cup down and headed upstairs to chat with Simone. "Good morning, darling," Stefan spoke.

"Hi," Simone replied with a smile, left the shower and wrapped a towel around her. She moved closer to Stefan.

"The cook made regular coffee this morning. He knows I hate regular coffee. I'm heading down to the coffee shop on the strip and get me a cup. Would you like anything?"

"What type of coffee did the cook make?"

"I told you, regular beans. It didn't have a flavor to its odor."

"No, you go right ahead and get your coffee. I'm going to enjoy what's down stairs."

"You do that. Don't say I didn't warn you when it taste horrible."

"Warning is heeded but thanks anyway." Simone reached to kiss Stefan, but he turned and left the room without looking back. *Typical!* she thought.

Simone selected a presentable outfit from her wardrobe, dressed and headed for the kitchen. She had breakfast, found her PDA in her office and reviewed her schedule of events, notes, emails, and documents. She made multiple calls to business clients and partners. She kept her hand into multiple types of businesses, like marketing, insurance, and property management. All of her current business contracts and partnerships were made a couple of years earlier after she received the inheritance. Simone, in the midst of her work, stopped for a moment to review her check list from years ago. While she figured success on one hand, she realized it was three hours that Stefan hadn't returned. *Boys will be boys.*

Simone closed her office door and called for the car to drive her to the beach. The chauffer pulled the large luxury car to the front, stepped out and opened the door for her entry. Simone looked up to the sky and saw the bright shining sun and felt the warmth on her face. She then decided to drive a convertible and sent the limo away. She walked to the garage, jumped in her favorite convertible and drove onto the main street from her home. The convertible top down, wind blowing, warmth, blue skies and sunshine all supported her decision to drive the convertible. "Beautiful, just beautiful," she exclaimed.

Simone drove down the main street on her way to the beach and passed her husband's car parked at a coffee shop. *At least he's socializing with the locals. He's truly a people person and I'm sure they're getting a kick out of him. He's such a cad. I'll stop after my time at the beach if I see he's still there.* The next block was at the beach's parking entrance, Simone turned into the parking lot, replaced the car top for storage and security, and exited the parking lot. She took her bag and headed for the sand, and strolled close to the water line. She found a spot in the sand where there were very few people, and gave a view to die for. She set up for a few hours of sunshine and

solitude while she heard ocean waves crashed along the shore. She
fell into a deep thought as she relaxed. She compared changes in her
life from years ago. *I'd never have anything of this stature in life if it
weren't for you Aunt Marge. I'm sad you're not with me to enjoy this,
but thankful for this change; and what a change.*

Simone's cell phone rang, and broke her thought. She answered
"Yes, this is Simone."

"Hi Simone, it's your lawyer Phil, how are you?"

"Oh, Phil, I'm fine. I'm out here at the beach and the weather is
awesome. It's such a beautiful day."

"I have news for you, some good and some bad. Which do you
want first?"

"I'll take the good news."

"Ok, ninety percent of our commercial real estate is full of tenants.
This is a change over the last year where sixty percent was the norm. I
don't know what's happened but whatever it is, we're happy. The
profit for the properties will exceed projections by twenty percent at a
minimum. You're making more money this quarter than I reported
earlier. And this is the great news. Are you ready for the bad news?"

"After hearing that, how can any news be bad?"

"Well, there's a hostile attempt to invade the business. There is
one stipulation Aunt Marge left in her will that we didn't take into
account. I didn't mention it because it wasn't a threat. Now, it's a
threat from the city and you need to look into it. I have all the
information leading to eminent domain for one of your major building
properties."

"Eminent domain; is this where the government buys property?"

"Yes, it's from the city where they take a property for the good of
the city or community."

"What property are they interested in?"

"The shelter your Aunt Marge started years ago. It's in the middle of the city and practically runs itself. Aunt Marge funded the effort for the past twenty years. They want the building and the operation shut down."

"Who wants the operation shut down?"

"The city leadership and a major developer want to revitalize the area with new amenities."

"I set up a meeting with them on the fourth. Can you make it? I think your presence will make a world of difference."

"I'll get back to you on this within the hour. I'll get Sabrina to join us."

"That's a great idea. The two of you with a solid front will make a difference. As well, the money you give the city will also challenge the developer. It's a political move but the developer stands to make a heck of a lot of money on the project. Let me know as soon as you can if you'd make it or not. I can reschedule for a later time but the risk is they'll move without us sooner than later."

"I'll get back to you soon. Talk to you later."

Simone disconnected the call and quickly dialed Sabrina. She watched the ocean waves crash against the shore, and waited for the rings. *I wonder what country she's in now?*

"Hey Simone, funny you're calling. I was going to call you tonight. What's up?

"Hey, where are you?"

"We're in Paris. It's beautiful and we're enjoying every part of it."

"Oh, when are you heading back to the States?"

"We weren't planning to right away. We were thinking of heading to the coast of Spain for a romantic week and then do a shoot in Prague. Why do you ask? Are you planning to visit with us? We'd love having you two along."

"No, the offer is nice, but not this time. I'm calling about Aunt Marge's shelter and helping the homeless program."

"She started what? I thought we knew everything about her work. Where is this program and what is it?"

"It's back in our home town; she started the program over twenty years ago. It includes an old warehouse she transformed into a boarding house. She supported the program with funding and little assistance from contributors. She did it practically alone from what I understand."

"Is it in trouble or something?"

"Yes, it's in trouble and need our help. There's a developer pushing the city government to execute a takeover of the property. The powers to be want to develop something like a civic center or shopping mall in the location, Phil wasn't exact on what's being developed, but I'm guessing. Whatever is in the works, the city thinks it will enhance interest for downtown. Unfortunately for us, they haven't made much of an effort to purchase the building, and Phil thinks we can head them off if we attend the meeting they're having. We have to be there when they present the need for eminent domain. When can you come back?"

"I guess if it's that important we can be back in a few days. I'll have to change a flight and coordinate with my agents. How long will it takes us to discuss this with the contractor?"

"Phil has a meeting scheduled in a few days. I can coordinate with him to make sure we're present and influence an alternate solution. I'd hate for Aunt Marge's work to end."

"Yes, I'd hate for that to happen too. I know she'd fight to help the homeless to the very end."

"Then plan on being home in two days. I'll meet you at the airport and we'll stay at a suite near downtown."

"Okay, Simone, we'll be there."

"Good. And tell James hello."

"You do the same with Stefan."

The girls disconnected the call on Sabrina's last comment. Simone picked up her things and headed back from the beach sand. On the walk back, she turned for a last glance the beauty of the ocean offered. *I'll be back in a few days,* she told the ocean and sand. In her car, she pulled into traffic reversed the route she took from her home. Along the way and near the coffee shop, she searched for Stefan's car. When she didn't see his car, she raced home.

Within minutes she arrived at her house and parked her car in the garage. There, she realized Stefan returned home with a few guests. There were two additional cars in the driveway. When Simone entered the house, she noticed the back sliding door was open and the butler had a tray of drinks in his hand and served people around the pool. She counted five ladies and three men lounging and swimming. Stefan was in the pool near one lady, deep in conversation while others are lounged in reclining chairs. Simone stepped through the doors and approached Stefan. "Hi, darling," she said. Abruptly and surprised, Stefan turned from his guest and responded.

"Hi, Simone, these are my guests from the coffee shop. Everyone say hello to my wife, Simone."

"Hi, Simone," they spoke in unison.

"Hello everyone, are you enjoying yourselves?"

"Yes," responded one gentleman on the lounge chair. The others nodded in affirmation.

Simone whispered, "Stefan we need to talk."

"What now? Can't you see I'm entertaining?"

"Excuse me young lady, can you give us a moment?" Simone asked the woman next to Stefan.

"Sure," she replied and moved away from Stefan.

"Stefan, don't be an ass, I'm not complaining about your guest. This is business. We have to meet my lawyers back home. Sabrina and James will meet us there in two days. I'll tell you the rest after your guest leave."

"I'd prefer not going and just enjoy my home. Your home isn't my home. My guests and I can have a wonderful two days while you're there."

"I'd not like to think as much. It's a serious reason to pull me back there. I wouldn't ask if it were something I can do alone."

"You can do this alone. Simone look around, you've accomplished all of this without me. I'm sure you can do whatever it is there without me."

"That isn't the point. We are in this together aren't we?"

"Yes, we're in this together, but whatever it is back there, you're in it alone. I'm not going." Stefan moved toward his guest and directed Simone away.

"You're an ass." Simone shouted.

Two days passed, Simone's plane landed as scheduled at the Richmond International Airport. Just as the plane doors open, she took her things and headed to pick up her luggage. She maneuvers though the airport and found her limousine driver. The driver picked up her luggage, and before they left for the car, she turned and looked for Sabrina. *Her flight was supposed to land the same time as mine. I wonder if she's late.* Simone pondered.

"Hey," Sabrina shouted loudly.

"Hey, Sabrina, how long have you been here?"

"Oh, a few minutes; long enough to get a cappuccino. And they're nothing like in the old country."

"Glad to see you. Where's James?"

"He decided not to come. You know, it's..."

"…Business," Simone finished the sentence. "Yes, Stefan said the exact same thing. So we're here alone without our guys. What a shame."

"Not in my eyes, its quality sister time and we'll take advantage." Sabrina smiled and moved towards the luggage.

"Is this all your luggage?" asked Sabrina while pointing at five suitcases in the cart the driver was pushing.

"Yes, they're all mine. Where's yours?"

"It's on my arm. I've learned to travel light. I thought you'd travel light coming here too."

"You never know what you may need and who you'll run into."

"Yes, I guess. You never know. Do you have someone in mind?"

"No. Not really."

"Sure sister, not really," Sabrina giggled.

"Let's go driver," Simone directed to the driver and nodded her head to Sabrina.

The girls walked to the waiting limousine, entered and left the luggage for the driver to place in the trunk. The driver took them to the Omni luxury hotel downtown. When they arrived, the bell hops jump to service as the limousine stopped. Simone and Sabrina walked to the counter, "Reservations for Whittingham," Simone told to the desk clerk. Immediately the manager arrived at the counter and interrupted the clerk. "Did I hear Whittingham?"

"Yes, you did," replied Sabrina.

"Welcome," he said with a smile and then added, "We have the Star suite penthouse floor. The entire floor is at your disposal."

"That's great," Sabrina smiled in reply. "Yes, my flight was long and I'm ready to relax."

"As you wish," the manager responded while he signaled the bell hop. "Take the Whittinghams to their room; the Star Suite."

"Please follow me," the bellhop directed.

The ladies followed the bell hop to the elevators. The entourage shadowed the ladies in a different elevator. Sabrina, Simone, and the bell hop arrived on the private suite floor and walked directly to the doors. "Ladies," the bell hop addressed them while he held the door open. Simone and Sabrina enter and drop their coats. The bell hop directed the following entourage to place the luggage just inside the door of the suite. "Ms. Whittingham, where would you like your luggage?" asked the bell hop.

"Leave it there, we'll get it," replied Sabrina.

"Sure thing madam. And the key?"

"Oh, you can leave it on the table by the door."

"Thank you, ladies," The bell hop left after Sabrina tipped a large bill.

Sabrina retrieved her bag and rolled it into the room while looking around for the phone. She picked up the phone on the way to the bed room and dials zero, when the operator answered, she instructed, "Front desk, connect me to a Paris, France Operator please." Sabrina waited for the connection, she unpacked as if the hotel was her new home. She asked the French operator, "Connect me to 8984747." When the phone connected, Sabrina rushed in greeting, "Hello, James?"

"No, James is indisposed can I take a message?"

"Indisposed? Tell him Sabrina is on the phone."

"No, James is indisposed at the moment. I can take a message for him, if you'd like to leave one."

"Who are you?"

"I'm his secretary. Who are you and what's your business with him?"

"I'm his wife. Did you not know of his marriage to a beautiful model?"

"Excuse me, you're the third woman today saying you're his wife. Sorry, you'll have to call back when he's available. Or, as I've told the others, you can have him call you."

In a heated response, "You tell that ass to call his wife Sabrina! He has my number." Sabrina ended the call.

"What were you yelling about?" asked Simone

"Oh, some bimbo's playing a game with me about James. Same jealous move to get my husband because he's a hot man."

"You have to fight the dogs too?"

"Yes, I'm afraid so. I never thought it would be so tiring but I love him and he's fun. I can't see myself living without him in my life."

"I never thought you'd go with him after his disregard for keeping in touch. He didn't talk to you for months on end. You surprised me. But you know, love is awesome and feels great when you have it?"

"We girls tend to forgive but not forget. He's mine anyway and it's going to stay that way for a long time."

"I feel the same about Stefan. He can be a pain in the rear, but he's one catch of a man."

"Aren't you going to call him?"

"No, I'll wait until he calls me. I don't have to check up on him."

"Check up on him? That didn't sound too comforting. Is he enjoying life too much without you?"

"Well, if you must know, he's living the life for sure. He hardly does anything with me except big events. Then he's on his own mostly. I can say one thing; he's a fantastic lover in bed. Without him, life is just a bore."

"You know it's nothing like we were years ago. My how we've changed; do you think it's because of this money?"

"We haven't changed. We've evolved into living the quality life Aunt Marge spoke of before she died."

"Oh, you know, if Aunt Marge were alive, we'd have different men in our lives." Sabrina smirked.

"Yes" Simone sighed, "we would for sure. Whatever happened to Lorenz the love of your life back then?"

"Last I heard, he went to South America to practice medicine. It was right after our break up. I didn't want the white picket fence type life or live as the trapped doctor's wife. I realized it after he was offered positions in Milwaukee, and then Minot."

"You didn't want to live in those cities?"

"No, not at all, it would have been difficult to retain the business. So I offered to take him to Paris, or Madrid where he can put his training to use. There I can stay in the business. I thought it was a compromise."

"I guess he didn't want it."

"No, he actually said he'd love to go."

"Okay, you're confusing me. He said he'd go and then you two didn't go. Why?"

"He came to Paris right after my shoot. I got there first for a few days and ran into James. Before I knew it, James and I were waking together the next three days."

"Oh, you're bad."

"No, I'm good." The girls laughed. "James showed me the way to live again and not think too much of tomorrow. I am not the type to take on the pains of others. Lorenz is a man of people and I'm not dedicated to helping others."

"You've come to grips with yourself in that manner. Again, we are not Aunt Marge."

"No we aren't."

"And because of her, we're back in this town. You know why we're here?"

"Yes, I know. So what are we going to do?"

"At first I thought we'd let the city buy it and be done with it. But, the shelter is a good program and a great write off for the business."

"I think we should sell it and give the money to a different organization. We'd get the same write off wouldn't we?" asked Sabrina.

"No, not quite the same but close," replied Simone. "We'll talk more about it in the morning with Phil. Meanwhile let's go see some of the town. We can at least go to Shockoe Bottom."

"Why not, I'm all for it. I'm sure there's a nice restaurant around there."

"Yes, I'm famished."

"Good, let's go."

Chapter 16

Meeting Again

Rodney's entered the art store as if a magnet pulled him in. He walked to another painting of embracing silhouettes reflected by moon light. He strolled around the multiple paintings, stopped at a picture in the park that reminded him of his date with Simone. "Damn, I can't stop thinking about her for some reason. It's been months since I had her on my mind. If I don't control my thoughts, I'll never get her out of my mind or out of my heart."

Simone and Sabrina left the restaurant and decided to stroll down the street. They whole heartedly laughed at the traffic complainers. "Those poor guys fighting traffic and caught in the rat race. Aren't you glad we don't have to do that anymore?" asked Simone.

"Yes, and my goodness, it's gotten worse over the years. At least we didn't have to sit in one spot for longer than a few minutes before the car moved a few feet. These cars haven't moved for the last three blocks." responded Sabrina.

"No, they haven't moved at all. I'm glad we decided to walk instead of using a cab."

"Good decision, Simone."

"Hey, here's that old art store I use to visit to dodge traffic. Let's look around.'

"Okay, we might as well; it's like another twelve blocks back to the hotel."

"We can use the breather. Who's in a hurry anyway?"

"Not us." Sabrina replied with a giggle.

Simone and Sabrina walked through the art store and looked at multiple paintings. Just shy of Rodney, Simone turned with her back to Rodney as she passed him. As usual these days, Simone hardly paid attention to others who were not in her direct view. Her attention was on her interest. "Hey," Sabrina whispers, "Isn't that Rodney you just passed?"

"Rodney who?" Simone replied.

"Oh, you've forgotten the man who fell for you after countless meetings?"

"Rodney. The same man who chased me for months and the man who supposedly saved Aunt Marge?"

"Supposedly actually happened and yes, one and the same Rodney."

Rodney heard his name softly spoken and not t thinking it's about him, he moved to the next isle of paintings. He looked intently at posters and became certain he recognized a voice amongst the two women. It dawned on him it's Sabrina. *No it can't be her. She doesn't live in the city anymore and it's not logical she'd return since her sister moved away tool.*" Without additional thought, Rodney placed focus back on the posters.

"Well aren't you going to talk to him?"

"Why should I talk to him? He was not the man for me and you know it."

"Who are you trying to fool? You fought your emotions for him like fighting a war of terror. I'm not saying you have to open a door to him, just say hello and catch up. Is that so hard to do?"

"If we ran into Lorenz, would you talk to him?"

"Without a doubt and intently so; especially after my last phone call to James, I sometimes wonder if I made the right decision."

"Okay, if we pass him again, I'll break the ice."

"Pass by? You are a Whittingham woman, beautiful, powerful, and smart. Why be nonchalant? Go, be direct and impressive as you are. I'm sure he'll respond to just the sight of you. Just stop him and be silent; works every time."

"You sound like you're still in the game."

Sabrina laughed as she responded, "No, I'm not but I still have skills."

Rodney turned at the end of the aisle as if headed towards the exit. Simone quickly maneuvered to intercept him without running and being so obvious. The rapid clip clap of her heels shattered the silence of the store. "Rodney!" she called. Rodney stopped, turned, and saw the well-dressed woman coming his direction. "Yes," he replied.

"Remember me, Simone Whittingham." Simone said while extending her right hand forward.

"How can I forget such a beautiful woman? Of course I remember you," Rodney smiled in return but thought, *It's the same woman I fight to forget.*

"How nice seeing you."

"Is it really you, Simone?"

"Of course it is. I think of you all the time."

"I wonder how you think of me these days."

"I've kept up with your career and you starting the firm. I'm waiting for you to take it public so I can purchase stock. You're such a good investment."

"Oh, really, I'm surprised you think of me in such a manner. How are you?"

"Oh, I'm quite happy and content. Life continually treats me well."

Sabrina walked up and nudged Simone. "Hi, Rodney," she greeted him.

"Hello, Ms. Sabrina, my dear friend and ally."

"Ally?" asked Simone

"Yes, ally," answered Rodney. "She was in my corner all the time. Too bad we didn't win."

"Oh, yes I remember; how nice of you two to team against me?" Simone smirked.

"It was nothing of the sort. I thought Rodney was the best guy for you." replied Sabrina.

"And so did I," Rodney agreed and then said, "I'm still the best, but situations change."

"Are you married now?" asked Sabrina

"No, that situation hadn't changed. Still single, and focused on my firm. How about you? Are you married…ah either of you?"

"Yes, two years and counting," answered Simone.

"Well, as it seems now, I am," responded Sabrina.

"What's that supposed to mean?" asked Rodney.

"It means I'm married but mad at my husband at the moment." Sabrina smirked.

"Oh, I hope it turns around for you. I'm sure Lorenz would be happier when you're happy."

"I thought I told you my husband's name is James."

"Wow, I must not have paid attention or did I miss something. You aren't married to Lorenz?"

"No, not Lorenz, James; Lorenz is in South America working for a medical assistance non-profit organization. You know, help the children or something."

"My goodness, what happened to you two? If anyone had gotten together, I thought for sure it would have been you and Lorenz."

"Long story, but let's just say, my heart opened to a wonderful guy. One from my past and I love him dearly."

"Okay. So what's your story Simone? As cold as you were to me, what made you decide to get married?"

"Cold to you, nonsense; I wasn't ready. After aunt Marge died, the inheritance, and the game you played, I didn't think we were a good match."

"What about the date and the intense flirting between us. Was that my imagination or something real between the two of us?" as Rodney as he gave a look of confusion.

"Your imagination."

"No way, you were interested too. Don't pretend you weren't and I know it because I know you." Sabrina commented. "As a matter of fact, he was in your mind long before Aunt Marge passed on. Why don't you admit it?"

"It's okay, water under the bridge. I'm glad you moved on.," Rodney regained his composure.

"Actually, there are times when I think of you and what if I made the decision to get deeply involved. I still think of a time that could become a reality." Sabrina stepped away and provides an avenue for them to search those emotions. *You go sis, and let him know you're still crazy about him*, she thought with a smile.

"Simone, I think of you too. Much more than I care to admit, but reality sinks in from the pain you left me holding. I've never fought to have a woman accept me with open arms. I hadn't shown anyone as much nor fell for anyone as hard as I had done for you."

"I never asked you to Rodney. I never encouraged you to do those things for me. I expected the normal guy."

"I am a normal guy. I think you deserve royal treatment. A man should give you total affection and attention as you truly deserve. I thought for sure you'd accept honest and sincere love. Since you deserve such focus, I hope you're receiving the things you desire most in your life."

"I do think you weren't so normal. As a matter of fact, you seemed to scare me with the attention. I've never had anyone show me so much, nor pour their hearts out over the small time we interacted. Stefan does it for me and I know it's a challenge to get all the things from him, but he does well."

"Stefan is a lucky man. Where is he? Didn't he come along?"

"No, he's home. He had other things to do."

"Business must keep him pretty busy."

"No, he doesn't work per say, he has his own way of enjoying life."

"What does he do if he doesn't work?"

"Oh, he makes me happy."

"If his time was available to come, why didn't you bring him? Has he been here before?"

"No, he isn't interested in my history. Not much of a history buff."

"Has he met Sabrina?"

"Yes," answered Sabrina, as she walked back to their location in the Art store.

"You've met Stefan I assume."

"Well, yes and I've talked to him over the phone. He's a nice man, full of life and surely a man worth Simone's heart"

"Sounds like a hell of a guy. Well, Simone it seems I've taken up enough of your time. I hope you enjoy your visit. I should leave before I ask too many questions"

"You shouldn't go on my part. You should go out for a drink with us."

"No thanks. One drink and I'll have to ask you to marry me."

"That wouldn't be so bad," answered Simone.

"Are you asking or are you trying to tell me something?"

"Neither, I'm realizing after seeing you again its time for change." Rodney moved closer to Simone, embraced her as a long lost love and whispered "I'm still in love with you. I've never stopped loving you or given up on the dream of having you in my life. You are my dream."

Simone, shocked at his whisper, broke the embrace, looked into his eyes and frowned. "I can't believe you. After all this time you come up with a line. As if you'd sweep me off into the blue. I can't believe you."

Rodney was surprised in her response asked, "What?"

"I can't believe you. You're trying the same old smooth act you present to every woman. Why can't you be who you are?"

"As if I'm not being who I am. It's crazy you're the only woman I reach out to and yet the one and only who holds my heart. How dare you accuse me of dealing with multiple women when you never gave me a chance?"

"I gave you a chance years ago. You had to be the good guy in everyone's eyes. Too bad you weren't the good guy in mine. It's too bad you didn't understand my needs or desires in a man."

"Now I'm a mind reader and I'm confused."

"Confused? How can you be confused as if I didn't show you and tell you over and over again?"

"Oh, you showed me interest, just like today; you tell me if this isn't confusing."

"You aren't paying attention to me. You never did."

"Pay attention. I nearly worshiped the ground you walked on and you don't think I paid attention." Rodney walked from Simone and beaded a   path for the store's exit. "You're a lunatic and this makes it easier to move on and heal from something so idiotic. I should have never opened my heart to you. Never!"

"Good bye foolish man."

"What the heck are you doing Simone?" asked Sabrina.

Rodney left the building and walked to his car. *Damn it she does it again. I can't believe I empower her to hurt me. Such a selfish woman; she can kiss my…no need to get vulgar. Just let her insensitive and screwed outlook drive her to Stefan. Heck, I don't know why she's needs my heart anyway especially since there are so many available women in the world. I guess good guys finish last when it comes to the heart.*

Sabrina swayed her head from side to side in disgust. "You are confusing. I agree with Rodney. Honestly does Stefan show you anything Rodney has shown you over the years?"

"No, but he's not the type to do so."

"Then why do you put up with the disrespect and harsh treatment?"

"You wouldn't understand."

"I understand. Believe me, there are times I wish Lorenz was in my life. Take today for instance, I don't think Lorenz would have a woman answer the phone and ignore me as his wife. Oh, I understand."

"Probably so, but I need a challenge, with my guy. If he gives me everything, treats me with the utmost respect and admiration he's a weak man. I have no room or need for a weak man."

"Weak? He's successful in many areas and a self-made millionaire. And you call him weak. If anyone saw him as weak or unexciting, it would be me. Why on earth...? It doesn't matter."

"I understand you and your taste Sabrina, but you don't understand me. I have to have a challenge."

"I know you aren't going to like what I say, but Rodney is better for you than Stefan could ever be. Why are you pretending to believe differently?"

"Because Stefan is my challenge and I can change him over time."

"You've lost it sis and as bad as I'd like to say it, you're right. You have to have a challenge to keep you on your toes."

"There you go Sabrina. Now you understand my view of things. The good guys finish last in my book."

A Note from the Author

Thank you so much for reading this novel. I hope you truly enjoyed the story and connected to the characters.

Good Guys Finish Last is my first novel, the one where life starts between pages, and carries in other books like; When Love Evolves, Against Conventional Expectations, and The Predictable End.

Please consider leaving a review. I take every response to heart, especially since I can only enhance my writing   with feedback.

Write your review on any of these websites:
      www.amazon.com
      www.amazon.ca
      www.GoodReads.com
or   www.ElevationBookPublishing.com
or   www.LonzCook.net

Join me on facebook: Lonz Cook Author
 www.facebook.com/Lonz-Cook-Author-168973854345/